PRAISE FOR LISA MOORE AND *FEBRUARY*

"Lisa Moore is an astonishing writer. She brings to her pages what we are always seeking in fiction and only find in the best of it: a magnetizing gift for revealing how the earth feels, looks, tastes, smells, and an unwavering instinct for what's important in life."— Richard Ford, author of *Canada*

"Luminous . . . Moore offers us, elegantly, exultantly, the very consciousness of her characters. In this way, she does more than make us feel for them. She makes us feel what they feel, which is the point of literature and maybe even the point of being human."　　— *Globe and Mail*

"[An] unusually philosophical, thoughtful narrative . . . Far more than just another great Canadian novel, *February* pieces together a life on hold."　　— *Irish Times*

"Loneliness is hard to write about without becoming maudlin or clichéd. But Moore never errs on the side of sentimentality . . . There's an economy in Moore's style that shows us how a once vibrant life can be whittled down by pain and loneliness. But, by grounding her writing in the physical world, Moore shows how life's everyday tasks and encounters create a comforting continuity that allows forward movement . . . You'll be surprised at this novel's ability to uplift."　　— *National Post*

"Moore manages to pull off a novel which takes a moment of catastrophe and focuses not only on the moment itself but on all the moments that surround it; that are altered, subtly or dramatically, by it." — *Guardian*

"Mesmerizing...A graceful meditation on how to survive life's losses." — *Marie Claire*

"A solid, unflinching, unsentimental study of grief...Moore's descriptive powers, her enviable ability to highlight defining elements of character (either individual or societal) by making perceptive observations, are, as always, in evidence." — *The Telegram*

"[*February*] is what great prose should be...a work of art...a moving narrative of risk, love, loss, and surviving." — *Newfoundland Quarterly*

"[Moore] uses a varied style to deliver content that's driven by powerful emotions...a beautiful testimony to the power of love and the devastation of loss....Moore's near-perfect structure keeps the story moving between memory and present-tense mourning, and the Newfoundland setting is evoked with loving detail." — *NOW Magazine*, NNNN

"Moore's writing resembles poetry...She expertly captures her characters' physical surroundings in sharp-edged fragments of colour and sensation...Helen comes across as a perfectly ordinary woman...But that's what [*February*] is about: a perfectly ordinary woman whose life is profoundly changed by an extraordinary event. This is a marvellous book." — *Winnipeg Free Press*

ALSO BY LISA MOORE

FICTION

Degrees of Nakedness

Open

Alligator

ANTHOLOGIES

*The Penguin Book of Contemporary Canadian Women's
Short Stories* (Selected and Introduced)

*Great Expectations: Twenty-Four True Stories
about Childbirth* (Co-edited, with Dede Crane)

FEBRUARY
LISA MOORE

ANANSI

Hardcover edition first published in 2009 by House of Anansi Press Inc.

This edition published in 2010 by
House of Anansi Press Inc.
110 Spadina Avenue, Suite 801
Toronto, ON, M5V 2K4
Tel. 416-363-4343
Fax 416-363-1017
www.houseofanansi.com

Distributed in Canada by
HarperCollins Canada Ltd.
1995 Markham Road
Scarborough, ON, M1B 5M8
Toll free tel. 1-800-387-0117

House of Anansi Press is committed to protecting our natural environment.
As part of our efforts, the interior of this book is printed on paper that contains
30% post-consumer recycled fibres, is acid-free, and is processed chlorine-free.

17 16 15 14 13   4 5 6 7 8

Library and Archives Canada Cataloguing in Publication

Moore, Lisa Lynne, 1964–
February / Lisa Moore.

ISBN 978-0-88784-962-6

I. Title.

PS8576.O61444F42 2010   C813'.54   C2009-906016-7

Cover design: Ingrid Paulson
Text design and typesetting: Ingrid Paulson

*We acknowledge for their financial support of our publishing program
the Canada Council for the Arts, the Ontario Arts Council, and the Government of
Canada through the Canada Book Fund.*

Printed and bound in Canada

For my parents, Elizabeth and Leo Moore.

EARLY MORNING

Sunrise or Sunset, November 2008

HELEN WATCHES AS the man touches the skate blade to the sharpener. There is a stainless steel cone to catch the spray of orange sparks that fly up. A deep grinding noise grows shrill and she thinks: Johnny is coming home.

The sharpener vibrates the counter beneath her fingers; John had phoned last night from the Singapore airport. The roar of a plane landing in the background. She'd sat up on one elbow, grabbed the receiver.

Her grandson Timmy stands before the bubblegum dispenser, transfixed. There is a cardboard sign written in pen promising a free skate sharpening if you get a black jawbreaker.

I've got a quarter in here somewhere, Helen says. Unzipping the beaded coin purse. She is the mother of one son and three girls and there are two grandchildren.

My daughters complied, she thinks, digging for the quarter. She thinks of a slap, stinging and loud; she slapped Cathy's cheek once, the white print of her hand flooding red — this was years ago, a lifetime ago. Helen demanded of the girls that they give in, do what she said; but Johnny had been ungovernable.

A boy just like Cal, is what she thought when she discovered she was pregnant with Johnny. The nurse didn't tell her the sex of the fetus that first time but she'd known it was a boy. The ultrasound was at five in the morning and she rode her bike. Lime Street covered in an early October frost. There were still stars at that hour. Her hands cold on the handlebars. Having to walk the bike up Carter's Hill.

How desperately her son had wanted everything when he was a kid. He had wanted that puppy he'd found behind the supermarket sitting on a scrap of cardboard. She had said about the cost and fleas and the exercise a dog needs. But Johnny wanted the dog.

The grinding wheel revs and squeals when the blade touches it, and Helen pulls out a handful of change and lets Timmy take a quarter. His mother will be furious. Timmy doesn't eat his vegetables, lives on macaroni and cheese. They have rules; Helen's daughters all have bitter rules. The fate of the world can hang on a jawbreaker. If you say no, you mean it.

All profits, Helen reads, go to the Canadian Mental Health Association. She watches the boy slide the quarter into the notch and turn the stiff handle and the jawbreakers slump against each other behind the glass. Timmy lifts the little gate with his finger. Black. A black jawbreaker rolls out into his hand. He turns to show it to Helen. His pale freckled skin, lit up. The blue vein in his temple. Orange hair. The spit of his mother. The very spit out of her mouth. It is joy, the colourless eyelashes, green eyes flecked with hazel. The sharpener on the second skate blade. The smell of burning metal. And the fan of orange sparks. Timmy holds up the black jawbreaker and the man behind the sharpener stops the machine and lifts his goggles and lets them rest on his forehead.

A free one, he says. He frowns, running a thumb down the blade.

Johnny called last night to say the sun was rising over Singapore. Rising or setting, he did not know.

I don't know what day it is, he said. He was coming from Tasmania and he'd slept on the plane, lost track of time. His cellphone kept cutting out, or there was a zooming in and out of his voice. He'd woken her up. A telephone at night scares the hell out of her.

It might be Monday, he said. Or it might be Sunday. A big red ball hanging over the palm trees at the edge of a landing strip.

Have you ever tried to figure out the difference between what you are, he said, and what you have to become? He said it softly and Helen sat up straighter. Sometimes his voice was perfectly clear.

Johnny was capable of grandiose philosophizing while encountering a sunset; that was all. Maybe there was nothing wrong, she'd thought. He was thirty-five. He was somewhere in Singapore.

She thought of him: a day at the beach when he was seven years old, his tanned chest, his shins caked with sand. Some bigger boys had been whipping him with strips of seaweed, forcing him farther out into the waves. She'd looked up from her book. Helen had been lost in a novel one minute, and the next she was knee deep in the water, striding, screaming her lungs out. The boys couldn't hear her because of the wind.

Bullies, she screamed. You big bullies. You should be ashamed of yourselves. Then she was upon them and they froze.

He started it, Missus.

Look at the size of you. Just look. Pick on someone your own size. And the boys took off, plowing through the waves, glancing back, half saucy but scared.

Where had the girls been on that day? Cal must have given her a break. A day at the beach long ago, three decades or more, and now here was the dresser, her perfume bottle pierced by a street light, the brown liquid full of a still fire, the fringe of the rug, her housecoat on a hook; Johnny was a grown man. She was clutching the receiver. She was fifty-five; no, fifty-six.

What you have to become, she'd said.

Johnny was the kind of guy who phoned his mother infrequently, but when he did he was by turns pithy and incoherent and, inevitably, he had a bad connection. Or else something was wrong. He wanted to share the sunset with her; that was all, she'd thought. The sun was going down. Or the sun was coming up. But no, it was more than a sunset. This time he had something to say.

The proprietor hooks bright red skate guards over the blades and knots the long laces so the skates can hang over Timmy's shoulder.

There you are, you're all set, he says. He gives Timmy a soft cuff on the ear. Timmy ducks shyly. Helen sees the jawbreaker move from one cheek to the other.

Going skating, are you, the man says.

We're going to give it a whirl, Helen says.

The ponds will be good soon, the man says. We've had a nice stretch of weather.

They all turn to look out the window. The street has been sanded away in a blast of wind and snow.

. . . . .

Basilica, February 1982

THE *OCEAN RANGER* began to sink on Valentine's Day, 1982, and was gone by dawn the next day. Every man on it died. Helen was thirty in 1982. Cal was thirty-one.

It took three days to be certain the men were all dead. People hoped for three days. Some people did. Not Helen. She knew they were gone, and it wasn't fair that she knew. She would have liked the three days. People talk about how hard it was, not knowing. Helen would have liked not to know.

She envied the people who knew that the winds were ninety knots and could still show up at the Basilica in a kind of ecstasy of faith. Three denominations were at the altar for the *Ocean Ranger* mass and the whole city came out.

They didn't call it a memorial service. Helen doesn't remember what they called the mass or if they called it anything or how she came to be there. What she remembers is that no reference was made to the men being dead.

Helen was not church-inclined in 1982. But she remembers being drawn to the Basilica. She needed to be around the other families.

She cannot remember getting ready for the service. She might have worn her jeans. She knows she walked to the Basilica. She remembers getting around the snowbanks. The snow had been shaved by the plows. High white walls scraped smooth, soaking up the street light. There was nowhere to walk. The statue of the Virgin with snow in the eye sockets and over one cheek and the mouth like a robber's kerchief. She remembers that because already something was rising inside her: the injustice of being robbed.

. And when she got up over the hill there were people out on the Basilica steps. They couldn't all fit inside because of the crowd.

But Helen pushed her way through. She was supposed to meet her sister but she doesn't remember seeing Louise first or last. People pressing in on all sides and the organ and candles and incense. She remembers the candles and the lilies. More lilies than you could shake a stick at.

Helen's mother-in-law, Meg, was also at the church, but Helen didn't see her either. Meg must have been at the front. Cal's mother would have wanted to be close. Meg had a dream the night the rig went down. She dreamt a baby: I got up and looked out the kitchen window and there was a little baby in the tree branches all wrapped up in a white blanket. I said to Dave, I said, Go out and get that baby before something happens to it.

Everybody had some kind of dream the night the rig went down. Every soul in the whole province knows exactly where they were on that night. One of Helen's friends was coaching tennis at the Boys and Girls Club in Buckmaster's Circle. Just Helen's friend and a child prodigy, a seven-year-old tennis star, alone in the gym, and the vicious smack of the ball, and they had no idea about the storm going on outside. They came out of the gym and the car was a blob under a drift, a single marshmallow in the empty parking lot. The whole city had shut down. Another friend was supposed to waitress for a Valentine's dinner that had been pre-sold. Every table with a candle burning and a rose in a miniature vase, and there was duck in blueberry sauce for the main course; but the restaurant had to close and the owner asked Helen's friend to join him in a meal before they went home. After they'd eaten, the owner went around to each table and blew out the candles.

There were men out on the rig who had said goodbye before they went out, that was the funny thing. Some men phoned their mothers. Men who were not in the habit of using the phone. A lot of the men weren't used to saying how they felt. They didn't think that way. They certainly did not say *thank you*. Not *goodbye* or *I love you*.

They were in the habit of turning those sentiments into actions. They chopped wood or they shovelled. A big pile of wood stacked under the blue tarp out by the shed. They brought over moose steaks. They put in an apartment for the mother-in-law. They got up on the roof with a bucket of tar. That was *thank you*. Some of them were so young that to say goodbye would never have occurred to them. They couldn't think that far ahead. But even some of those kids in their early twenties phoned home. Called girlfriends. Said they were heading out to the rig and just wanted to phone before they went.

A lot of the men who died on the *Ocean Ranger* had gone out of their way to say goodbye, and it was strange. That's the way it got remembered. That's what everyone remarked on years later. *He called up just before he left.*

On the night of the *Ocean Ranger* mass Helen walked up the steps to the Basilica and said, Excuse me. She shouldered her way in and nudged forward and she was unapologetic.

She doesn't remember Louise and she didn't see Cal's mother or father anywhere in the church but they must have been there.

The organ thrummed a long, low note like a human moan. She felt that note in the soles of her feet; it vibrated between her legs, in her pubic bone and in her gut, turning her insides to water, and in her nose. It made her nose hurt and her eyes filled. The organ music went through her.

She was not church-inclined but some part of her must have been hoping for a hint about how to get through what was coming. She was numb and unbelieving, but she had three children and a kind of intuition about the pregnancy though she hadn't even skipped a period yet. Or if she had, she hadn't noticed.

Louise says, I was there. We said about the crowd and I gave you a tissue. I had a tissue in my sleeve. But Helen doesn't remember Louise.

The candles — there must have been hundreds on the altar, each in a little red glass, all slipping sideways in a blur when her eyes filled. She blinked and the candle flames became sharp stars and the stars threw out spears and her eyes filled and the flames became a wall of sluicing light.

This is a big cathedral, the Basilica, with vaulted ceilings and usually a chill, and that night you could not move because of the crowd. And the organ music was loud. People probably heard it on Water Street.

And the voices were just as loud. When people started to sing, the candles held their breath and then blasted brighter. Or the doors at the back blew open and the cold wind went all the way up the aisle and the candles flared.

Who came over to watch the kids? Helen didn't bring the kids to the church. She regrets that. Johnny was nine and Cathy was eight and Lulu was seven. Bang, bang, bang, one right after the other.

Three youngsters on the floor in diapers, her mother-in-law Meg had said, as if that was a plan. She should have kept the children awake that night, got them into their snowsuits. She wishes she had.

The kids should have been with her at that mass, but she wasn't thinking that way at the time. She doesn't know what way she was thinking. She had an idea she could shield them. Ha.

The candlelight moved in time to the organ music. A bank of golden light behind the priests — or whatever they were; ministers, an archbishop for sure — in their white gowns with their arms raised. The singing began and she had to get out.

The wavering high-pitched voices of the old ladies in the front. Those voices are distinct, they don't blend, they're on key but reedy, and they just don't ever blend or harmonize or join in; they lead is what they do, old ladies who come to church every morning, walking up from Gower Street or King's Road or Flavin Street after putting out some food for the cat and a dishtowel over the tan bowl with bread rising in it. They come in rubber boots with zippers up the front, boots that slide over indoor shoes and used to belong to the husbands, who are dead, and the old ladies have plastic rain hats they tie under their chins and wool coats with big buttons and permed hair and rosary beads in their pockets beside balled-up tissues. Those old women couldn't believe they had to look at so much sorrow so late in their lives. That kind of thing should have been over for them. They sang and the reedy sound was resignation. It takes seventy or eighty years of practice to master resignation, but the old women know it is a necessary skill.

And there were male voices, deep and full of the texture of trying to think. The men were trying to think of how to get through the hymn and the mass and find the car afterwards and drive back to the church to pick up the wife and youngsters so they wouldn't have to walk in the weather — I'll come back to get you, no need for you to get wet, you just wait on the steps there, look out for me — and these men were thinking of the traffic, and whether their sons or brothers were dead. Knowing they were dead — they all knew — but wondering if. Holding the hymn books out at arm's length, these men, because they were far-sighted, and squinting and nodding as if they agreed with the words they were singing, or were just glad to be able to make them out.

The men holding the hymn books had their brows furrowed and their wives were standing next to them. The cathedral was full of the smell of wet wool and winter, cold stone, incense, and near the altar there was the smell of candle wax and lilies. In some of the pews were whole families, little girls with ringlets or braids and dresses that hung out over their snowpants, red-cheeked, yawning, swaying back and forth. Toddlers asleep on their mothers' laps.

Here's why Helen left the church in the middle of the mass: Some of those people were full of hope. Insane with it, and the lore is that hope can bring lost sailors home. That's the lore. Hope can raise the dead if you have enough of it.

She was glad she hadn't brought the kids. What kind of people would bring their kids to this, she thought.

Helen knew, absolutely, that Cal was dead and she would be lucky to get his body back.

She wanted his body. She remembers that. She knew he was dead and how badly she wanted his body. Not that she could have put it into words then.

What she might have said then: She was outside. The best way to describe what she felt: She was banished. Banished from everyone, and from herself.

· · · · ·

Outside, 1982

BECAUSE OF THE children Helen felt a great pressure to pretend there was no outside. Or if there was an outside, to pretend she had escaped it. Helen wanted the children to think she was on the inside, with them. The outside was an ugly truth she planned to keep to herself.

It was an elaborate piece of theatre, this lying about the true state of where she was: outside.

She pretended by making breakfast and supper (though she often relied on chicken nuggets and frozen pizza) and she did the children's homework with them.

John bit the erasers off his pencils, chewed the gold metal until she could see his teeth marks, and there was nothing left but a bit of saliva-coated rubber that fell off the tip of his tongue when she held out her hand. He started chewing things after the rig went down. His teacher said John ate his pencils during class. He ate a pencil a week, the teacher figured. It can't be good for him, this teacher told Helen. He also chewed the cuffs of his shirts until they were in rags. He came home, and his cuffs were damp with saliva. And he ate his lunch with his mouth open, showing the food.

The teacher said, Kids will make fun of him. Just gently remind him, she said. Chew with your mouth closed. This is basic. One day I went into the cafeteria and he was sitting by himself. Big table.

Helen told this to John, and then he ate with his lips pressed hard and tight, eyes wide and fierce with the magnificent strain of being polite.

Helen did math with John, and she told him: Your fives are backwards.

They made a project about penguins with photographs from *National Geographic* and bristol board and Magic Markers. Penguins keep the one mate for life. They slide off the cliffs of ice on their bellies. Every now and then one will get eaten and the other will be left alone. These were the maudlin, sentimental facts about penguins. Johnny cut out photographs with his round-nosed scissors and glued them onto the bristol board and he made slanting lines with a ruler for the captions. His printing was atrocious.

Helen made the children sit at the table together for the evening meal. Always. Sitting at the table together was the cornerstone of her act.

She didn't bake. Helen put store-bought pastries in their lunches, and she put in cans of pop. She put in a ham sandwich with mayonnaise and Wonder bread. All the families of the drowned men were waiting for the settlement, because how do you feed four kids and pay Newfoundland Light and Power?

After a while she got a job bartending. Meg babysat and Helen worked when the bar called her in, and she found she couldn't count change. She'd look at the change in the cash register drawer and the change in her open palm and the five-dollar bill in her other hand and she had no idea what it all meant.

She got the orders wrong. Some people had tabs and she didn't know which people. Once she refused to serve a man and he offered to blacken both her eyes for her. Then you won't think you're so smart, he said. He picked up the phone and called the owner and gave her the receiver and the owner said, You're there to serve beer. Now serve the goddamn beer.

She cleaned up puke in the bathrooms and she'd leave at four in the morning and walk home. Cars crawling beside her on Duckworth Street. Men asking did she want a lift. Do you want to get in? I got something for you.

Once she screamed in a man's face and burst into tears and demanded to know: Where is your wife? Where is she? Don't you have a wife? The mirrored window rolled up with a whir and she saw her blotched face and the snot and tears and the halo of her hair lit from the street light and she didn't know who it was. Screaming as the car burned rubber. The smell of the tires and her face streaking in the glass.

The money from the bar was enough to keep her family in groceries until a man smashed a beer bottle on the corner of a table and held it to his girlfriend's face. The bouncer broke the man's back tossing him out and then Helen quit.

She called to the children from the foot of the stairs, her hand on the banister: Supper is on the table.

Johnny got a paper route and on winter evenings she and the girls followed him, waiting on the street while he banged on doors collecting change. He was ten and the baby, Gabrielle, was in a carrier on Helen's back. John had the idea that he should support the family. Saucy as a crackie, a corner boy. She'd watch him ring the bell and be asked to step inside.

Johnny chatted up the old men who came to their doors in bathrobes and scuffling slippers. Helen listened to the screech of their screen doors and watched as the old men looked up the street for a parent and saw her and the girls, and then they ushered John in.

Come in, my son.

Or there were the housewives digging through their purses. Ten years old, and Johnny would notice a new haircut or he'd say the supper smelled good.

He worked them for a tip, ten years old. He patted the dogs and stood talking while he handed over the paper.

Helen and the girls walked all over the neighbourhood while Johnny collected for the *Telegram*. When she got home she'd sit on a chair and Johnny would hold the backpack while she undid the straps, and when she had worked her shoulders out it felt like she was floating. She would put Gabrielle in the crib without taking off her snowsuit. Even the sound of the zipper could wake the baby.

She thinks of the smell of the *Telegram* bag John carried over his shoulder, the smell of frost and ink. The change spilling out of his wallet onto the kitchen table. Slamming his hand down on the rolling quarters before they got away. He wanted to buy groceries, so she let him. He bought tubs of ice cream and cookies. He'd give the girls a spoon each and they'd all eat from the tub there on the kitchen table. Once John bought her a steak. He was very proud of himself.

What a maniac Helen was if the children didn't come immediately for supper — I am putting supper on the table down here and I expect you to come when I Jesus call and I expect you to come immediately.

The girls flung themselves into their chairs. Laughing, talking over each other, reaching for the ketchup. Gabrielle learned to go up the stairs, her pudgy diaper wagging in the faded yellow sleeper. *Watch she doesn't fall. Are you watching that baby?*

Johnny would get up when Gabrielle woke in the middle of the night and bring her a bottle of milk. He was afraid of the dark but he made his way down the stairs into the kitchen, and Helen would hear the fridge and she would hear him coming back up the stairs as fast as he could. He would give Gabrielle her bottle and climb into bed with Helen, his cold feet on her shins. He always had a pain in his tummy. Rub my tummy, he'd say. It was stress. A little kid with stress. Nobody said *stress* back then. Growing pains, they said.

Elbows, Helen said at supper. Not on your sleeve. Use your napkin. Do you want to crack the legs off that chair? How many times do I have to tell you? Don't lean back. Don't bounce the ball off the walls.

She would not have the TV on during supper. She had an idea of what a family was and she would make them be one. Turn off that TV, she said. If she had a quarter for every time she said, Close the door; we're not heating the street.

John forgetting to use his fork. Use your fork. Use your goddamn. I'll cut it for you. Do you want Mommy to cut it? John hated to sit in his chair at the table. Can I be excused? No, you can't. I'm finished. You're not finished until everybody is finished; this is a family. Gabrielle is finished. Lulu is finished. Can I go now? Go then. Go. Go on if you want to. Go on out of it. Go for the love of God. Jesus, Mary, and Joseph.

And John tore around the corner and down the hall and out the door. Shut the door. Shut the goddamn.

Or John would wolf his food and then bounce a basketball. That ball is marking the paint. What did I say about the ball? I said don't bounce the ball off the. Look at the wall! Look at the mark on the. What did I say?

Standing by the table, dribbling the ball. She would not have any sauce, Helen told her children.

Don't back-answer me, young lady, if you know what's good for you, she said.

I'll tan your arse, she said.

John was this kind of kid: You'd have to say *Stop bouncing that ball*. The loud spank of it had an echo and the light over the dining room table would vibrate from the noise. This was a light with a fake electric candle and four plates of smoked glass around it and a bronze-looking chain that wrapped around the cord. It hung from the ceiling, and when John bounced the basketball, small rectangles of light jiggled on the tablecloth. This is a boy, ten, eleven years old.

Bunny ears, his sister Lulu told him. You make one loop, then you make the other loop and you fold this loop under that loop and you just pull tight. But John could not tie his shoes.

The girls drew on the sidewalk with coloured chalk — flowers and hopscotch. Cathy knotted elastic bands together in one long rope and put one end around the telephone pole and the other around Lulu's knees and she would jump onto the elastic and hold it down under her shoe. Or the girls played with a Footsie. One October the family had to listen to the screech of Lulu's violin for a half-hour every day after supper. Lulu had formidable discipline, her chin crimped up against the little plastic cup, the raw squawks so shrill they buzzed in Helen's teeth.

In the summer they bought ice creams and sat by the fountain in front of the Colonial Building. At dusk, fans of shooting foam burst up from the bottom of the shallow pool. Sheets of mist drifted in the breeze, covering their hair in a netting of tiny beads. No woman should be left alone to take care of four children, Helen had thought then, the baby with a wasp sting that made one eye swell shut like a prizefighter's. The music, faint, coming up from downtown, and the smell of barbecues, and kids on skateboards floating past — a Friday afternoon at suppertime after a day in the park.

She had John bouncing the basketball and Gabrielle in a high chair slopping food. Cathy and Lulu were capable of sitting still at the supper table. The girls could use a napkin. John wiped his face on his sleeve.

By *outside* Helen meant that there was a transparent wall, a partition between her and the world. She could be yelling her head off — *Stop with the goddamn ball* — but nobody heard her.

After the *Ocean Ranger* went down there was a very long wait for a settlement. People always want to know how much the families got, and Helen is in this camp: none of your goddamn business.

People who want to know about the settlement seem to think a life has a figure attached to it. A leg is worth what? An arm? A torso? What if you lose the whole husband? What kind of money do you get for that? They think a husband amounts to a sum. A dead husband does not add up to an amount, Helen is tempted to tell these people. People who want to know about the money don't know what it's like on the outside. They are still inside. Or they have never been in love in the first place. Helen watches those people with interest.

What she would like to tell people is that she and her four children waited a very long time for the settlement. There was a charity fund for the families, yes, and people had the best intentions, they were generous, but the charity didn't go far. She doesn't say that to anyone. But that money didn't go far.

It would be best if people don't get her started on that subject. Her sister showed up with groceries, is what she would like to say. More than once, and Louise didn't have extra either. Louise just showed up and started unloading the car and she didn't want to hear thank you. A week's worth of groceries.

Louise wouldn't hear thank you. It was a terse business between two sisters, putting those groceries away in the cupboards. Louise had gone into nursing and she was just getting started and didn't make much money then and she had two children of her own.

This is, Louise said. Don't mention it.

Thank you, Louise, Helen said.

Do me a favour and shut up.

Helen folded laundry. Matching socks was an act that looked very much like matching socks. She looked exactly as though she were in the world, engaged in the small work of *Here is one sock, now where could that other sock be?* And when she was done there would be an actual pile of socks.

She had the radio on all the time. Or she turned it off.

That's one mouth we can shut, she'd say. And snap the radio off.

The more time passed, the more convincing Helen became. There was the smell of chicken nuggets; there were bread crumbs under the toaster. She made lunches and had the oil company fill the tank and she went to the children's Christmas concerts. Her lowest point ever was when the pipes froze. Down in the basement with its earthen floor, low ceiling, and damp stone walls, going at the pipes with a blowtorch. The hawking sputter as the flame shot out, strange blue, and the hiss. It frightened the life out of her. She couldn't afford a plumber.

Louise did not miss one of Helen's children's Christmas concerts. Husbands and wives sit together at Christmas concerts, so Louise went with Helen. There was a program that went on for three hours, and there were costumes, and silver snowflakes hanging from the rafters, and the exuberant, insistent piano, and the dramatic gestures of the music teacher with her baton directing the overly animated, dead-serious kindergarten choir, *and now, and now*, and the children enunciating the syllables. Louise dying for a smoke. Louise falling asleep. Louise crying when Lulu played her solo on the violin.

But the girls became sophisticated fast, and harder to fool. So Helen took another job, she started sewing again, and she went to yoga. Nobody said, Have you thought about meeting somebody else? For a long time nobody dared.

. . . . .

John Likes to Phone Her, November 2008

HELEN SLEEPS WITH an eye mask to block the light. The phone: Singapore. She thought for a minute that it was Thailand, but it was not Thailand. Singapore was China. Or was it Hong Kong? It was a stopover. John was on his way to New York. He said about the sun. We're just touching down, he said. Getting fuel.

I'm having a little espresso, Johnny said.

The phone had rung and it might have been Louise with a heart attack, or God knows. Helen lifted the eye mask and saw how different the two kinds of darkness were. She could believe the world was made of atoms that buzzed and jostled, and if she wanted to, she could put her hand through the dresser, murky and insubstantial, and rub her nylons between her fingers, rub them away like fog on a mirror.

Her black cardigan hanging on the closet door. Always there is that high-pitched terror when the phone rings at night: Is someone hurt? Louise has had a few scares with angina. An ambulance last winter. Helen is frightened of the phone.

Her cardigan looked like a presence, a ghost. She was old, after all, and yes, years had passed. The bed flying over the edge of a cliff and a siren ringing out across the water and her body seemed to fall at a slower rate than the bed and she felt the bed hit with a *plosh* and then she hit the bed and began to sink, but it was just the phone, not a siren. The phone. Answer the phone. I'm certainly not old, she thought, snatching the receiver before she missed the call.

It was just the phone; it was just her cardigan.

Where are you, John, she said.

Mom, you're screaming in my ear. John could speak blandly when he wanted to make fun of her. He could be dry. She was not screaming. But she would try to speak more softly.

I'm in the Singapore airport trying to get myself an espresso, he said.

Helen heard a cash-register drawer snap closed. John had been all over the world on business. Tasmania was the most recent place. Meetings in Melbourne and then an adventure vacation in Tasmania. Some outdoorsy package. If you go all that way you want to take a few days, see the place, he had explained to her.

And now you're on your way home? Helen asked.

. . . . .

There's a Baby Coming, November 2008

TWO DAYS AGO I was feeding peanuts to a wallaby, John told his mother. Now I'm in the Singapore airport.

He had been reaching into his pocket to pay for the espresso and he'd pulled out a candy wrapper and wondered how it got there. A purple wrapper with an illustration of a comic-book princess brandishing her hand — on her hand was a giant ring she wanted someone to kiss — and John thought of the wallaby nursing its baby. How the mother wallaby had seemed both lulled and dangerous as the baby nuzzled at her teats. The mother had rocked and swayed while the little one suckled. Splotches of scouring light had fallen through the rainforest onto the hard-packed earth and boulders.

There had been a Japanese girl beside him, maybe eight or nine years old, in a yellow sundress. Her parents were a little farther down the path. John could hear their voices through the leaves. The little girl reached out to pat the baby wallaby and the mother wallaby hissed. Drawing back her lips to reveal mottled gums and yellow teeth. John put a hand on the child's shoulder. Shadows flickered across the ground like the raggedy end of a film in an old projector; there was a rush of wind high up, a shuddering light.

He'd made the little girl take a few steps back, his eyes on the wallabies. They were animals no bigger than mid-sized dogs and appeared to be as innocuous as teddy bears, springing up and down the trail. But they were not cute; they were wild — maybe rabid, for all he knew.

John was sure the mother wallaby would pounce and tear out the little girl's throat. Big eyes with thick, feminine eyelashes. John looked the mother wallaby in the eye, but if there was intelligence in the animal — something he could bargain with — John did not see it. The eyes were amber, a splintering of darks and lights, browns, rusts, golds, and devoid of anything other than dumb instinct. The mother shivered. The muscular tail thwacked a bush. Then the baby sneezed. *Ker-chew*. It rubbed both paws over its nose, eyes shut, a headshake, a clownish unclogging of water droplets and snot and mother's milk that startled them all, put things right, and both wallabies leapt through the underbrush and were gone. The little girl rolled her shoulder to release it from John's grip. Then she was running up the path away from him, her straight black hair flicking from left to right.

It was a five-hour hike to Wineglass Bay, and how white the sand of that beach had appeared when seen from the lookout above. And that's when John's cellphone rang.

They were a small crowd of tourists on the lookout platform. The sibilant *shuck-shuck*ing of cameras, the crescendo of surf from far below. It had been a hard climb, and now an eerie solemnity fell over the group. They felt mounting awe, and the inevitable dip from awe to irritation. What did any of them have in their ordinary lives that could measure up to the stark virginity of that beach? They'd seen signs down on the beach requesting that they not remove the seashells.

It seemed to John that the parents of the Japanese girl were bickering. They hardly spoke to each other once they reached the summit of the hike, and when they did speak their words were horked out, guttural and crisp, spat in the direction of their shoes. The mother lowered a pair of red-rimmed sunglasses from her hair and crossed her arms tightly over her chest.

The other fifteen tourists glanced at one another when John's phone rang, a techno-drone that brought back offices and subways and busy streets and cancelled the otherworldly whisper of criss-crossing palm leaves. John slapped at his pockets as if he were on fire.

He thought it must be his mother, but it wasn't his mother.

It was a woman he'd slept with months ago. A woman he hardly knew.

It's Jane Downey, the woman said.

John tried to think of her face and drew a blank. There was a hint of eucalyptus in the cloying heat. The smell made him think of Vicks VapoRub, the dark indigo of the glass jar. The *plock* when the metal lid was unscrewed and the welling aroma that cleared the fog of a half-sinister, seductive dreaminess. His mother had wiped a slick of it over his top lip and smeared it on his chest. Someone had told her to put it on the soles of his feet. This was when he was eleven and had a fever that kept him home from school for three days. He had missed a math test on that occasion. Dysgraphia — that's what the specialists called his condition later — made him see all numbers and letters backwards and sometimes upside down. John had overcome this, compensated, faked his way through. He could always get to the answer by going the long way around. He took engineering in university out of spite. He'd gained from his mild disability an unshakeable certainty that things were not always what they appeared to be.

Are you good? Jane Downey asked. John said about the beach and the climb. He talked about a zip ride he'd tried out a few days before — a long cable stretched across the roof of the rainforest, how he'd worn a crash helmet and how it had felt like flying.

Just so fast, he said. Once you jump off that cliff there's no turning back. Everything he said sounded as if it were translated from a dying language. Why did he talk about not turning back? The more he tried to keep the conversation light, the heavier it became.

I had some work in Melbourne, he told Jane Downey, and I took an extra week. A ferry to Tasmania. Thought, I'm here, check it out, right?

Absolutely, she said. Tasmania. Wow.

It's been a tremendous year, he said. And then: I thought you would be my mother. He turned around as he said this, half expecting to see Jane Downey stroll up behind him and tap him on the shoulder. He moved away from the cluster of tourists on the platform but the little Japanese girl followed him. Perhaps she'd heard the mewling tone that had crept into his voice. Like everybody else he had a phone voice, but he was not using his phone voice. His voice sounded guilty.

He had stopped himself from speaking to Jane about the feeling of accomplishment that came with taming a fear. He did not tell her how the zip-ride cables had squealed and sagged under his weight during the plummet. There was a video camera, he told her instead, in the crash helmet, and he'd purchased a DVD record of his ride.

They gouged me for it, he said.

I'd like to see that, Jane Downey said. She spoke with false gusto.

John could not remember anything false from the week he'd spent with Jane in Iceland six or seven months before. He had a presentiment that she was going to tell him something true and inescapable. He did not want to hear it.

Jane Downey had perfect skin, John remembered, pale and freckled and lit with honesty. There must be some inner virtue, he'd thought when he met her, to account for the uninjured beauty he saw in her face. He had been reading pamphlets that promised a dirty weekend in Reykjavik, blondes in bikinis cavorting in the Blue Lagoon. Jane was not Icelandic. She was from Canmore, Alberta.

John had been in Scotland on business and a friend had suggested Finland. He'd only spent a few days there; Finland was too austere for him. The people in Finland were either morosely sober or blind drunk, he decided. But from Finland it was a short flight to Iceland, and he thought, Why not? He liked islands. He'd heard you could run into Björk on the sidewalk.

Something old-fashioned, a rogue honesty Jane Downey probably wasn't even aware of and couldn't control — that's what he'd seen in her face. A girl from Alberta who was writing a PhD thesis in anthropology. She was in Iceland for an academic conference and they met in a bar.

The little Japanese girl on the platform in Tasmania reached into the pocket of her dress and took out a cellophane packet, and she tore it open with her teeth. She let the packet flutter to the ground, and although John had no memory of doing so, he must have bent and picked it up.

Littering is bad, he must have thought. He must have engaged the adding machine of morality, the subconscious work of ticking through the rights and wrongs he had committed recently, in case there was a need to defend himself. Jane Downey's false tone induced in him a vertigo similar to the vertigo he'd felt when he leapt off the cliff a few days earlier to zoom and swoop like some heavy-headed bird over the rainforests of Tasmania. He had not enjoyed the ride while it was happening. It had been something — he realized as soon as his feet left the cliff — he needed to get through. But immediately afterwards — legs rubbery, a crusty line of drool on his chin from breathing through his mouth and yelling his guts out over the treetops — he'd felt a luxurious clap of solitude, the sense that he would always be happy in his own company.

And now, as he reached into his pocket in the Singapore airport to pay for his espresso, there was the purple candy wrapper.

Inside the packet had been a plastic ring with a giant candy jewel. The little girl had put on the ring and sucked the candy, and it was faceted and red like a ruby, and the dye from it had stained her lips. The sun in Tasmania had caused the candy-jewel to pulse, and in the harsh light John had thought of it as emotion: the dull red light in the ring going flat and bright by turns, like a twist of love or fear.

John had felt pretty sure that when he and Jane Downey said goodbye at Heathrow almost seven months ago, it was with the firm understanding that there would be no phone calls. He had tried to work that former understanding into his conversation with Jane Downey. A slight reference — nothing crude or cold — to the fact that maybe she should ask herself what the fuck she was doing phoning him up out of the blue.

And now he was striding through the Singapore airport, and he desperately wanted his mother's advice. He had phoned his mother's number without giving a thought to what time it was at home. He had a desire, he realized, to be absolved. John wanted his mother to be indignant on his behalf, avenging. He wanted her to leap at the throat of the world.

The Singapore sun was blasting through the glass wall of the terminal. The airport was cool but a heat haze lifted off the tarmac, and it made the plane rolling slowly towards the building look wobbly. John took the candy wrapper he'd found in his pocket to a garbage bin and tossed it, but some sugary resin or static electricity caused it to stick to him. He shook his hand over the bin and the wrapper clung to the cuff of his shirt and slid down his pant leg and worked its way to the sole of his shoe. He walked with it attached to his shoe towards the endless expanse of glass that looked out over the landing strip. The sunrise or the sunset — whatever it was — and the disintegrating darkness above. The girl behind the coffee bar was calling to him — Sir, Sir — because he had her cup and saucer, but he ignored her.

His mother was groggy and panicked all at once.

The thing is, John said. I think I got somebody pregnant. Then he felt the candy wrapper under his shoe. He stepped on the wrapper with his other foot and the cup jiggled on the saucer, and he lifted the first foot and looked around to see who was watching him. The wrapper peeled off and then it was stuck to his other shoe.

John, his mother said.

She says she's having a baby, John said.

Who says? his mother asked.

A woman, John said. Who I slept with.

Whom, his mother said. She was half asleep.

With whom I slept, John said. He bent and removed the candy wrapper from his shoe and looked hard at it. The princess in the illustration had an oversize, threatening grin and the print below was in Japanese. He slid the wrapper through a vent in the air conditioner built into the ledge under the window. The wrapper rattled violently and was sucked from his fingers to become trapped in some flickering gadget inside the ledge. It created a low, sick whir deep down in the cogs.

My God, his mother said.

The shock in his mother's voice sent a shiver through John. He could see her sitting up in bed. That silly mask she wore pushed up on her forehead, her hair mashed flat on one side. Out on the landing strip several men in white suits were sauntering towards the plane. One of them was holding a wand lit fluorescent orange, and he turned towards John and waved it slowly back and forth. Who was the man waving at? It seemed to be a warning from a dream: *Get out of the way.* The plane was bearing down on the man with the wand, its white wings tinted pink with sunlight. The orange wand swished through the moist heat, back and forth, and then the man ducked his head and trotted out of view.

What did you say to her, John? his mother asked. The sun was as red as any sun he'd ever seen. Tropical pollution made it redder. The sun was shedding its beauty in spurts and jolts. The palm trees at the edge of the landing strip looked as if they were scrubbing the sky.

John had said to Jane Downey: Why didn't you get an abortion?

It was the first thing he'd said. Did that make him a bad guy? He had said it knowing it was too late for an abortion. He had said it knowing it was a useless thing to say.

And Jane Downey had hung up on him. There was just the platform and the giant boulders and the pale yellow dress of the Japanese child and the red candy ring catching the light.

It was uncanny: a woman so far away with his child in her womb. John had believed her, of course. He knew the world could be this way: A stranger might call you to account, wreck your life.

The Singapore sun bored into his skull and he was in the clutches of full-blown bafflement. Dazzled by how wrong it seemed. He had been wronged, and maybe he was wrong too, but his mother might absolve him. Everything around him — the chrome and black-vinyl furniture, the silver carpet, the white espresso cup — was stained red, a creeping blush.

On the platform overlooking Wineglass Bay John had glanced away from the little girl when Jane Downey announced she was pregnant, and he saw that the little girl's parents were making out. The man's hand under his wife's shirt, the shirt bunched over the man's wrist, the small of the woman's back. Her black, black hair cut in a straight line hanging just below her shoulder blades. John could make out the woman's panties through her tight white pants. The elastic on her panties, a lurid pink, rode up over the top of the low-slung waistband of her pants, cutting into the cheeks of her bum and making a voluptuous dent on her bare hip. The parents had not been fighting. They had been aching to touch. The air on the platform had blown in from Antarctica and it was the purest, cleanest air in the world. It made everything look too sharp. John had gasped. Then he'd blurted into the phone: Why didn't you have an abortion?

He wanted his mother to say that the pregnancy must be the result of an elaborate trick. Especially since he had been generous with laughter and good feeling and even money; he'd bought Jane an expensive necklace after a long discussion with the artisan who had fashioned it. Hardened volcanic lava, chunks of it. The kiss-off present, he'd admitted to himself on the platform in Tasmania. The necklace had been a way of saying he would remember the week for a long time. Or that he wanted Jane to remember it.

There'd been a tacit understanding, sealed with the necklace, that nobody would come out of a seriously fun and even deeply affecting week of fucking and eating and drinking fabulous wine and bombing around glaciers on Ski-Doos and putting white mud on their faces in eerie blue hot springs and dancing to live samba music in Iceland — that nobody would come out of that with anything but fond memories.

There had certainly been an agreement that there would not be a baby or anything remotely like a baby.

But Jane was six months pregnant. What the hell kind of thing was that to tell him on a cellphone? The little Japanese girl had pulled her candy ring out of her mouth with an audible *pop*. Jane Downey hung up, and like a fool John said, Hello, hello, and stared at the tiny instrument in his hand and then put it back to his ear.

Everybody knows wallabies are herbivores, the little girl said. And then: What's an abortion? John had assumed she didn't speak English.

The red Singapore sun shot out a fist and it socked John in the eye. Why couldn't his mother say that Jane Downey must be inferior in some way, a succubus, an old hag. Or an independent and beautiful woman — he remembered her face exactly: freckled, a wide smile, impish — who would be just fine on her own.

John wanted his mother to dig deep into the secret womanly knowledge buried in the pheromones and cells and blood of that murky, heady thing he thought of as femininity, and to report back: John, you owe that woman nothing.

A baby, his mother said.

· · · · ·

Dawn in St. John's, November 2008

HELEN THREW OFF the covers and pulled her cardigan off the hook and put it on over her nightdress. She went downstairs and switched on the fluorescent light while she listened to

John on the phone. The kitchen bounced up and fluttered out of the dark.

She listened to John breathe. Even on a cellphone, calling from the other side of the world, they could let long bouts of silence stretch between them. She would be babysitting her grandson, Timmy, today, and in the early afternoon there would be a trip to Complete Rentals for a staple gun, and then a trip to get skates sharpened. She had a carpenter coming tomorrow. A pork chop thawing on the counter.

But John had got some girl pregnant. There was going to be a child.

Two months after the *Ocean Ranger* sank, Helen's mother-in-law had told Helen she'd had the dream again about the baby in the tree. It was the same dream Meg had when the rig went down.

I think you're pregnant, Meg told her. And Helen realized her mother-in-law was right. She'd been throwing up every morning since Cal's death.

It was a beautiful little baby girl in the branches of that tree out there, Meg said. All wrapped in a white blanket, and it was snowing, and I said to Dave, Go out and get her, and he did.

Helen switched off the overhead light and sat in the alcove in the kitchen with one knee touching the cold window. It had been snowing. The black branches and the telephone wires and all the roofs and the railings of the fences had a white trim.

God, Johnny, she said. Remember when Gabrielle was born?

Gabrielle had arrived in late September. Helen's water had broken on the sidewalk outside Bishop Feild School, where she'd gone to pick up the children. The water leaked into her nylons in a cold, chafing patch. Cathy and Lulu with their Cabbage Patch Kids knapsacks and patent leather shoes; John with a Star Wars light sabre that glowed blue. He ran ahead of them and stopped suddenly, swinging the sword in big circles with both hands, holding off an invisible foe.

Don't cross without us, young man, Helen called out. Don't step off that sidewalk, Johnny. Helen walked mincingly along Bond Street, pausing during the mild contractions. There was a sky piled with gold cloud over the South Side Hills. It had rained all day and then cleared just before she had to go get the children. Every puddle reflected cloud and a white burning sun the size of a quarter. As Helen walked past the streaks of water on the asphalt, the white quarters slid along the length of the puddles until traffic sent a shiver through and broke the reflection apart in concentric rings so that the water became, for an instant, transparent and she could see the mud and cigarette butts and brown leaves beneath.

Helen had called Meg to come and take care of the children. Then she made a plate of crackers with peanut butter and jam. The shadows from the maple trees in the backyard stirred over the cupboard doors and the floor and the table. She just stood still at the kitchen counter, the butter knife upright in her fist, her giant belly tightening hard. The strange thing was that all the pain was in her thighs. Helen felt the contractions mostly in her legs and they were crippling. She lowered herself onto a chair beside John.

He had been watching her intently. Since Cal died, John had become watchful. He'd been sent to the principal's office a few times. There had been phone calls from the school. Johnny was watchful and his glass of milk was held quite still, just before his lips. He didn't move.

This is it, she told him. Helen wasn't speaking to him, but as she spoke she was looking into his eyes. The two of them were alone in the kitchen. What a thing to say to a child. This is it.

Then John put the glass of milk down carefully. How earnest he looked. A ten-year-old boy.

He drew his sleeve across his mouth. Helen was sitting in front of him with the butter knife, chilled by the breaking of a light sweat. Someone walked past the house with a boom box and the racket filled the hallway and thumped into the kitchen. A blast of racket zooming in and zooming out.

It is an afternoon that comes back to her. Not the birth itself; that was so fast. What's to remember? The butter knife in her hand. The weather. How the street glistened after the rain on that walk back from the school with her children. Johnny watching her, so full of fear he could hardly breathe. The shadows.

I can't, she said. Why had she said that? She remembered saying it.

I'll go with you, John said.

No, you absolutely won't. Helen retrieved some scrap of herself long enough to sound curt and dismissive. The child needed to be dismissed.

The taxi arrived and there was another contraction and she lowered herself to the front step, leaning her forehead against the rail. She could not stand or walk or get to the door of the cab, so she carefully lowered herself to the wooden step for a rest.

The taxi driver wasn't having any part of that. He took Helen's arm and eased her back on her feet. The slack, alcoholic features of his face winched tight to one corner, one eye crinkled shut, in an effort to keep his cigarette tilted up out of the way.

This is a fine state you got yourself into, he said. You're a piece of work, Missus, I'll tell you that. What did you go and call me for, he said. I'm just minding my own business. My lucky day, this is.

He lowered Helen into the back seat — she clutched both his hands — and he lifted her feet in since she couldn't move them herself, and he closed the door. The taxi was too warm and smelled of the wigwag of blue cigarette smoke hanging over the steering wheel and the pine-scented air freshener. Helen opened the door and threw up over the road. The driver jumped back out and ran around the back of the cab to hold the door for her. And then, careful of his polished shoes, he reached over and gathered up her loose hair and held it out of the way, his fist at the nape of her neck.

Nice one, Missus, the driver said. Heave it out of you, my love.

She swatted him away, so he stood looking off down the street until she leaned back into the cab, and then he closed the door and trotted around again to his door and got in. He tilted the rearview, and touched the cardboard pine tree hanging from a thread to stop it from twirling. When the pine tree was still he took his fingers away from it. Helen saw that he was rattled, and what was important to him was to appear composed, and he had better hurry up and get that way because they needed to go.

Then Johnny slapped his hand against the window.

Don't let him in, Helen said.

The driver leaned over and opened the front door. Get in, my son, the driver said.

This baby is coming now, Helen said. She clenched her teeth and hissed, Now, now.

A slow stream of smoke poured from the man's nostrils and the corner of his mouth.

Not in my cab, lady, the guy said.

. . . . .

Cab Ride to St. Clare's Mercy Hospital, 1982

GOD, JOHNNY, HIS mother said. Remember when Gabrielle was born?

John remembered the cab driver, with the greyest face he had ever seen and the most watery brown eyes. The eyes had squinted against cigarette smoke, and those eyes were calculating. There had been a school photo of a little girl taped to the dash of the cab. The kid was grinning like a maniac, her two front teeth gone. She had a red bow.

Years later, John had run into the guy at the Rose and Thistle and bought him a soda water. For a while the man and his mother had exchanged Christmas cards. In the pub, the man told John that he had gone to AA and become an electrician under the TAGs program. His daughter was going to sing at the open mike. John realized then that the man was a lot younger than he had thought back in 1982. Or this cab driver was the sort of person who could transform himself to survive. He could pull that sort of thing off. It was something John had thought at the time of Gabrielle's birth — that the two adults in the cab had transformed themselves. He'd thought that his mother was possessed by the devil, or something more ordinary and worse. And if there was to be a guide through the evil spirit world it might be this man with smoke streaming from his face.

Seat belt, his mother had screamed. Then she screamed it again. The driver and Johnny looked at each other.

Put on your Jesus seat belt, the driver said.

John's mother had thrown up in the car and in the elevator at the hospital. Bits of apple peel and a foamy pink spew that stank. She and John were separated as soon as the elevator doors opened. There were two nurses and a wheelchair waiting. They got his mother out, and she was sobbing and gasping for breath and telling them it was now, it was happening now. The elevator doors shut and he was still in there, and the elevator went down and it took a long time, and when the doors opened on the ground, there was his Aunt Louise. He stepped out of the stink and the doors closed behind him. Louise shouted his name.

What are you doing here, his Aunt Louise said. She slapped him on the arm. That's for nothing, she said. Don't try anything.

John pressed his face into her camel-hair jacket and hugged her so tightly he could feel her ribs moving with every breath. That's enough, Louise said. Let's get up there and see what's going on.

Gabrielle was born as soon as his mother hit the hospital bed, she told him later, and the baby was cleaned up and swaddled and the bloody sheets removed before John and Louise came into the room. Louise had tipped back the tiny white receiving blanket and stared. She had put her face close to the baby, to feel the infant's breath. Louise with her eyes closed.

Come see your little sister, his mother had said.

They're calling my flight, John said now. I've got to go.

Now, listen, John, his mother said. Are you listening?

I'm listening, Mother, he said. He said *Mother* with a brittle irony.

What did you say to her? his mother asked.

The espresso was thick and textured, full of velvety grit. His mother would not be absolving him. He could feel her taking the side of a woman she did not know, taking Jane Downey's side over her own son's.

She was going to make him take responsibility.

Watching the red sun over a runway in Singapore, John felt tears welling. He was exhausted, of course, jet-lagged and trapped. But he was also relieved. His mother would force him to do the right thing, whatever that was. She would know. They had been through this before, in a way. His mother had been possessed that day in the kitchen long ago. She had a butter knife in her fist and her mouth was open, and her eyes got big and shocked and she looked like she wasn't there any more. The sun struck the butter knife and made a square of jittery light fly over the table and flit across the ceiling. Her soul had fled and she had been taken over.

And she'd left him in the elevator. It was unforgivable. John's father had already done the impossible: His father had died. What he had thought, moving towards his mother's hospital room with his Aunt Louise: His mother must have died too. His aunt was holding a scrap of paper with the room number that the woman at reception had given her. Here we are, his aunt said. She rapped on the door, and then turned the handle and stuck her head in. John pushed in behind her. There was a bed in the centre of the room surrounded by a white curtain.

If the death of his mother was behind that curtain, John realized, he was unequal to it. He knew he was just a kid and that he should not understand about being unequal to anything. Most people didn't have to face that kind of realization until they were well out of childhood; he knew all that. But he had learned too early that you could be unequal to your situation.

Helen, are you in there, Louise asked. John saw a shadow waver, stretch tall, and shrink as the nurse, behind the folds of the thin curtain, moved in front of a concentrated oval of light. Then the nurse ripped the curtain back with a pragmatic flourish. The metal curtain rings on the chrome bar above the bed sounded like the spill of a brook. A delicate tintinnabulation announcing something big. A strong white lamp with a chrome shade was knocked askew and the light hit John in the eyes. The white of the white light: he closed his eyes against it.

He'd seen, just for a few seconds on his closed eyelids, the shape of his mother sitting up in bed, a floating bright orange shape with a violet aura. Then he'd blinked and a buzzing darkness had rushed in from the periphery and dissolved, and the nurse had switched off the big lamp with a loud *snap*. It took only a few seconds, and then the fiery insubstantial outline of his mother became solid. His mother had been restored to John. She was his everyday old mother, only more haggard and happier.

Come and see, she said. John moved in close and knocked against the table on wheels lodged just behind the gathered curtain. There was a basin with the placenta on the table. A solid mass of purplish blood, and he smelled it too — pungent, mineral, ozone-tinted, fishy and rotting smelling.

Don't mind that, the nurse said, whisking the bowl out of the room.

Over here, his mother said. Wet black hair, blinking black eyes, the tiny wrist with its hospital armband. Gabrielle had been his from that moment. She belonged to John. The little baby had been his to protect and love.

He was in the lineup now to board the plane. He should have called his sister, he realized, not his mother. Any one of his sisters would have been a better choice. But the mistake had been made. He was tired of the red sun, and tired of his mother.

How is Gabrielle, he asked.

She expects you to buy her a ticket home for Christmas, his mother said.

Gabrielle was in Nova Scotia studying art. She had made John a painting out of a red vinyl raincoat with the brass buttons still attached. It was ugly and he'd paid a fortune to get it framed and she had been pissed off.

Glass kills it, she'd wailed. You want to make it palatable. It's not supposed to match your frigging couch, she said. John had been mystified and hurt.

Call me when you get to New York, his mother said. We'll talk about the baby.

RENOVATIONS

A Blast of Wind, November 2008

WHY NOT LET the boy have a jawbreaker, Helen thinks. Then there is a blasting howl of wind and the world is whited out. The skate blade touches the sharpener and the sparks fly.

Helen had been to Complete Rentals earlier in the afternoon to pick up a staple gun and sixty clips of staples. There was machinery in neat rows all over the floor at Complete Rentals and a woman in a grey sweatshirt served her. A sign on the wall, beside a real cannonball attached to a chain and shackle, said RENT A TRIAL MARRIAGE.

So they were jokers, Helen saw, in the rental business.

The girl in the grey sweatshirt paused to look out the window. The snow required a pause. It hurled itself at the glass and the wind rattled down the eavestrough, and the girl said, Do you need a compressor?

Helen didn't know about a compressor.

If the guy you got working for you never said nothing about a compressor, you probably don't need a compressor, the girl said. They usually says if they wants a compressor. He's putting down a floor?

A man strode out of a back office and also paused to take in the weather.

A silence occurred and then there was a siren, far away.

There's a fire, or someone has had a stroke or heart failure, Helen thought. There was a spat of domestic violence or a holdup in the west end.

Last night she'd bought gas after Christmas shopping at the Village Mall, and it had been cold on her hands, working the squeeze nozzle. She'd gone into the glass booth of the station to pay and the young man behind the counter was reading *Anna Karenina* and he turned the book over on the counter regretfully. She saw the big Russian saga drain out of his eyes as he took her in. Helen and the smell of gasoline and a freezing gust of wind.

The coldest weather in fifty years, the radio had said. They would have snow. She had watched as the gas attendant dragged himself from a cold night in Russia, full of passion and big fireplaces and lust, back into the cold, lonely night of St. John's to take Helen's debit card, and she had felt motherly. The gas attendant was John's age, she guessed, but he was nothing like John.

If there's a compressor involved they usually says, the man at Complete Rentals agreed.

He didn't say compressor, Helen said.

Is he a good carpenter?

He seems to be good, Helen said. She thought of Barry hooking the metal lip of the measuring tape over the edge of a piece of two-by-four, marking it with the pencil he kept behind his ear, then letting the tape skitter back into the case with a loud *snap*.

Then he got his own compressor, the girl said.

After the skate sharpening, Helen drives her grandson to a shop to buy a second-hand helmet. Children aren't allowed to skate without a helmet these days, and at a red light she angles the mirror so she can see Timmy's face, and his cheek holds the jawbreaker, round as a moon.

· · · · ·

Water Everywhere, February 1982

SOMEHOW HELEN HAD picked up the idea that there was such a thing as love, and she had invested fully in it. She had summoned everything she was, every little tiny scrap of herself, and she'd handed it over to Cal and said: This is yours.

She said, Here's a gift for you, buddy.

Helen didn't say, Be careful with it, because she knew Cal would be careful. She was twenty and you could say she didn't know any better. That's what she says herself: I didn't know any better.

But that was the way it had to be. She could not hold back. She wasn't that kind of person; there was no holding back.

Somewhere Helen had picked up the idea that love was this: You gave everything. It wasn't just dumb luck that Cal knew what the gift was worth; that's why she gave it to him in the first place. She could tell he was the kind of guy who would know.

Her father-in-law, Dave O'Mara, had identified Cal's body. He told her this over the phone.

I wanted to catch you, he said. Helen had known there wasn't any hope. But she felt faint when she heard Dave O'Mara's voice. She had to hold on to the kitchen counter. She didn't faint because she had the children in the house and the bath was running.

It gave me a turn, her father-in-law said. I'll tell you that much.

There were long stretches in that phone call where neither of them said anything. Dave O'Mara wasn't speaking because he didn't know he wasn't speaking. He could see before him whatever he'd seen when he looked at his dead son, and he thought he was telling her all of that. But he was in his own kitchen staring silently at the floor.

Looking at his dead son must have been like watching a movie where nothing moved. It was not a photograph because it had duration. It had to be lived through. A photograph has none of that. This was a story without an ending. It would go on forever. And Helen was trying not to faint because it would scare the living daylights out of the children, and besides, she had known. She'd known the minute the bastard rig sank.

Dave said, It was Cal.

Helen lost her peripheral vision. She could see a spot about the size of a dime in a field of black. She tried to focus on the surface of the kitchen table. It was a varnished pine table they'd bought at a yard sale, and in that little circle she could see the grain of the wood and a glare of overhead light. She had willed the spot to open wider so she could take in the bowl with the apples and the side of the fridge and the linoleum, and then the window and the garden. Her scalp was tingling and a drip of sweat ran from her hairline down her temple. Her face was damp with sweat as if she had been running.

Dave said, They had bodies down there with just their ordinary clothes on and a few men who weren't fully dressed like they'd just left their bunks and there were some had their eyes open.

One man in particular, Dave said. Looked right at me. Draped in white sheets. Dave said, They looked alive, those men. He'd half expected them to move.

I can't get over it, he said.

Helen could think only of how frightened Cal must have been. He couldn't swim. She felt such a panic. She wanted to know exactly what had happened to Cal. She wanted that more than anything else.

Only twenty-two bodies, Dave said.

Helen was in a panic as if something very bad was going to happen, but it had already happened. It was hard to take in that it had *already happened*. Why was she in a panic? It was as if she were split in half. Something bad was going to happen to her; and then there was the other her, the one who knew it had already happened. It was a mounting and useless panic and she did not want to faint. But she was being flooded with the truth. It wasn't going to happen; it had already happened.

You don't want to see him, Dave said.

Helen was in the kitchen looking out the window over the backyard. She had the phone cord scrunched up in one hand and her other hand slipped a little on the Arborite counter and made a squeak. The tap was dripping, sharp pings in the stainless steel sink. She pushed the faucet so the drip would hit a dishcloth. She watched the faucet shine with wetness and watched as the wetness gathered into a drop and hung at the rim of the threaded washer and jiggled and fell and hit the cloth with absolute silence.

I wanted to catch you, her father-in-law said again. Before you left the house.

Helen had kept her own last name when she and Cal got married. Not many were doing that then. Nobody she knew. There'd been a dinner before the wedding and Dave O'Mara had said, I don't know what's wrong with our name.

It was all he'd had to say on the subject. He'd half lifted his wineglass and put it back down without drinking.

Helen had kept her own name, and when she found out she was pregnant with Johnny she decided to give the child her last name. Cal had been fine with that. He had liked the idea. He was all for women's lib. But her father-in-law had come by to fix the faucet over the kitchen sink. She'd been without the sink and the dishes were piling up. Dave had fixed the faucet and dried his hands and folded the pot cloth and patted it.

I'm going to ask you to do something for me, he said. I want the baby to have Cal's name. Our name.

Dave turned and put his tools back in the toolbox and closed the lid and flicked the two latches shut. He was down on one knee and he put his hand on his leg and pushed himself up from the floor. He hefted the toolbox and everything slid to one side with a *clang* and he met her eyes. Will you do that for me?

It was the only thing he'd ever asked of her during the ten years she was married to Cal. He had treated her just like a daughter. He'd fixed her plumbing and loaned her and Cal money and co-signed their mortgage when they finally found a house and he'd driven her to work. Helen couldn't drive. She didn't have her licence back then.

I can walk, she'd say.

You just hang on, Dave would say. I'm coming to get you.

He'd show up in the rain and wait outside and give the horn one toot, or later he'd call to say he was picking up the children from school, or he'd drive Helen to the supermarket and he'd wait outside with the newspaper crammed up against the steering wheel, the windows fogging. Her in-laws had walked in the rain when they were raising a family and they said there was just no need for it. Dave would call to say he was coming and Helen would hear Meg in the background.

Tell her to wait, Dave, until you get there. She can't walk in this.

Be watching out for me, he'd say.

The cars Dave and Meg bought always had the new-car smell, and the two of them were vigilant about upkeep and oil changes and winter tires. They would not let Helen spend money on taxis.

Tell her to save her money, Meg would say.

Hang tight, Dave would say. They would not let her walk the length of herself. Don't be dragging them youngsters out in the weather.

Her mother-in-law had babysat for Helen and offered to do her laundry and sent down cooked meals when the babies were born and had the family over for Sunday dinner every week.

Dave had called about Cal's body and Helen had leaned against the kitchen counter with the phone. She was looking out the window as she listened to Dave speak about the bodies in a voice that was intimate and far away. Dave had called to spare her. He wanted to tell Helen there was no need for her to go. He seemed to want to talk.

I took hold to Cal's hand, Dave said. His hand was there under the sheet. Had his wedding ring on. You'll want that ring, Helen, and I'll make sure you get it. I said to the man there, My son's wife is going to want that ring. I took Cal's hand and held on to it. I held on to his hand. I don't think you want to see him, Helen. I said the same thing to Meg. I said to his mother, I don't think you should go over there. That's all. That's what I said to her. That's all there is to it. Some of the bodies, I said. I said to Meg. I don't think you want to see. The place is all a shambles. It's orderly over there but there are a lot of bodies. I said goodbye to him, Helen, Dave said. That may sound foolish.

He was silent for a while and Helen didn't speak either. She could see through her window, over the back fence, the deep yellow square of light from her neighbour's kitchen. The neighbour — she was some kind of actress — was at the sink washing dishes. Helen watched her putting plates in the rack. Then a man was standing beside her. The actress turned from the sink and she and the man spoke. Not long, just a few words. The woman left the sink and followed the man into the dark hall at the back of the kitchen. Helen felt a welter of jealousy. The couple framed in all that yellow light, the white plate in the woman's hands as she paused to listen, and the man turning into the dark hallway. Why Cal? Why her husband? Why Cal? Then Dave spoke again.

I don't think we're going to get over this one, he said. This one is a hard one. Meg is in there in the bedroom. She went in to lie down.

It doesn't sound foolish, Helen said. Holding his hand and saying goodbye. That doesn't sound foolish. A giggle escaped her. She was so far outside of everything. Some half-hysterical sound came out and she covered her mouth with the back of her hand.

The light went off in the kitchen across the yard. The garden was dark now and Helen could see snowflakes. It was still snowing.

Dave kept talking and didn't know he was talking, but it was also an effort to talk; Helen could tell. Dave sucked in air through his teeth the way someone does when he is lifting something heavy. He kept saying the same things. He kept saying about holding Cal's hand. Not to worry about the ring. She would get the ring, he'd make sure. That Cal's glasses were in his pocket. That Cal had on a plaid flannel shirt. The receiver felt sweaty and it was dark early in the afternoon because it was February, and it would be dark for a long time. It was silent out in the dark except for the wind knocking the tree branches together.

Helen hadn't ever believed that Cal had survived, but the news of his body was a blow. She had wanted the body. She had needed the body and she could not say why. But the news of the body was awful.

There were people who went on hoping for months. They said there must be some island out there, and that's where the survivors were. There was no island. Everybody knew there was no island. It was impossible. People who knew the coast like the back of their hand. But they thought an island might exist that they hadn't noticed before. Some people said there might be. Those people were in shock. Some mothers kept setting the table for an empty seat.

Someone on one of the supply boats had seen a lifeboat go under with all the men strapped into the seats, twenty men or more, with their seat belts on, going under.

The morning of the fifteenth, Cal's mother had phoned the Coast Guard and argued with them.

She shouted, You've got the wrong information. The company would have informed the families if the men were dead. Meg hoped for the whole day and well into the next day. A great rage had blistered over the phone between Helen and her mother-in-law because Meg said there was hope and Helen didn't say anything.

I know he's alive, Meg said.

Helen had no hope at all, but like everybody else she had needed the body of her loved one. She had needed Cal's body.

She listened to her father-in-law talk about the bodies he'd seen, and her purse was on the counter and she picked it up and clutched it to her chest as if she were about to go out, but she just stood there listening. She thought about Meg lying down in the bedroom. Meg would not have bothered to take off her clothes. Maybe not even her shoes. The curtains would be drawn.

Helen had wanted Cal's body and now it had been found and she was afraid of it. She was afraid of how cold it would be. What kind of storage facility was it in? They must keep the temperature low. She was, for some reason, afraid of Cal's being very, very cold. Her heart speeded up as if she'd just run down the street, but she was stuck to the kitchen floor.

She wanted to ask someone what to do about the body and the person she wanted to ask was Cal. She was going over it with him in her head. Not thinking it out exactly, but telling him about the problem. She wanted to get off the phone so she could ask Cal what to do.

You don't want to remember him that way, Dave said. She heard a loud spank of water, a great gushing *slap*, and looked out into the hall. She had let the bath run over and the water had come through the ceiling. There was water everywhere. The children came out of the living room where they had been watching TV and stood at the end of the hall looking at her on the phone. Mommy, they screamed. The water poured down in fat ropes and thin sheets that tapered to a point and got fat again. Sheets of water that slapped the linoleum, and Helen shouted, Get out of the way. She told Dave she had to go. She ran up the stairs two at a time. When she came back downstairs the receiver was on the counter, buzzing hard.

She would call her sister Louise to drive her to Cal's body, she decided. She did not have to tell Dave or Meg she was going. She wanted to hold his hand too, no matter how cold it was. Maybe she would just sit outside the facility. Maybe she didn't have to look at the body. But she had to be near it.

. . . . .

The Carpenter, October 2008

HELEN SPILLED THE cleanser onto a sponge and went at the bathtub.

Helen had waited for Barry one month exactly. Back in the summer. He had come into the house and they had introduced themselves but they did not shake hands.

How strange, she thought, that they did not shake hands. Barry walked into her living room with his thumbs hooked into his belt loops, and he looked at the ceiling. For a while he didn't speak.

I'm going to tell you straight, he said. He stamped his foot twice. You're going to need a sub-floor, he said. His eyes were grey.

There's no way around it, he said.

Helen got under the bath with the Swiffer. It was a claw-foot tub. She didn't care half as much about the kitchen, but she liked a clean bathroom.

He's an excellent carpenter and reliable and you'll like Barry a lot. This was Louise's daughter-in-law Sherry. Sherry had said, He is very good. Sean's wife, Sherry: You'll like Barry a lot.

Had Sherry been trying to set them up? Helen froze at the thought, her outstretched arm still under the tub. Of course she was. Helen heard the reciprocal saw downstairs. The saw tore through, a revving up and dying down. But that's silly, Helen thought. She waved the Swiffer back and forth, big sweeps. She heard Barry walk to the foot of the stairs and she felt a hot flash.

I'm going to step out for a coffee, Barry called up to the bathroom. She imagined him on one knee, tugging on his steel-toed boot. She stood and saw herself in the mirror and she was bright red, with the sheen of a fast sweat on her forehead.

Okay then, Barry, she called.

Sherry had imagined her to be lonely. Helen was flooded with shame. The blood rushing to her head, making her ears ring. She would not be pitied.

· · · · ·

The Valentine, February 1982

THERE'S SOMETHING IN the mailbox, Helen said. A bright red envelope, big enough to hold the lid up about an inch.

Louise was leaning forward, holding the wheel. She wore her fox-fur hat and black suede coat and matching gloves, and she had on a dark lipstick. They had come from Pier 17, where the bodies were, and Helen had not gone inside to see Cal's body.

Louise had pulled into the parking lot and they had just let the car idle. Helen couldn't go inside. But she was glad to be there. Louise had picked her up and hadn't said much, and they'd just stayed there is all they did. They stayed for a while. The radio was on, and after some time Louise turned it off. She wasn't in a hurry. She took off her hat and put down the visor and smoothed her hair and put the visor back up. They didn't have to talk.

Louise reached over and opened the glovebox and rooted around, and there was a packet of tissues and she slit the plastic with her nail and tugged one out and Helen took it. Louise opened her purse and got out a cigarette and pushed in the lighter and waited until the lighter glowed orange and popped out.

She lit the smoke, her cheeks caving, and pushed the button so the window went down a crack, and she blew the smoke out the window. After a while she threw the cigarette outside into the snowbank.

Cancer sticks, she said. They watched an ambulance pull up and park, and someone got out and went into the building and the door closed behind him. After a very long time a woman came out and there was a man with her and he had his arm around her. He brought her over to a Buick and opened the door and the woman got in, and the man trotted around the front and got in himself and started the car, and they drove off.

Helen said, Okay.

Okay?

Let's go, Helen said.

You're not going in, Louise said.

I should get home, Helen said. She blew her nose as hard as she could. Jesus, Louise, she said.

I know, honey, Louise said. You're my baby sister.

And now they were sitting in the car outside Helen's front door. Louise's husband was a car salesman and they'd always driven a Cadillac because Cadillacs were big and safe, and Louise liked a luxury car.

A pickup truck came up behind them. The road was narrow because it wasn't plowed properly, and the truck waited for them to move.

Louise watched the truck in the rearview. She narrowed her eyes.

The guy tapped his horn once.

Go around us, you bloody fool, Louise whispered. Then she pressed the button and her window rolled down and she put her hand out and waved him around. Her hand outside the window did two slow turns and she pointed with one finger. The finger looked stern and mocking in her black glove. She drew her hand back inside the car. The cold air came in and all the noises of the street. She took two fingers of her glove in her teeth and pulled it off and then she tugged off the other glove, one finger at a time.

The driver of the pickup didn't attempt to go around them because there wasn't enough room. Only one side of the street had been plowed. Louise opened her purse with a loud *snap* and found the pack of cigarettes again without taking her eyes off the rearview.

Look at that fool, she said. There was a group of teenagers coming down the hill too. They had their coats open and their breath was visible in the air and they were bright-cheeked and loud. A scrawny girl at the back was full of shrill giggles. She was running to catch up with her friends and her boots slapped loudly on the pavement.

Helen knew the mail in the mailbox was a valentine from Cal. He always sent a card on Valentine's Day. He liked to mark all the occasions with a card. He liked the card to arrive more or less on time.

The lighter popped and Louise lit her cigarette and turned her head and blew smoke out onto the street. Then she tilted the mirror to watch the guy in the truck.

He pressed his hand into the horn. He kept the horn blaring for as long as he could, and then he let up and then he pressed it again. There was traffic behind him now and he couldn't back up. And he couldn't go around. The kids coming down the hill had stopped and gently collided with one another, their heads all turned, trying to see what was going on.

I guess I better go on inside, Helen said. But she didn't move. She felt like she couldn't move. Or that she *had* moved, had got out of the car, had lived out the rest of her life, and had died and was dead and was back in the car, a ghost, or something without musculature or bone. Something that could never move again.

The guy was out of the truck now and he slammed his door. He was in a fury and he brought the flat of his hand down on the roof of Louise's car and it made a hollow *boom*.

He bent down to look Louise in the eye and his face was very close. But Louise kept looking straight ahead. She took a draw on her cigarette and blew smoke at the windshield. The man might have kissed her temple if he were a couple of inches closer. His eyes were a pale watery hazel and he was bald, a pale face with high cheekbones and a weak chin, and his lips were pressed tight.

You're blocking the goddamn road, he said.

My sister's husband was on the *Ocean Ranger*, Louise said. We were just up identifying the body. But actually she didn't go in.

Louise, Helen said.

The man stood back from the window.

We're just sitting here now because we're worn out, Louise said.

The man looked back at his truck.

I don't even smoke, Louise told him. She was looking at the cigarette as if she didn't know what it was. She dropped it out the window.

It's a dirty habit, she said.

I should help you, the man said.

Oh, we'll be fine, Louise said. Helen put her hand over Louise's hand. Her sister was holding tight to the wheel. Louise always drove leaning forward slightly, gripping the wheel. She drove as if she required the seat belt to hold her back from something she wanted.

I'm going now, Louise, Helen said.

The man came around the front of the car and he opened Helen's door for her and he held her by the elbow as she walked as if she were an old lady. Or as if she was leaning on him. Helen was leaning, because she had a feeling she couldn't walk. She felt drunk. It took her a long time to find her house keys in her purse. Finally the man took the purse from her and dug out the keys and he opened the door and put the keys back, and he was standing there holding the purse. The traffic all down the road was backing up bit by bit and turning around and finding side streets. When the door was open, Louise toot-tooted and drove off.

Helen let herself into the house and it was quiet. The kids had gone to school that morning. They must have discussed it amongst themselves because they hadn't awakened Helen. They'd let her sleep. She took off her coat and hung it on the banister and she put her boots by the heater. The heat was off in the kitchen and she turned it on high. She put on the kettle and dropped a teabag into a cup, and she drank the tea without taking out the bag because she forgot to take it out. She had taken a butter knife from the drawer and it was lying on the table next to the red envelope. There was also a phone bill and some kind of flyer from a pizza shop. Then she just opened the red envelope.

There was a card with a picture of a big bouquet of red roses on the front. The words were in gold swirling italics and they said *For My Wife on Valentine's Day.* Inside there was a greeting-card poem that didn't rhyme about love. The poem touched on the meaning of a life and generosity and kindness and all the good times, and on the back, in extremely small print, it said the card was a product of China. Cal had written over the top of the poem, *My Love*, and he'd signed it at the bottom, *xoxo Cal*.

. . . . .

Baptism, October 1982

YOU SEE YOUR life but it's as though you are behind a glass partition and the sparks fly up and you cannot feel them.

You know it's your life, because people behave as though it is. They call you by your name. Helen, come shopping. Helen, there's a party.

Mom, where's the peanut butter.

There are bills. You wake in the middle of the night because you hear water and there is a leak in the kitchen roof. The plaster has cracked open and water is tapping on the tiles, faster and faster.

She did not want a tree the first Christmas after Cal died but Cathy demanded a tree.

Mom, we have to have a tree.

Hit the sauce. Do not hit the sauce. Gain weight. There are two outfits in her bedroom closet and they are both black because black is slimming. Because you didn't notice there were only two outfits and you didn't notice what colour; thirty pounds and you didn't notice.

Stop believing in meaning. Hurry by staying very still. There is no meaning. The unheralded velocity hidden in not moving; watch all of time flick by. *Tap, tap-tap-tap. Tap, tap-tap-tap* on the kitchen tiles. Hear the pause and the speeding up of time. She has spent many precious hours of her life helping her toddler (which one?) sort Cheerios on the high-chair tray. You fall into a kind of doze where the blue of the high chair looks more blue. It bristles with blueness. There's a pattern in the distribution of the Cheerios over the vibrant blue and the time between each drip from the tap, and then the big spoon comes down and all the Cheerios jump and skitter.

Don't cry in front of the children. Cry all the time. Eat meat loaf. Beg for forgiveness. Beg to go back to the wedding night or the birth of the children or an ordinary moment cooking in the kitchen or when there's a bill to figure out, a snowfall, skating on the pond. She thinks of an afternoon when they all went skating on Hogan's Pond. The wind blew the children and they sailed forward with their arms out.

John could skate. Johnny was in hockey. Cathy's eyes are exactly like Cal's, a medium blue with flecks of a pale blue and the iris rimmed in black, and the white of her eye is very white and she has his freckles — black Irish, Cal's mother said, the O'Maras from Heart's Content — and the trees were full of ice and the sun ran itself all over, sparking, flaring, and the wind crashed the treetops, knocking the ice off, and it shattered and rained down on the snow.

She and Cal liked the heat on bust. Sometimes they put in a fire. It was always stifling when Cal was home. He fell asleep on the couch. Shift work messed up his sleep and Helen would hear him in the early hours plugging in the kettle. He read in bed and she'd have to go to sleep with the light on. He slurped his tea and this infuriated her. Could you stop making that noise?

The youngsters want a tree: What are you thinking? Haul your sorry ass out of bed. Are you thinking you won't have a Christmas tree?

The phone company believes you exist; they cut off the phone. How dead a phone can sound when it is dead. It's time to shape up. It's time to smarten up. Get up, for the loving honour of God.

There is nothing on the other end. No sound at all. No buzzing. Just silence. Has there been lightning or something? Has the wind knocked down a pole out there? They cut off the phone and Helen was there with four kids; it was a safety hazard. And she couldn't even phone to find out what had happened; she had to go to Atlantic Place and use a quarter, only to hear them say, Oh yes, that phone's been cut off.

Fall apart. Take note: You are falling apart. Fat cow. You are now, my God, look at you, fat as a cow. You're listening but there's nobody there. Are you hearing me? I'm screaming at the top of my lungs here. How long do you imagine that money will last? Try harder.

Someone said, Get a grip.

Someone said, You have children.

Pretend it all matters. See this sneaker? It matters. See this violin? See this sale on prime rib? The earnest karate instructor. The earnest art teacher. Supermarket coupons. And this is how you make a mask from papier mâché. Look at my painting, Mommy. The whisk matters. Where is the whisk?

Do you smell something? You left the pot on the stove. You turned on the pot and you walked away. One of the children has an earache. There is fever; there is heat.

Let me tell you something: There are things you don't get over. But what matters is a tree. What matters is that you have to laugh if there is a joke. Look like you're having fun. And you can go to your room, young lady. You can't talk to your mother that way. I am your mother. You want a god-damn tree, I'll get you a goddamn tree.

There's a seventy-five-dollar reconnection fee. You received three notices.

Did I?

Absolutely; we never send out our field staff until three notices are delivered.

What did the notices say?

They said, Disconnect.

Where is her husband? Listen intently, even in your sleep, in case, just in case, he sends a message from the grave. This is what Helen expects and longs for. It's her due.

She sleeps and sometimes she dreams him, and it is wrenching to wake up. There is no talk in these dreams, no actual words in these dreams, but she knows what he wants; he wants her to follow him.

How awful. Death has made him selfish.

Forget the children. This is what he means. Forget yourself. Come with me. Don't you want to know what happened?

And she *does* want to know what happened. She wants to know so badly, but something is holding her back — the children, the roof, the phone. Is there a way to go and come back? Why can't Cal come back?

When she wakes up she is full of guilt because she decided to stay. Something rigid and life-loving and unwilling to cave in takes over. She betrays him in this way, every single night of her life, and it's exhausting. She denies him, she forgets him. Every time she says no to him in a dream she forgets him a little bit more.

She remembers the time he poured boiling water on his foot and the blister was as big as the palm of her hand, and how he left his sneaker unlaced and the tongue hanging out and he could not walk for a week, but she doesn't remember if that happened before or after the children.

She will never forget his face. She won't forget the green cotton scarf he had. Or the time he patched the canoe and there was the smell of Varathane.

To remember his voice she has to think of him speaking to her on the phone. She could feel if the phone was going to ring. She'd have a feeling, and the phone would ring and it would be him, and they'd say just a few things. About groceries, or did she want to get a babysitter and go out. Did she want to go to a movie? Helen thinks of Cal on the phone and she can hear his voice perfectly. Or she can remember his voice if she thinks of him singing.

If they were in the car she'd say, Sing me a song, and he knew Bob Dylan and Johnny Cash and every single thing Leonard Cohen had written, and he mimicked whoever the singer was because he was shy about singing, even when it was just her.

Or she remembers the way he held her hand when John was born, nearly breaking every bone, and how he wasn't afraid.

Or she remembers the times when they had to push the Lada to get the motor to catch. The guy who sold it to them saying the car didn't have reverse. He was going to charge an extra twenty-five bucks for reverse. They'd leave the two doors open and lean in and feel the weight of the car, and then when it started to roll they had to half-jog and jump in and pull the doors shut, and the car coughed and backfired and shook and the engine came on and there was a hole in the floorboards. She could see the asphalt under her feet.

She does not forget making love. She remembers Cal's smell. What he tasted like. The texture of his hair and his curls and the freckles over his chest, and if he had been out in the garden the tan line of his T-shirt sleeves, how creamy his skin was above that line. She licked his belly at the top of his jeans. She licked the waistband of his jeans and his belt buckle and the leather belt. And then she undid the belt and the snap of his jeans and the zipper, and she put her tongue on his cotton underwear and then her whole mouth.

He made her come, and waited and made her come again; this went on and on, she remembers. She does not forget that. And she remembers his legs wrapped around hers and his feet digging into the bed and his face with his eyes closed and the colour coming up in his cheeks.

She listens for his voice or a sign or advice. But there is nothing. She lives through the disaster every night of her life. She has read the Royal Commission report. She knows what happened. But she wants to be in Cal's skin when the rig is sinking. She wants to be there with him.

ONE AFTERNOON IN that first year after Cal died, Helen left Gabrielle with her mother-in-law so she could do some shopping. The older children were with Louise. She took the bus back to Meg's at the end of the day and she knocked on Meg's door and waited, and there was no answer.

It was mid-October and her breasts were leaking and they were hard as rocks and her nipples hurt; one of them was cracked and bleeding. It was still warm that late in the season and she could smell barbecues somewhere in the neighbourhood, and she went around the back.

Meg had her laundry out and the garden had been mowed. The geraniums had dropped their coral petals on the dark green deck. It was very still in the backyard and Helen opened the back door and went through the house calling, and then she stopped calling. She could hear water running. Water bashing hard against a deep sink, and a washer was going.

She came upon Meg with the baby in the laundry room. Meg was holding the baby over the big sink, and she had the baby dressed up in a long white dress that hung down over Meg's arm and a little beaded cap, and she had her eyes closed and she was praying with the tap running. Meg prayed and took a handful of the water and dropped it over Gabrielle's forehead, and Helen crept out quietly, unseen, back down the hall, and she opened the back door, careful not to let the spring screech, and ran down the street and around the corner and waited. She came back ten minutes later and Meg had changed Gabrielle back into her sleeper and there was no sign of the baptismal gown. Helen unbuttoned her blouse and Gabrielle latched on fast and her other nipple squirted fine threads of milk all over the kitchen table.

I've got a nice stew, Meg said. I'll heat you up a bowl in the microwave. It won't take a minute.

I'd love a bowl of stew, Helen said.

That little girl was as good as gold, Meg said.

Cal had refused to have the children baptized and there had been a fight. He had refused. Meg had been angry and hurt. What harm, she had asked Cal, but he would not relent.

Gabrielle snuffled in and sucked hard and the other breast was dripping fast and there was a drop of blood, bright red, on her other nipple and it slipped down her breast.

. . . . .

Wedding, December 1972

HELEN THINKS OF Cal's hands on his coffee cup: big, clumsy hands. Cal was tall, six foot two, and there was a kind of grace in his awkwardness. It was the dumbstruck objects, the things that leapt into the path of his hands and arms and knees, that were entirely without grace. Cal was just moving, just getting through, loose-limbed and unwilling to take into account the corner of the coffee table.

On their wedding night he broke a full-length mirror in the Newfoundland Hotel.

He must have touched it, knocked it in some way, but it seemed to spread with cracks all by itself. Helen wasn't looking, and when she did look there was mirror all over the carpet.

It broke by itself because Cal had glanced at it and all the bad luck to come was already in place. Everything was in that glance and it smashed the mirror.

Helen had left the reception in her wedding dress. She and Cal left their friends, and they left Helen's new mother-in-law in a shiny purple dress with a big corsage. Meg with her glasses reflecting the ceiling lights — this was at the Masonic Temple — and Louise smoking on the fire escape out back. Helen had wanted Louise to catch the bouquet. But Louise had been outside smoking.

They'd done the bride-and-groom dance at the beginning, everybody tapping spoons against their glasses, and they were out there on the dance floor all by themselves and Cal couldn't waltz himself out of a paper bag; neither of them could. So he just draped his arms over her and they did a couple of shuffling circles, self-conscious as hell, with the lights roving over them, and then he went under her big skirt to get the garter.

She lifted the front of the skirt, yards of satin, and the place went up with catcalls and clapping and someone pulled a chair out to the centre of the dance floor so she could put her foot up on it. Cal got on his knees, inching the garter down, and the men were clinking beer bottles together, and Helen dropped the skirt over his head. She let the whole thing fall over him and he, like a clown, stayed under a long time, just his shoes sticking out.

He put his mouth on her. There on the dance floor. His head a lump under her skirt, and she put her hands on that lump, both hands. His fingertips just barely touching the front of her thighs. Stroking her thighs. He breathed hot breath through her panties while she stood there. She had to close her eyes. She played along, fanning herself like crazy, and everybody cheering and laughing. Everybody whooping it up. And when he came out he had the garter swinging around on his finger.

After a while, Helen wanted to go. She found Cal on the dance floor and dragged him out by the bow tie. She tugged one end of the black shiny bow and the thing came undone with a little *pock* and she seesawed it against his neck and he caught the end of it in his teeth, and then she dragged him, step by step, off the dance floor by the bow tie.

Everybody cleared a path and the band tapped the drums with each exaggerated step Cal took, as if he didn't want to go, as if she were a temptress, as if this were it, the big night, and she was going to chew him up and spit him out and he was frightened to death. He made big terrified eyes and kind of growled, and then he leapt off the dance floor and the band drum-rolled and they were gone out the door and down the steps.

They had his parents' car for the night, and how conspicuous they were, checking in at the front desk of the Newfoundland Hotel. Helen had a going-away outfit but they hadn't bothered to change. The chandeliers and Persian carpets and a waterfall in the lobby. Cal's tux with black satin trim on the lapels and the bow tie already undone and the shirt with the big frills, and each frill with a line of black piping, and the whole thing untucked because he hated the tux and couldn't wait to get out of it.

They were just kids experiencing adult luxury for the first time, and it was a lark and utterly serious. Helen marvels at how serious they were.

Just twenty and twenty-one.

She was knocked up, but that wasn't why they got married. Or maybe it was. They didn't choose to get married; they did it for their parents or they did it for the big party or they did it because deep in some not-often-used part of their brains, they believed in ritual. Lapsed Catholics, they believed subconsciously that a wedding could weld them together. But they were already welded and Helen had missed her period and she'd told Cal and he'd held her.

Just put his arms around her, and she could tell he was wishing it wasn't happening so fast. Cal wanted a little bit of time before they had youngsters, Helen could tell that.

But he didn't say.

Wow, he said. Or he said, Great. Or he didn't say anything. He moved his hand vigorously up and down her back as if she were a friend in need of consoling. A good buddy who had lost a big bet.

And she had put her arms around him, too, when she told him about the pregnancy. They had been standing in the kitchen. Cal's sweater smelled of cigarette smoke and she pressed her face into his chest and felt the roughness of the wool against her forehead, rubbed her face against that roughness. This was his Norwegian sweater with the suede patches because he'd worn out the elbows and his mother had said, Leave that sweater with me. Let me fix those holes.

This was, Will you marry me? Or, I guess we should get married? Or there was a slight pause while Cal gathered himself together. After all, this was a baby. They were talking about a baby. For Helen, twenty years old had felt very old, very mature, but for Cal it felt as if the two of them were just starting out.

Wow, he said.

In the Newfoundland Hotel the bellhop scooped up Helen's train to help her into the elevator. Someone winked. A businessman opening a newspaper on the couch in the lobby winked at Cal. Helen remembers the bellhop, careful with all the satin. He had a cotton ball in his ear.

The doors of the elevator closed quiet as could be and Helen put her hand on the ruffles of Cal's shirt and pushed him back against the elevator wall and stood on tiptoe and kissed him, pressed against him; and the doors opened. There was an elderly couple waiting, and they saw her kissing him and saw the dress, and they took a step back and didn't even get in the elevator.

Cal was so tall that sometimes in the kitchen Helen would stand on a chair to give him a proper hug. She would haul the chair over and get up and he'd turn from the eggs frying on the stove and bury his head in her breasts and put his arms around her and squeeze hard, and she'd kiss the top of his head. And then he'd go back to the eggs. He would always have the music blasting when he made breakfast.

Cal put the key in the hotel room door and opened it; the room was big and they looked out the window and they could see the whole city. It was snowing. Snowing over the harbour and the ships tied up with their rusting flanks and sharply curving bows and orange buoys piled up on the deck, covered with snow; and snowing over the white oil tanks on the South Side Hills and the cars on Water Street, their pale headlights catching narrow fans of falling flakes; and snowing over the Basilica. And the Christmas lights looped across Water Street.

Then Cal inched her zipper down, all the way to the small of Helen's back, where he had to jerk it because it was caught. He threw himself onto the big bed. Helen crunched the whole dress down, stamped her way out of the mountains of scratchy tulle with her patent leather spikes.

And Cal had glanced at the hotel mirror. His face with its freckles and sharp intelligence, and his gangly arms and unfamiliar clothes—he was naked beneath the tuxedo shirt, and he'd dropped the pants on the bathroom floor, the jacket over the desk—and his black curly hair and his big blue eyes, and the gentleness and humour in them, and all the lovemaking to come. Helen remembers the unadulterated energy it took to keep the enterprise in motion from that moment, one baby after another, and the jobs, the bills, snowsuits, dinner parties, disappointments—sometimes she had been immobilized by disappointment—nights on the town, staggering home in each other's arms, dragging each other up the hill, and the stars over the Kirk, graffiti on the retaining wall; all of that was in the mirror in the Newfoundland Hotel on their wedding night, and—*POW*—Cal glanced at it, and the mirror spread with cracks that ran all the way to the elaborate curlicue mahogany frame, and it all fell to the carpet, fifty or so jagged pieces. Or the mirror buckled, or it bucked, or it curled like a wave and splashed onto the carpet and froze there into hard, jagged pieces. It happened so fast that Cal walked over the glass in his bare feet before he knew what he was doing, and he was not cut. It was not that the breaking mirror brought them bad luck. Helen didn't believe that. But all the bad luck to come was in Cal's glance, and when he looked at the mirror the bad luck busted out.

They didn't even think about the mirror then because they were making love, and afterwards they ordered spare-ribs and put on the terry cloth robes and steamed up the bathroom, soaping each other in a shower so hot they turned pink, and they lay on the bed and tried the TV.

They were just kids putting on a kind of maturity. Trying it on for size. No idea what they were getting into. Acting big.

But it was like Helen's mother said: Get that look off your face or the wind will change.

Helen and Cal ate the ribs and had sex and let the heavy door close on the world and smashed the mirror or walked through the mirror to the other side, and then they were mature overnight. They had changed overnight, or in an instant. They were married.

Helen can bring herself to the point of weeping just thinking about Cal's yellow rain jacket that came to his thighs and the rubber boots he wore back then and the Norwegian sweater with the elbows out of it and how he rolled his own cigarettes for a time, which was unheard of (he had other pretensions: he made his own yogurt and tofu, grew pot, experimented with tie-dye), and how he wanted a house around the bay for the summers, and how the children came by accident, every single one of them. Cal was a reader, of course; he read everything he got his hands on. They both read. Helen had a book in her overnight bag and so did Cal, and after they'd had sex and showered and looked through the TV channels and eaten and drunk some more beer, they each got out their books, and they had the bedside lamps on. They fell asleep like that. Cal with a book over his chest.

Neither of them had paid any attention to the Church; whatever the Church said about birth control they had ignored entirely. The trouble was that they simply could not keep the idea of birth control in their heads. The smell of latex and spermicide — they'd done that the first few times, maybe. The idea of birth control had been a hard one to keep hold of. Have you got a condom? I thought you had them. I thought you had them.

And Helen had thought, when she was pregnant, It's a boy and he will be like Cal, and my son will be like that: black hair and blue eyes and thousands of mirrors smashing in his wake.

But of course John looked nothing like Cal. He was not clumsy and he looked like her, exactly like Helen.

· · · · ·

Jane Telling John, November 2008

JANE IS AT the airport in Toronto. She'd been on her way home to Alberta and she had discovered, in the terminal at Pearson Airport, that she could not go home. She'd been sitting at a crowded Tim Hortons with an apple-cinnamon tea and her laptop. There had been an email from her father. The baby had jabbed a toe into her spine. A toe or a drill bit.

A young woman with drawn-on eyebrows is working the Tim Hortons counter. She has the sweet smile and shiny scalded complexion of someone on antidepressants, and there is a scar, a soft white wrinkle, running from her nose to the top of her misshapen lip.

The customer in front of Jane had wanted an oatmeal raisin cookie, and the girl, whose wide backside was squeezed flat in polyester pants, could not see the oatmeal raisin cookies.

Right in front of you, the customer said. The girl's plump hand with the square of wax paper hovered over the donuts and a blush crawled up her neck.

Oatmeal raisin, the customer said. She was wearing a glossy black plastic coat that squeaked when she lifted her arm to point. A clean, uncomplicated sound. Jane felt glad to be back in Canada. She was sick of New York, the grime and abrasive twang and the poverty she had documented — *unflinchingly*, her supervisor had said — in her master's thesis. She was leaving after four years, just as things were about to change for the better.

Second shelf from the bottom, Jane said. Three trays over. No, three. One, two, yes. Jane listened to the woman unfold her arms, the moist plastic making kissing sounds. She thought of the snow over a field of stubble back home, and the Rockies off in the distance, smoky and white-capped. She was at the peak of a euphoric hormonal surge.

Oatmeal, the customer said again.

Raisin?

Oatmeal. Raisin.

The Tim Hortons girl snatched up a cookie and dropped it in a paper envelope. Anything else, she said. A gold ring hung from her nose like a drip. Then the girl got Jane's tea and stood with it in her hand, staring forward with what might have been paralyzed awe or a prolonged yawn. She gave herself a little shake and put the cup on the counter.

When's your baby coming, the girl asked.

February, Jane said.

I got three at home, the girl said. My brain went out with the placenta. But it's not too bad because I live near the airport so I get to work easy. My mom helps out.

Jane got a table and pried the lid off the tea and the steam smelled of apples, and she felt the baby's hand — she thought it was a hand — wobbling her tight tummy.

Then she read her father's email. Jane would not be staying with her father after all. She pressed her eyes, first one, then the other, with a crumpled paper serviette.

We'll go it alone, Jane whispered to the baby. What she had actually thought, throughout the six months of the pregnancy so far, was that her father might help her. Maybe he would drive her to prenatal classes, she'd thought. Jane's father might let her stay with him until she was on her feet. But it turned out that Jane's father wondered, as he stated clearly in his email, what in the name of God Jane had been thinking.

Jane's New York friends from university had been titillated when she told them she had not contacted the baby's father. These friends had thrown her a shower in her colleague Marina's tiny apartment — just ten or so women from Anthropology — and they'd lowered their voices when they mentioned the subject of single parenthood. They'd sounded reverent. They were all in their mid-thirties and most of them were childless because they'd lost themselves to academic careers.

But they were excited about the shower. In the spirit of parody they'd resurrected old games. One of them, Lucy, brought a video camera because she wanted to use the resulting material object in her FemCrit class. They ate retro appetizers. Cucumber sandwiches on white bread with the crusts removed, an aspic mould with tinned fruit cocktail, pigs in a blanket. Jane was forced to put on a pair of stockings over her jeans while wearing oven mitts. Her friends dressed her in a shotgun-wedding dress made of toilet paper. Everybody was given a chance to design some part of the dress, and the prize — a hand-held cappuccino foamer — went to Elena, who constructed a bustle over Jane's ass that took an entire roll.

Someone passed a crystal platter of devilled eggs and the faintly sulphuric smell reminded Jane of the water from the taps in the Reykjavik apartment where she and John O'Mara had spent the week together months earlier. The shower and kitchen tap in Reykjavik stank, even after they ran it for five minutes, but John had assured her it was good to drink. The devilled eggs made Jane feel off kilter.

It's your body, absolutely, Jane's friend Rhiannon said. The guy knew he was taking chances, right? I mean, he wasn't a total dummy. Rhiannon popped half an egg into her mouth and seemed to swallow without chewing.

Jane lay on the floor while another friend, Michelle, held a needle swinging from a piece of thread over Jane's belly. The needle circled and stopped and swung in a line and circled again. The needle would not make up its mind.

Maybe it's a little hermaphrodite, Gloria said.

Michelle told Jane about a cousin whose baby's head had been stuck in the cousin's pelvis for eight hours of pushing.

That's apparently when the pain is greatest, Michelle said.

Imagine — too big, Rhiannon said. She made a face as if the egg had lodged in her chest. She thumped herself with a fist.

What size is your baby's father's head, Michelle asked.

Jane got up off the floor and began unwinding her toilet-paper wedding dress. Marina stacked the paper plates, and removed one end of a blue streamer hanging over the entrance to the kitchenette and began rolling it in a tight coil.

You don't even really know the guy, Elena said.

After the shower was over, Jane had phoned her closest friend since childhood, Keri Farquharson, a marine biologist with three golden labs and a new husband, who had recently moved to Maine. Jane had put off telling Keri about the baby.

It was one week with the guy, Jane said. Almost seven months ago.

Phone him, Keri said. The dogs were yapping in the background and Jane heard Keri open the door and the dogs burst out into what sounded like a wide, open space. Then a screen door slammed.

Jane was surprised by a weeping jag and she could not trust herself to speak.

Jane, Keri said.

Yeah, Jane said. But it came out as a high-pitched wheeze.

Phone him, Keri said. She must have moved into the kitchen, because Jane heard boiling water and a pot lid crashing into the sink.

I would be better off by myself, Jane said. A profound welling of sorrow had ballooned in her chest. She could speak only in chuffing spurts. Keri could be lacerating. This was why Jane had finally called her.

Don't you think your kid is going to want to know her father, Keri asked.

The baby kicked and wedged an elbow under Jane's rib. I'm as big as a bloody whale, Jane said.

You need to think about the baby.

I *am* thinking about the baby. But Jane had been thinking of John O'Mara, and the night the two of them had been together in the bar with the Cuban musicians. Reykjavik at four in the morning, and the light still bright with long shadows, but there had been a chill in the air and she and John were both drunk. Arm in arm in the courtyard outside the bar. The next day they'd woken up in the early afternoon and all of Reykjavik had been out on the streets for a big parade. It was Independence Day. The crowds waving tiny flags and, near the harbour, a strongman strapping himself to a transport truck. The man planned to move the truck several yards simply by putting his back into it.

I want to be independent, Jane said to Keri. But the truth was, she could not face the idea that John would be angry or sullen or sarcastic or anything other than — but she could not imagine. Her girlfriends in New York had been right: Jane hardly knew him. Her imagination migrated to her ribs, and the baby wedged an elbow under them and made them go numb, and she could not imagine John at all.

The extra week in Reykjavik had been John's idea. Jane's conference had ended and she was ready to go back to New York, where she was finishing her PhD thesis, and John said, Stay with me. I've got a little apartment for the week.

Light pouring in slanted shafts through the dusty windows of the bar, and cigarette smoke hanging above their heads like pulled taffy.

I'll pay for everything, John said. Later, when they were both coming out of the bathroom at the same time, John backed her against a grungy wall and wedged his knee between her knees, gently prying them open. He worked a thumb under the button on the cuff of her blouse and he moved his thumb in circles on the inside of her wrist, hardly touching. It stirred her all through. It was like stirring a lump of sugar through a cup of tea. He was stirring horniness through her sluggish drunken self. Back at the table he held on to the end of her long silk scarf, playing with it, flicking it with his fingers. He took the very end and let it touch his lips. Someone at the table said there was going to be a volcano in the sea. You'd get to see an island rise up out of the ocean. Someone said the glacier was magnificent.

And out on the sidewalk in Reykjavik, the windows of buildings across the square were bright pink and winking, and Jane allowed John to throw his arm around her shoulder.

It had been one week. That was all. And so, for a long time, Jane had decided not to tell him about the baby. She stood at the kitchen counter in her New York apartment and heard herself practising his name, as if she were about to call him and casually mention *I'm pregnant*, and his name had sounded more like a sound than a name, a sound shaved of all meaning.

Just do what you think is right, Keri said. She was banging something, a ladle, against the sink. Three sharp raps. It sounded like a gavel dismissing court.

I've got to clean up here, Keri said. Bill will be home any minute. And so Jane said goodbye to Keri and phoned John, and John said about an abortion — *Why didn't you have an abortion?* — and she hung up on him.

The idea had formed itself almost at once after that: Jane's father would let her stay with him. Jane's father was going to be a grandfather. He could help. She had sent her father an email and packed and got a flight back to Canada the very next day.

Jane's mother had died five years before of breast cancer, and a little more than a year later her father had married a woman named Glennis Baker. Jane's father had told her this in an email — the first she had ever received from him: that he was marrying a woman who wrote climate-modelling software. He made a comment, not without innuendo, about getting a firm grip on the newfangled technology and lots of other new things.

Glennis Baker was unassuming and not cold to Jane but they had met only once, during a brief Christmas visit when Jane was home between semesters. When Jane thought of Glennis she thought of gloves sitting on the dining room table. Black leather gloves that still held the shape of Glennis's big hands, the knuckles shiny, fingers curling up, and in the palm of one glove, a set of house keys. Years ago Jane's mother had bought a handmade plaque for keys and it used to hang in the back porch. The plaque was varnished wood and it had the family name burned over small brass hooks. It had been crafted at the penitentiary where Jane's mother had been a social worker in charge of rehabilitation. The key holder was now gone from the back porch, but the paint was less faded where the plaque had been and the screw holes in the wall looked raw. When Jane had returned home for the Christmas visit, she'd found her father doing all sorts of chores he'd never done before: sorting laundry, stacking the dishwasher. His wardrobe had changed. He had answered the front door wearing a pink sweater-vest.

Jane's father owned a riding stable with more than forty trail horses and four full-time employees. Jane had mucked out stalls and hauled water and hay bales and managed the cashier's booth in the summer, handing the tourists insurance waivers before they headed into the paddocks where the saddled horses waited with their reins looped over the rails.

It had been a sun-struck childhood spent outdoors in all seasons. Jane had never heard her parents quarrel. Theirs had been a marriage marked by a lack of turbulence, lasting forty-five years. Jane's father was a vigorous man with a demanding, satisfying business. He had moved with shocking ease into a new relationship a year after his wife's death.

But three years ago there had been an accident with rodeo horses during a six-day trail ride to the Calgary Stampede that had left him frail and unfathomable. A train had spooked the herd as they were going over a bridge on the outskirts of the city, and nine wild horses had fallen into the swollen, charging river and the animals had broken their legs or backs or necks.

Jane's father had been hired for the ride to oversee the tourists. The deaths of the wild horses seemed to have affected him more than the death of his first wife, which he had weathered with a distracted grace. After the accident with the horses he phoned Jane and wept for a long time. Her father described the frothing mouths of the animals, and their terror, the whites of their eyes as they tried to keep their heads above water, and how finally they had gone under for good and there had been nothing he could do but stand on the bank and watch them die. I had a bad feeling, her father said. That ride should never have happened.

Several months after the accident, Jane had received another email from her father. It seemed he had thrown off his torpor; he had joined the Knights of Columbus. He followed this statement with three exclamation marks. Things are much better, he wrote. He typed *much* in capital letters. He was seeing less and less of Glennis, he said, because her work absorbed all her attention. He mentioned that he had begun donating money on a monthly basis to an animal rights agency in the name of Jane's mother. He had visited Jane's mother's grave that very morning, he said, with a bouquet of roses he had picked up from the supermarket.

I like the idea of a nicely kept grave, he wrote. I am thinking of commissioning a new stone, he said. They have a new grey speckled marble at a masonry store downtown, and it's softer looking than the solid black. I'm thinking of a gloss finish. Your mother was a classy lady, he wrote. Graves have to be maintained!

Jane felt sure he'd crafted the last statement, with its single exclamation mark, as a kind of plea. But she could not give herself over to the shrill calm in the email. She was working on her thesis. He has a new wife, Jane thought at the time. Let her take care of it.

Jane was at the Tim Hortons in Pearson Airport when she opened the email from her father about the baby.

The baby needs a father, he wrote. As far as he understood Jane's situation, he said, she was by no means financially secure. She could not expect others to assume the cost of her carelessness. It was that kind of thinking that had the whole world in the mess they were finding themselves in right now. Had she thought of the state of his portfolio, he wondered. Had she realized every penny he had made over the years had been saved and invested, and he was watching those investments shrivel on a daily basis, and soon he might have to sell off some of the horses. Maybe let somebody go, too. Those boys have been loyal, he wrote. They've been like sons.

He also told Jane that Glennis Baker had moved out and that Glennis had taken an end table Jane's own mother had refinished in a course she'd done alongside the inmates at the pen, and that was an end table Jane's father had meant to leave to Jane. He asked Jane: Do you ever think about anybody but yourself? She had not finished her studies, he reminded her. Jane was making a mistake. Adoption is the only recourse, her father wrote. He hoped that she would do what was best for the baby. Thank God your mother was spared this, he wrote. I'm glad your mother is not around.

Now Jane looks for her phone, but when she finds it she just presses it against her chest.

The girl from the Tim Hortons has wedged herself out from behind the counter and is methodically spraying the tabletops with a squeeze bottle of blue disinfectant. She stops by Jane's table and puts one hand on the chair back opposite Jane and leans in. Her slowly blinking eyes take in Jane's face and the cellphone in Jane's fist and the fist pressed to Jane's chest. The girl breathes in through her teeth and sighs deeply.

Can I get you something, she asks.

. . . . .

John Lucid Dreaming, November 2008

JOHN WAS IN a youth hostel in Tasmania the evening after the astonishing phone call from Jane. He had paid extra for a private room but in the kitchen down the hall there was a woman from Sydney, Australia, along with her daughter, cooking a meal. He wandered into the kitchen, and when he sat down the chair scraped over the tiles.

He said at once about Jane and the baby. He said about Iceland. He told the whole story. The woman from Sydney chopped onions, one hand on the knife handle, the other on the top of the blade. The knife rocked hard, up and down, and the finely shredded onion piled up, and John's nose hurt and his eyes watered.

I've been to Iceland, the woman said. I had my throat slit in Iceland. John looked and saw that she had a thick white scar across her neck.

He had dreamt, the night before, a pedal-operated flying machine, creaky, with some kind of animal skin stretched over the wings. In the dream he had decided to land on the roof of Atlantic Place at home in St. John's. This was how he practised lucid dreaming. He became aware that he was dreaming and he tried to change the course of the dream. He tried to make it bend to his will. This time he wanted to land the flying machine on the roof of a building a few streets up from his mother's house. Then he would climb down the fire escape and walk home.

He had managed to fly, in the dream, to the outskirts of the city. But at the last moment the dreamscape morphed out of his control and he'd crashed in a marsh of bakeapple bushes.

When I was a student, the woman in the kitchen said, I worked in a cod factory in Iceland. This was years ago. I had a station on a conveyor belt that ran over a light table. I was checking for worms in the cod.

She took the chopping board to the stove and scraped off the clump of onion and it fell in the pan and the hot oil roared. Checking for worms, fillet after fillet after fillet, she said. She slid the spatula under the onions and they hissed and stuck and she tossed them over.

Last night, John suddenly remembered, he had also dreamt a fish on a chopping block and he had forced himself, in the dream, to examine the fish very closely so he could see each individual scale, opalescent and silver, tinged with blood. But when he got to the gills of the fish, the skin lost its scales and became pink and wrinkled, and the fish had a baby's face. He had awoken exhausted.

The woman's daughter was chewing gum and she was about seven years old. The child sat with one knee drawn up on the chair, reading a comic book.

A bloke from England, the woman said. Comes in, decides to joke around, turns the hose on me, he had no idea about the pressure. This was a pressure hose used for cleaning the concrete floor. Everybody in the factory just stopped, the woman said. The machines shut down all at once. She was cupping a pile of bean sprouts and she opened her hands and let them fall in with the onions.

They were all looking at me, she said. I reached up and touched my throat and looked at my fingers and there was blood, and next thing, I couldn't breathe. The water from the pressure hose had cut my throat and I couldn't breathe and I passed out.

After his father died, John had a vivid recurring nightmare. Every night, for a long time, a presence would seep through his bedroom door. An evil presence, in the form of a cloud, wet and cold. It swirled over his bed, full of weather and stars, and settled on his chest, and as it grew heavier, John felt a paralysis creep through him until he couldn't move. Then the cloud took on the form of a naked old woman who squeezed her hands over his throat. He'd feel himself suffocate. Sometimes it was an old woman, sometimes it remained a cloud, but always he'd felt awake, alert with terror, and he could not breathe.

Then John would wake for real, soaking wet, his hair stuck to his face, sometimes screaming. If he screamed, his mother would come and hold him. He began to sleep with his bedroom light on and insisted all the bedroom doors in the house be left open at night. An old woman whose face changed shape; or sometimes there was no face, but she climbed on top of him anyway.

John's mother had sent him to the guidance counsellor at school. The counsellor said John had been visited by the old hag. He said that in outport Newfoundland they used a thing called a hag board. A piece of wood with nails driven through one side that you could strap to your chest, nails standing out, and the hag couldn't sit on it. It was folklore; it wasn't true. Nobody really used a hag board, the counsellor had said, but the old folks talked about it.

There was a hag board, the counsellor had said, made by an artist, in the Newfoundland Museum on Duckworth Street.

John could also see, the counsellor had said, the doeskin dress and moccasins of Shawnandithit, the last of the Beothuks. Shawnandithit's skull had been taken off to the British Museum and lost during the bombing of London, along with lots of other skulls that had been collected from all over the world like trophies. Hundreds of skulls, the man had said, in glass cases, and the roof caved in and the glass popped and all the skulls rolled together and that was it, you didn't know who was who.

They got me to the hospital, the woman told John. She was slicing a deboned chicken breast into thin strips. And sewed me up.

I have a bottle of wine, John said.

Wine would be nice, the woman said. The child turned a page of her comic book and blew a bubble that burst over her nose and chin like a mask.

It was dark all day and all night in Iceland, the woman said. She was reaching up into a cupboard but could not reach. She drew a chair over and climbed on it and got the plates. I never saw the sun, she said.

John knew he should have helped her but he was thinking about Jane's phone call. He was thinking about Jane hanging up and how he had no way to get in touch with her.

The woman put three plates on the table along with forks and knives, and she lifted the lid on a pot of basmati rice. A huge billowing of steam lifted up. The lid was hot and it clattered into the sink.

Just watching all day for worms, the woman said. The stink of fish. And then my throat. The British guy on top of me, his hands around my throat. Holding my throat together.

The school counsellor, it seemed, had wanted John to know he was right to be afraid. There were very real things in the world to be afraid of. He had taught John some lucid dreaming techniques. These will help you cope, he'd said.

There's more, John had told the counsellor. He shifted in his chair, one leg kicking the desk in front of him rhythmically. She does stuff.

Sexual stuff, the counsellor had said.

It's terrible, John had said.

You orgasm, the counsellor had asked.

Yeah, that, John had said.

I hope you like ginger and chili, the woman said. This is a dish with lots of hot spice.

Where's the father, John asked. The little girl's father?

I don't have a father, the little girl said. She turned a page of the comic book.

When I was in Iceland, John said. It was twenty-four solid hours of light. We never slept.

. . . . .

Joke, 1981

CAL WOKE TO somebody hammering on his door. Men shouting the rig was going down. She's going down. He leapt out of bed to hit the light switch and his feet were wet. Water rushing under the door and more water through the door frame and the door was jammed. Something was holding the door shut and he banged on it with his fists and must have hit the lamp because the light was rocking on the bedside table, and he shouted, Let me out, there's a man in here, let me out.

Cal told Helen about it over a plate of spareribs. The door gave and there were the boys, killing themselves laughing. They were doubled over. They had poured a bucket of water through the crack and held the door shut, listening to him bawling.

There's a man in here, there's a man in here.

Killing themselves, Cal said. Laughing on the other side of the door.

Helen put the plate in front of him. She had parboiled the spareribs and then dumped a full bottle of barbecue sauce over them and left the ribs in the oven on low heat for the whole day, and the house was full of the smell. It was his favourite meal.

Often it was just the two of them in the kitchen and Helen would have a beer. Cal would look down at the plate before he touched it. His arms resting on the table.

It looked like he was giving thanks, Helen thought, but he was taking the time to recognize that the floor was solid under his feet.

The rig was big enough that the men could not feel the water moving beneath them, but they felt a marked difference in their balance when they came on shore. Cal would let the plate sit in front of him and he would notice how solid the floor was, and the table and the house and the ground beneath the house.

Then he would pat down the mashed potato with his fork. He always started that way, patting the potato, rallying the peas into one corner with the side of the fork.

Helen made sure to feed the kids early on the first night Cal was off the rig. The children would practically knock him over when he came through the door. They'd tackle him. John climbing onto Cal's neck, Cathy with her arms and legs wrapped around his leg, Lulu flat on the floor clutching his ankle. He'd stagger into the living room with them clinging to him. Or he'd come through the door and they'd keep watching TV. They'd move towards him with their heads turned towards the TV. They would keep watching and they'd hug Cal loosely without even knowing what they were doing.

There had been a bad list on the rig a few weeks before it went down and the men all went running for the same lifeboat. They ran to the wrong boat. Each man had an instinct about the direction to take and it was the wrong instinct.

The rig was the size of two football fields, and try to imagine how small in relation to the ocean around it. The crew had scheduled safety drills but they didn't show up. They slept in. Men who had been on the night shift stuffed towels over the speakers so the announcements about safety drills wouldn't wake them. They slept through.

The men were afraid of the helicopter, especially when the fog was thick. If they muttered in their sleep it was about the helicopter. Nobody could imagine the rig going down. The men broke bones or lost a finger. That was common. They were expected to keep on working if it was just a bad sprain or a minor break. A severed pinkie didn't get a lot of sympathy. That was an occurrence they saw every month.

There are men who would kill to have this job: that was the wisdom they worked under. And: the helicopter was a terror. But it was impossible to imagine the whole rig capsizing.

If the men did imagine it, they did not tell their wives; they did not tell their mothers. They developed a morbid humour that didn't translate on land, so they kept it mostly on the rig.

Cal patted the potato and told Helen about the men pouring the water through the door so that his feet were wet, but Helen didn't get the joke.

That's not funny, she said. And Cal looked up and saw her and didn't see her.

They all knew they weren't safe. Those men knew. And they had decided not to tell anyone. But it leaked out of them in larks and pranks and smutty puns, and it leaked out sometimes in a loneliness that made phone calls from shore hard to handle. A man would get his wife on the phone and have nothing to say. Great swishes of static and silence.

Helen was busy with the girls. She could not think about the rig because she could not think about it. And John was a handful. Cathy was having problems with schoolwork too. Helen made sure the spareribs were so tender the meat was falling off the bone. She had a case of beer and she made sure the kids were in bed early. It wasn't for Cal exactly. It was so she could sit down opposite him and watch.

This was not a meal they had together, because she'd eaten already. She'd eaten with the kids because she was hungry and because she preferred to just watch him.

He would look down at the plate before he picked up the fork and he was still on the rig in that moment and he could feel the ocean under him, though it was a kind of motion he never noticed when he was actually on the rig. It was a motion he felt only on land, and usually when he was dreaming. He could feel the bed sway while he slept, but only on land. It was the absence of the motion that he felt.

He picked up the ribs in his fingers, pulled the meat off, and he licked his fingers. He licked his thumb first and then his index finger and his ring finger, and he took his time. He was mostly absent while he ate, not aware, intent on the food. He put the bones on a saucer.

Cal had two separate lives, and when he and Helen had the money together they were going to buy a convenience store with gas pumps. They had gone over it, and if they both worked at a business like that they were pretty sure they could make ends meet. They were certainly putting money away. But they didn't speak of those plans. Because if they talked about Cal giving up the rig, they were admitting the risk. And it was something they had agreed never to admit.

. . . . .

Jane, November 2008

JANE TAKES A bus into Toronto from the airport, and then a streetcar towards a hotel she remembers staying in before, but she goes the wrong way. She gets off and crosses four lanes of traffic, dragging her luggage. It is almost dark and very cold and she has a number of books in her suitcase. The sidewalks are full of ice and the wind is at her back. Her hair stands out straight around her face. Snow swishes across the asphalt in thin veils, coiling and twisting up towards the sky.

She had asked a man pushing a shopping cart for directions and now he is following her. His cart brimming over with garbage bags full of pop cans and plastic bottles, the wheels plowing through slush. Jane had given him money and he'd shoved the bill into his jeans pocket without looking at it.

The man speaks in a kind of stage whisper, his eyes shooting back and forth, watching the crowd on the sidewalk, his words a melodic, insistent patter about dolphins and the beauty of marine life, the sway and flow of the ocean, and the creatures that break the surface, flying up out of the water and splashing down. He makes an undulating gesture with his hand, whistling through his teeth, blowing hard bursts of breath through his wet lips like the sounds of a dolphin frolicking in the waves. Coast of Mexico, he says, shaking his head as if he can see it stretching out in front of him.

Jane excuses herself and ducks into a grocery store. She is hungry for something raw and sweet. Mist shoots down with a hiss from an overhanging shelf onto a bank of red cabbage and pale lettuce and bok choy and fennel. It drifts down onto the dirty beets and broccoli, and she runs her hand over the ruffle of wet herbs, the smell of earth and cilantro.

Jane passes over the green apples and buys a single peach that comes in a fluted paper cup of dark purple. She is ravenous. There are three tables gathered under the sputter of a nearly broken fluorescent light and she takes a napkin from a chrome dispenser and rubs the fruit. The peach is so soft it is almost rotten and she bites it right to the centre. The pit bleeds a deep crimson stain into the orange of the flesh. She tries not to think of the texture of the peach skin; the fuzz gives her shivers like someone walking on her grave. Juice dribbles down her chin and she can feel a flutter from the baby. Her chin is sticky, and her fingers, and they smell like summer. The tips of her ears sting from the cold, and as she rubs them they begin to burn. It is as if the baby has felt the erotic pleasure of the peach and has kicked out to tell her.

Back outside, the man with the shopping cart is waiting for her. The wind takes the heavy door of the store from her hand and smacks it against a cinder-block wall, and Jane struggles with the suitcase. One of the wheels is stuck in an iron grating. The man leaves his cart and grabs the suitcase, twisting it through, and then the shoulder strap of her laptop bag breaks.

And *boom*— she knows. She does not want to have a baby by herself. The world is full of suffering. It is dark and cold. She is afraid of all that could go wrong. She needs a father for the baby. She needs John O'Mara.

She thinks of that morning with John in Reykjavik, the Independence Day parade streaming past him, the brass and the drums and a glockenspiel, the crowds jostling against them both. How exhilarated they had been. He'd gone back to find her scarf. She'd dropped her scarf.

The dolphin man is going up the stairs of a streetcar backwards, dragging her suitcase.

What about your shopping cart, she shouts. The suitcase bounces and jitters up the steps, and the streetcar's folding doors clamp shut on it and open and clamp shut again. Then the dolphin man is inside, knocking his way to the back, the suitcase smashing against knees and hips.

Mexico, yeah, Mexico, he whispers. He squishes his way through to the back of the streetcar, and he sits next to a woman who gets up and moves, and he slides to the window seat and slaps the seat beside him, and Jane sits next to him. The man has a pitted complexion and he is unshaven. His front teeth are grey and soft looking and a few are missing. He speaks to Jane as if they are deeply involved. He speaks as if his life depends on convincing her of something obvious and urgent.

Surfing off the coast of Mexico with a pod of dolphins, the man says. Hundreds of those babies, they were just playing with me, man, leaping out of the waves, they were dancing, those fellas, they really knew how to have fun.

Jane saw so much of this craziness while writing her thesis on the homeless in New York. She interviewed two hundred vagrants, an ethnography of indigence in the slums and projects. She discovered that the cold and the rain, hunger and loneliness, made people delusional. It was no more or less complicated than that. The world fell away from them or it blew through them. Scraps of dreams blew through.

This man will sleep outside tonight, Jane knows. The streetcar's brakes wheeze and there is a crowd waiting at the next stop. Someone dings the bell and the cold rushes in and swirls down to the back.

Jane thinks of John the morning after she first slept with him. She'd wanted a lamb kabob and he had found her one and then he said: Your scarf. Where's your scarf? And she touched her neck. The booming drums, and then somehow he ended up in the middle of the marching band, and he bent down, and when he stood up he got knocked on the head by a tuba. The members of the brass section scattered and the parade got backed up. There were unharmonious groans from the trumpets, and then they reformed the tight marching lines, eyes bulging with consternation, cheeks full of spittle, and John had her scarf. His fist shot up in triumph: the scarf of shantung silk she'd bought for herself in Santa Fe.

More dolphins than you could imagine, the man on the streetcar says. I was filled with wonder. Coast of Mexico, coast of Mexico.

John had dragged her into the National Theatre of Iceland after the Independence Day parade. How dark after all the sunshine. He'd found a back door because someone had said *architecture*, someone had said *closed to the public*, and there was a ballerina in the middle of the stage in a tutu and a mask of silver glitter. She raised her arms and spread two giant wings of white feathers, and she rushed towards Jane and John, and just as quickly rushed away on her toes. The janitor threw them out at once. He reprimanded them in Icelandic and then told them in English: Get out, damn you.

More dolphins than I've ever seen in one place, the man says. His eyes are glistening with tears, or perhaps because he has spent the day in the wind, or maybe his eyes are infected. His cheeks are wet and his eyes rheumy and bloodshot, lids puffy. I'm a marine biologist, he says. Or I was. It was the most beautiful sight I ever saw, them dolphins. He wipes one of his cheeks with the back of his hand.

They accompanied me, the man says. He is looking deeply into Jane's eyes, an unblinking scrutiny, and of course she is tired. But she feels close to this man. She is astonished by how much she feels for him. She loves him. It might well be love. Perhaps she is coming down with something. A profound tenderness. She wants to be accompanied, that is all.

A little-known fact, the man says. Dolphins often try to have sexual intercourse with their trainers. He smiles at their audacity.

Yes, Jane says. I've heard that.

The Independence Day parade in Reykjavik had flooded into a town square at the bottom of a hill, and there was the transport truck: a black cab and silver grillwork and a lengthy cargo container as big as a bungalow. A strongman had stepped out of the crowd. He wore black Lycra and his head was shaved and he had a strut. He raised an arm and curled his fist and turned the fist in towards his own forehead as if it were a threat he had to protect himself from by staring it down. The muscles in his arm were bowling balls. Two men in white overalls came out from behind the truck. They were carrying a huge tangle of straps and ropes and chain, and they strapped a leather harness onto the strongman.

Jane wants to call the father of her baby again. That's what she wants. Jane will call him. What if she needs him? What if raising a child requires the kind of strength she does not possess?

The strongman had leaned away from the truck and the chains went taut. Then he staggered, one step, another, then another. A cheer went up, a roar, and the transport truck rolled several yards.

I have to call someone, Jane says to the guy on the streetcar. She whispers so as not to startle him. But she wants to explain. There's a guy I have to phone, she says. She clicks her purse open and digs for her cellphone.

Dolphins try to have sex with their trainers, the guy whispers back. But of course they don't have the right appendages for that. They don't have, you know, those things, but they've been known to try.

I've got a card, Jane says. She takes John's card out of her wallet. She presses in the number and lets it ring.

Hello, John says.

It's Jane Downey again, she says.

Don't hang up, John says.

Okay, she says.

Promise you won't hang up.

Okay, I won't hang up, she says. The streetcar pulls up to another stop and the man beside Jane leaps up and past her, and stands in front of the doors looking at his feet, and then the door swings open and he turns back and calls to her: There's a storm coming.

Where are you, John says.

I'm in Toronto, she says. She looks out the window as the shops slide slowly backwards and begin to flick past.

Actually, she says, I'm lost.

. . . . .

The Empire State Building, Late November 2008

SO YOU'RE BRINGING her home, his mother says.

We're going to meet up, John says. In Toronto, and come on home from there.

But he is thinking about his childhood. Those moments of almost paranormal sensitivity a child feels. The sinister shimmer—a child intuits the toaster; he feels the toaster being a toaster. He looks at the toaster and the toaster looks back. He sees how things were put in place before he arrived. Small things. An eyelash on his mother's cheek. The adding machine *ka-chunk*ing with a vengeance on the dining room table late at night. His mother lost a contact lens and it fell through the veranda floor and his father found it in a spider web.

I love you, his father would say, and then shake his head at the enormity of it. Don't you ever forget it.

John's father would tell stories at night, lying on the bed between John and his sisters; they were all squished in and you couldn't move. Someone was always falling into the crack between the bed and the wall. His father's hands tucked under his head, elbows jutting up, as he told stories about princesses and monsters and journeys through enchanted forests and buried treasure. Stories about bravery and trust, enduring love.

John sees that all these things existed before he came along — the eyelash, the toaster, the parties — and it is a revelation of rock-your-world proportion: each object and moment belongs to itself, has always done so, and this is not something he can put into words. But sometimes he feels left out, outside of the world. It is late afternoon in New York. John has arrived from Singapore. Somewhere he has heard that if you drop a penny from the top of the Empire State Building it can kill a man on the sidewalk below.

I thought telemarketer, his mother says. But it's you. You're in New York now.

The truth is, John says.

Last night when you called, all I could think was, his mother says.

John remembers being in the back seat of the car with his sisters and going down Garrison Hill. Coming up over Bonaventure, his father would gun it, saying they were going straight for the harbour. He and Cathy and Lulu in the back and his mother in her red wet-look hotpants suit. His stomach would lift when they went over the top of the hill and came down, like being in an elevator. The little bounce the car made. The girls screaming. His mother wore big sunglasses and hoop earrings and she had long legs, and his father tended to her hand and foot. Flying over Garrison Hill, the east end lost in fog. The bells of the Basilica.

Or the washer overflowing. John thinks of that. The washer gagging and spewing with every grinding revolution of the parts inside. His parents in the bedroom with the door shut.

Don't come in, Johnny, we're napping.

But there's water all over the floor in the laundry room.

Don't come in here, Johnny. We're asleep.

But John had felt their wakefulness seeping through the door. He had felt their urgency. What John sees, when he looks back on the half-forgotten intensity of childhood, is the bald innocence of his parents.

So what we thought, John says, we thought we'd come home. And stay at your place and just get this sorted out. Jane says she's almost seven months and I think we have to sit down.

Yes, and talk, his mother says.

For some bloody reason, John says. And strangely, he feels as if he could cry. He is standing at the foot of the Empire State Building, looking up. The building tilts over him. It seems to slant. He feels as if a force coming from the centre of his chest is holding the building up. He feels the weight of the building, but it is only jet lag and a hangover from drinking on the plane. Drank his face off on the plane. There's a baby coming.

He has a meeting in New York and another plane to Toronto tomorrow night. Then he will meet up with Jane Downey.

How foolish his parents were to love like that. How foolish to have so many children. They had no money. He wants to ask his mother, What were you thinking? Didn't you know what you were getting into? Why did you love each other so very much? It destroyed you. Don't give that much, he wants to say. People don't have to give that much. How foolish to keep going.

And in childhood he had felt it: something is going to spill over. This is what he would ask his mother: Was it strange before Dad died? Did we know what was coming? Even back then, John had known it could not last.

Of course you can stay here, his mother says.

She's smart, John says.

A smart person, his mother says.

Attractive too.

I'm sure she is.

I don't know what she is, John says. I hardly know her.

It has nothing to do with knowing. His mother sounds irritated.

What she's like. Jesus, Mom, John says.

There's nothing to know, his mother says. Just come home.

I'm looking up at the Empire State Building, John says. His parents had believed what people said about risk back then. They had believed that there was a new science devoted to the assessment of it. Risk could be calculated and quantified. The risk, they had believed, was worth it.

· · · · ·

Putting Down Hardwood, November 2008

THE SKATES ARE sharpened and Helen is taking the kids skating at Mile One Stadium. Family hour. Timmy has run across the street to get Patience.

A family of Sudanese had moved in across the street: Patience, Hope, Safire, Elizabeth, Melody, and an older brother, Michael. Their mother is Mary. Helen first saw seven-year-old Patience standing in the middle of Long Street with her head tilted back, trying to catch snowflakes on her tongue. Her dark face even darker circled in the white fun-fur of her winter jacket. Patience with her eyes closed and her tongue out, and then she skipped around the corner.

Later she knocked on Helen's door, collecting for a school marathon.

Put me down for five bucks, Helen said.

Patience played with Timmy when he was over, or Patience would knock when she needed help with her homework. Drawings in her science exercise book: the sun, the flowers, the soil, the rocks, all the layers of the earth labelled neatly, and beneath, the boil of lava.

Timmy did his best to beat up Patience, but she gave as good as she got. They rolled in the grass, tearing at each other's hair, kicking and punching, and when they heard the front door they'd jump up and get away from each other as if nothing had happened.

What is going on over there?

Nothing.

Just playing.

Timmy, what are you doing?

He's not doing nothing, Helen, Patience would say. But they looked as if they might kill each other. Once Patience came downstairs with a wad of bloody toilet paper held to her nose. Timmy came down after her with a bump over his eye.

What happened?

Nothing.

Or they'd get under the blankets in the guest bedroom like an old married couple and play Nintendo.

Or once they let the basketball roll into traffic and Helen heard the screech of brakes and the angry horn. Or they climbed the new scaffolding next door: Get down, Jesus, get down, do you want to break your necks?

They scraped their knees and hands — finely shredded filaments of skin curling over bits of gravel and stone, blood coming up in little red beads — taking turns with the skate-board.

Today Helen takes them to Mile One and Patience clings to the boards. Then she skates with little steps that slip backwards as much as forwards and she grips Helen's hand. She swings her arms like windmills and falls on her bum with a *thump*. Timmy zips past, pretending he's never seen Patience or Helen before in his life.

The ice is etched with swirls and cuts, the faint colours of beer ads and soft drink logos under a pale blue. Helen runs into Gary O'Leary, whom she's known since high school. Still at Aliant, he says. Gary has a daughter who plays in the orchestra. And Sylvia Ferron and Jim, they are here with their granddaughter, same age as Timmy. A cashmere hat with kitten ears and a knitted strap under the chin. Helen has a chat with Mike Reardon; she heard Mike on the radio talking about solar panels and geothermal furnaces. She says about the renovations.

The men sway from side to side in cable-knit sweaters and eiderdown vests, blades whispering *shick, shick, shick.* Couples hold each other by a light touch on the elbow, moving in unison. The smell of the cold air and french fries and vinegar from the canteen. Carols over the loudspeaker.

Her ankles hurt when Helen hobbles into the dressing room and unlaces her skates. The ground feels inert and too hard. Her toes are cold. She drops Patience at home and takes Timmy back to his mother. It is dusk. The snow of the morning has lost its bluster. There are big flakes now that fall in a slant and loop up with the breeze like handwriting.

Helen unlocks her front door, holding an armful of groceries, and there are three empty floors and silence. It is a relief. Solitude, she thinks, is a time-release drug, it enters the system slowly and you become addicted. It's not an addiction; it's a craft. You open the closet doors very carefully so loneliness doesn't pounce out.

There's the war in Afghanistan and some woman held prisoner in Mexico without a trial for laundering money, Obama and Clinton, and then just Obama, a volcano in Chile. The *Globe and Mail* hits the screen door every morning with a *thud.* The guy throws it from his car window. She gets the *Telegram* too. Forty thousand died in an earthquake in China. Helen cannot conceive how that many can be lost at once. What does her life add up to in the face of that?

She has paid off the house. She and Louise have gone to Florida three times. They went to Greece last year. She has Patience and Timmy, and there's a houseful of young men who play in a band just two doors up. The boys in the band have a Newfoundland flag hanging in one window and Che

Guevara in the other. Helen hears the drums and the bass late on Saturday nights. They shovel her out after a storm.

The television says there's a problem distributing aid in Burma, just a few roofs left in each village after the cyclone. She sees a clip, a long line of men handing cartons of bottled water to each other down a line, a mass of people waiting behind a rope. Then something about polar bears. A mother bear collapsing on top of her cubs, suffocating them.

Helen cleans the cupboards. She cleans the fridge. She listens to the radio and she scrubs a pot and the yellow of her rubber glove looks weirdly yellow and the colour seems separate from the glove. The doorbell.

Just a second. Just let me find my purse. The yellow is a separate thing all on its own and she has tears in her eyes. She is lonely after all. Her eldest child is going to be a father. John is coming home and there will be a baby.

I know I put that purse somewhere. The paperboy is a grown man with a disability and he bangs on the door. He hits the aluminum screen door with the flat of his hand and the sound rings through the house.

I had it a minute ago. If I just put the damn thing where it belongs.

That's all right, Missus.

No, I have some change.

I'll come back later, Missus. The man's mother, she must be seventy, parked on the hill with the engine idling and her headlights coming through the door so her son is lit from behind, like an angel of some sort.

Here it is, she shouts. And what do I owe? What do I owe. Patience's father was killed by the Janjaweed, Helen has come to understand. She gives the paper a little snap and holds it out to read. There on the front page: Genocide in Darfur.

Keep the change, Helen says. She closes the door and locks it. A car swings past and long rectangles of light and shadow slide down the hallway to the kitchen. The house smells of sawdust. The sub-floor has been laid. Thick sheets of opaque plastic over the sofas and dining room table. Louise had demanded that she renovate.

You've got to put down hardwood, Louise said. Do something about the kitchen. You want to keep up the property value, you're going to have to renovate. You have to hire somebody.

Cal has been dead twenty-six years and she is capable sometimes, for a stretch of time, of forgetting Cal has died and how he died. She talks to her daughters every day. She is taken up with the house and her yoga. She sews wedding gowns, a kind of business venture that grew from a hobby.

I'm a young fifty-six, Helen thinks. Her grandchildren need her. She plays bridge. She took up curling but she hated the bloody curling. Her sewing gives her satisfaction.

Helen has mastered loneliness; nobody thinks of her as lonely any more.

You want something light, Louise said. On the floor.

A bloody fortune, Helen said.

Something with shine.

You're talking cosmetics.

I'm talking basic upkeep. I'm talking, do you want this place to be condemned or what?

But if Helen is, say, driving or sleeping or stretching on a yoga mat, she'll remember and live through a fresh fierce wallop of grief. It can take her by surprise. Knock her silly.

I'd get rid of these walls, Louise said. She was standing in Helen's living room, her hand raised, and gesturing in the direction of the bookcases.

I'd open this place up, she said. It's too goddamn dark in here.

And now there are two ragged gaping holes on either side of the fireplace where the bookshelves had been.

. . . . .

The Dog, 1975

HELEN AND CAL were walking along a beach and there was fog and the dog was with them. The dog flew, his paws barely touching he was going so fast, lunging with his head and neck, gathering all that muscle and shine, hardly marking the dimpled sand. Then he snagged to a stop. He yanked back as though on a chain, and circled, half-crazed, and started digging. A concentrated fury, the forepaws sending up arcs of sand.

Helen was thinking that whatever the dog found would be putrid and half decayed. The skin or feathers or fur fluttering in the breeze, detached or softening, coming apart, and an ugly truth protruding like the teeth still attached to the jawbone, a relishing grin.

The dog would lie down in it and press his shoulder in, squirming in the filthy stink. The dog's hindquarters moving in a half-circle while the one shoulder pressed into whatever kind of carcass, emitting bitter snarls and coaxing whimpers. The dog would be panting, crazed by the smell that floated towards them, tail thump-thumping, and they should get over there and haul him out of it.

Cal took off his shoes and his jeans were rolled up, and the waves crashed and foam rushed in over his feet. He bent down and put his fingers in the water and then put three fingers in his mouth to taste the salt. He sucked the salt water off his fingers. That was all.

But Helen felt his mouth tugging on his fingers, the fast suck of it, over her pelvic bone, and it was the baby, moving for the first time. She felt it.

A swatch of a memory that has held together only because of the sun burning through the fog that day. Or because her senses were torqued by the pregnancy, the bliss factor, and how sensual Cal's fingers looked in his mouth.

Were they having an argument? She remembers the dog and how it stank of death. How they drove home with it in the back seat and her eyes watered.

But they were full of bliss. There might have been some minor rage earlier that day, odd rages took them over sometimes, but in the wake were utterly ordinary moments, or there was bliss.

Is this what a life is? Someone, in the middle of cleaning the bathroom, remembers you tasting the ocean on your fingers long after you're gone. Someone draws that out of the fog, draws out that memory, detached from circumstance, not locatable on a timeline. Was it her third pregnancy? Or her second?

It was an afternoon long before Cal had applied for the *Ocean Ranger*, Helen thinks. They had heard about the jobs and Cal decided to apply. It was not what he wanted to do, but he had three children and a wife. He decided. He went to the office on Harvey Road twice a week for two months. It was all about who you know, he'd been told. He had a cousin put in a word. But everybody had a cousin.

Cal pulled his fingers from his mouth and Helen can't even remember the season — was it September?

Tasting the ocean. She knows they had the dog then, and they were broke and didn't care about money. They had thought about university, but they didn't go. Odd jobs and cobbling together a life. Trips to the beach. Cal could wire a house, though he didn't have official papers. He painted in the summer, renting the scaffolding. He did construction. Three children, and then they started to care about money. They had Cal's resumé typed professionally.

There was a guy behind a desk, big fat guy, taking the applications, Cal said. He would come home and Helen would be cooking or getting dressed for work. She was waitressing then.

Every day you hear something different, Cal said. She remembers him heading up the hill towards the office on Harvey Road. He walked with his hands drove into his pockets and his jacket open to the wind and snow. She thinks about the fluorescent light, greasy looking on the high-gloss walls of that office, the big cylindrical ashtrays on either side of the row of wooden chairs, and how he would have had to force himself through the double doors because it was like begging.

Going with my cap in my hand, he said. But if he got a job on the rig they could buy a house.

For the first little while they'd had the apartment on Lime Street. The snow used to come in under the back door. They'd gotten drunk in a bar and gone home together and they were all caught up in each other. They were caught up. Caught. Cal's apartment on Lime Street in the candlelight. Sometimes she babysat for a couple she knew.

They'd had a condom break. People say that doesn't happen, but it does. He'd had his back to her, sitting on the edge of the bed, and he was doing something. Fiddling with the condom.

It broke, Cal said. He let all the implications settle in. He held out the broken condom to her and there was a tear in it, and it was flat and milky looking on his fingers and wet.

It broke, he said again. She remembers him saying it twice. His face was flushed, and she felt the rough wool of his sweater that she had bunched up under her head. She sat up on her elbow to look and the sweater uncrumpled, slowly, moving by itself.

Helen had wanted to hold on to him, but she didn't know if he was the sweater, rough against her hot cheek, or the translucent bead of wax dripping down the candle, or the sex smell, or the date crumbles from his mother that were in a cookie tin lined with waxed paper on the bedside table, or the book he was reading.

Cal liked to drive by dilapidated old houses around the bay, with rippled glass in the windows and a storm door with blistering paint and a sagging roof, houses that had been built by hand and left with the kettle still sitting on the oil stove and all the dishes in the cupboard. He'd wanted one of those houses; he would fix it up and they could be in the country on the weekends or for the summers. He had wanted a view of the ocean, and he'd wanted the long grass and the root cellar. He felt an affinity for silvered wood and cobwebs and the battered suitcase under the feather bed with old receipts written by hand and spelled wrong.

Drop in later in the week, the man at the Harvey Road office had said.

There would follow, after the rig sank, a lot of talk about risk assessment. The oil companies held a symposium.

The oil companies were all about acceptable levels of risk and they always had been. They spoke of possible faults in the system and how to avoid them. Here, here. They advised strongly against intuition when assessing risk. If you were scared shitless, they said, that was only intuition, and you should ignore it. They asked the public to consider the overall good to be achieved when we do take risks. They spoke in that back-assed way and what they meant was: If you don't do the job, we'll give it to someone who will.

They meant: There's money to be made.

They meant: We will develop the economy.

They meant there isn't any risk, so shut the fuck up about it. Except they didn't say *fuck*, they said: Consider the overall public good.

Helen had not for a minute thought she was pregnant. She hardly knew Cal (although she knew everything important). She hadn't thought it was at all probable that she would fall in love. Love was a fault she easily could have avoided if she (1) hadn't been tipsy; (2) knew about risk assessment then and all the ways to avoid risk; (3) wasn't in love already.

She and Cal had been drunk their first night together, and it was all still so new, and she liked him a lot but she didn't want to say *love*. Or, they had been slightly inebriated and had made light work of the date crumbles. The hole in the condom had struck them as kind of funny, because how likely was that? But they were lucky people. They had flopped back down on the bed and the candle flame had wagged back and forth and they had recounted for each other personal stories of fabulous luck. He had won a hundred dollars off Nevada tickets. She had been born with a caul. They had both had their throats blessed — two cool candlesticks tied in the middle and opened to form an X at the throat, and a Latin prayer — and then they were safe from telling lies or getting throat cancer.

I love you, she said. It had just popped out of her mouth. It had been exactly the wrong time of the month to have a condom break but she hadn't thought she was pregnant because that wasn't the sort of thing that could happen to her.

Cal just happened to be in the Harvey Road office at the right time.

Look what the cat dragged in, the fat guy said when he saw Cal.

Cal was in the right place at the right time. And he was lucky. He happened to have his shirt ironed, and it was the same guy on the desk, and the guy was sick of looking at him. Helen had missed a period and thought nothing of it.

What comes over Helen when she's tired is a kind of fog.
A day at the beach after a long drive. How the yellow grass
caught the light and the edges of the blades gleamed like
steel. The end of a season. A haze hanging over the breakers.
A whiff of something dead, there and not there, in the breeze.
The foam rolling out, tinted yellow, thick as whipped cream.
Those jeans Cal wore.

We were young, Helen thinks. The clear, cold ocean roiling up and dragging back, encircling Cal's bare ankles like
chains. And he bent and dipped his hand and put his fingers
in his mouth.

. . . . .

Jane, November 2008

YOUR ROOM WILL be covered, and all the other things, John
said. Jane heard a horn blast somewhere near him. He was
on a street in New York and she was in a streetcar in Toronto
and they were going to meet up. He was on his way home
for Christmas. They were going to talk about the baby. And
he would pay for a four-star hotel.

I just go into the hotel off the street, she asked.

Your incidentals, he said, will be covered.

When the call was over she rode the streetcar a couple
more blocks and found the hotel and dropped off her suitcase,
and now she is walking until she finds a mall. She wants a
food court. French fries and cheeseburgers and the shushing

of cash registers, fake storefronts themed like a frontier town or a global village, thatched huts or cedar shingles, moulded plastic furniture and blinking neon. She needs to pee and then she wants to plunk down in an orange chair that can swivel from side to side, a chair that is attached to a table with a metal bar. She has a craving for grease and noise.

People do not say *failed* any more, Jane thinks. They say other things. A whole movement has risen up to avoid the acknowledgment of failure. People want to learn from failure, they want to embrace it.

But failure isn't good, she thinks. If something can be redeemed it isn't really a failure.

Jane is failing spectacularly. She'd had an eighty-thousand-dollar scholarship at the New School in New York to do a PhD in anthropology on the rituals and practices of modern spirituality as seen in New Age sects all over North America. She'd made a stir with her master's thesis, an ethnography of street people living in New York. She'd hung out with street people who slept outdoors or who lived in squats; she had been equipped with a little digital recorder that she could turn on discreetly.

Jane had shaped the material because she'd felt for a while that she knew what it meant. Or she'd pretended she did. Conclusions were necessary and she had come up with them.

But she had also learned things she didn't put in the thesis. The street people had frightened her. Some poor people were right-wing and violent. Some were avaricious. They were hungry and cold. They had runny noses and glittery snot-caked sleeves. They ate with their mouths open. They had glazed eyes and addictions. They were illiterate and they had lice. Or they were brilliant and meticulous with their appearance and saintly. They could see ghosts. They were fair-minded. They shared what they had. They had nothing. They fed the pigeons. They were full of wisdom. They were full of worms. They were full of AIDS. They were spiritually bereft. They were luckless. They were a *they*. Best of all, they knew the scope of a single lifetime and how not to make a mark.

When Jane had finished studying the street people, she experienced a glimmer of what it might mean to be invisible, to live without a trace, to hurt nothing. A kind of passivity that harkened back to an Aquinian notion of grace. One had to be empty to experience grace, empty or uncertain, and even then it was not a sure thing. She had kept all of that out of the thesis. Her master's thesis had made a mark. She was not willing to be empty.

A woman Jane had interviewed frequently saw a dead boyfriend at the bottom of her bed. This was an eighty-year-old woman who had six cats and a collection of thirty dolls still in dusty cellophane bags lined up around the baseboards of a temporary bed-sit. The room stank of cat litter and empty wine bottles and human shit because the woman hadn't gotten out of bed for three days. The old woman's abdomen was swollen — hard with cancer, she said — and she was drunk and she had a foul mouth and her boyfriend, Archie, had died last week.

Right here in the bed next to me, she had said, spanking the covers. The woman had a brother in jail for stealing a chalice out of a church and she was afraid of Satan and she gripped Jane's hand.

Make me proud, she said, over and over.

She spoke to Jane and then focused on a spot just over Jane's shoulder and said, Don't say anything, Archie, until the little girl is gone.

Jane returned with her little recorder ten times and asked questions, and the woman answered. Jane changed the sheets, of course, and cleaned the cat litter and put out the wine bottles. She cooked food.

That thing on, the old woman would ask, composing herself. Preparing the story of her life. She was obsessed with the chalice her brother had stolen and she wanted to know if they would all go to hell. She had asked Jane to feed the cats and to bring her cigarettes and to move the dolls around.

Once Jane had put a doll with black curly hair and a red velvet dress with gold braid and a matching parasol on the bedside table, leaning against the lampshade. The old yellowed cellophane around the doll crackled like the sound of a fire starting. The woman watched from the bed and lifted her hand with effort and moved one finger to point, tapping the air, and then the arm dropped. Jane saw that the woman wanted the light turned on, and when she pressed the switch the doll's eyes blinked shut.

The woman died shortly after, and Jane listened to her voice on the recorder, rewind, fast-forward, rewind, fast-forward, for a week while she transcribed. Each ragged breath audible.

Jane had also interviewed a man who argued that since the populations of Africa had the highest mortality rate, that was the place to outsource toxic industry — those industries whose toxins collect over the years in the lungs and blood and bowels and turn into full-blown cancer when most of the population turns, statistically speaking, fifty-five years old. Many Africans weren't going to make it to fifty-five, was the logic of this completely insane litigator-turned-street-person. He had grabbed her breast and squeezed it hard, twice, like you'd toot a horn.

They had all been famous something-or-others in another life, the street people she met. Or they were retarded. Or they had been abused as children.

Toxic industry wouldn't affect the Africans, the former litigator had said. They would be dead by the time the toxins kicked in anyway. They'd never know.

This had been a conversation over a fire in a burn-barrel under a bridge in some industrial park on the outskirts of New York. There was a man dressed in a robe made of burlap sacks with *Jesus Saves* in red paint across his back. He had healing hands and he laid them on Jane's head and she felt a definite zap. A current of some kind zoomed through her skull and the man told her she had painful memories knotting the muscles in her back and calves, and her scalp was tight. He had loosened those memories, he said, and she would become very sick for several days but it would be her body releasing those memories for good.

The profanity used by the street people Jane interviewed was dazzling, and Jane broke it down, counting the number of times certain words and phrases appeared in each given sentence. She made charts. Polyglottal and euphonious, and full of waste and sex and death. The profanity was a casual encryption of despair. She made graphs.

All of this had looked very good on paper, but now Jane was studying New Age spiritualism throughout North America and she had lost her bearings. She had her digital recorder and a laptop. She had method and theory. But she was disoriented by the calm belief these New Age followers — followers of every sort — brought to utter nonsense. It unnerved her. She was charting the unassailable certainty of the subject who gives up logic. In the midst of their canny, bitter arguments, Jane had lost faith.

Jane buys a container of french fries and she holds four miniature paper cups, one after the other, under a pump nozzle, and ketchup squirts out. She puts each little cup in a line on her orange tray, and she thinks she might faint with hunger. She goes at the fries with the bottle of vinegar, slippery with other people's fingerprints, and she tears open two packets of salt.

Not good food for the baby, she thinks.

All afternoon she has been thinking about the pregnancy and the state of her thesis. She'd known from the beginning that she wanted the baby. There had been some spotting in the first month and the doctor had said it was nothing to worry about and to take it easy, and yes, she could keep on with her work.

Jane devours the french fires and rides the escalator up to the street, and the mall is full of Christmas music and artificial trees and there is a giant moose with a candy basket. The moose hands her a candy cane. There is an entire face, a woman's face, at the back of the moose's throat, under the big snout. A strip of pink felt, the moose's tongue, is like a runway leading to the woman's chin. She is an elderly woman with bright orange lipstick and glasses.

What's it like outside, the woman says. I'm baking in here.

Jane passes a tattoo shop, bright and clean as the inside of a fridge. There is a bald man with a crown of thorns tattooed on his head. He has an elastic band stretched between his two index fingers with a pen hanging from it and he flicks the pen so it twists up and twirls out. Jane feels big kicks over her pubic bone and stands still for a moment, watching the man with the pen.

Then she comes to a pizza place with a single customer sitting on a stool. She stands on the sidewalk to watch the cook throwing the dough into the air. She watches it fly up off his raised fists and spin around in the air and stretch bigger.

She is thirty-five and doesn't have a boyfriend. This was her chance, she realized when she'd seen the two pink lines on the pregnancy test almost seven months ago. It had been a *yes*, and she hadn't believed the yes. She had read the little folded sheet with illustrations and some print in red. The sheet said there was such a thing as a false negative, but a false positive was impossible. She let her shoulder hit the metal stall of the public bathroom she was in and tried to think about what that could mean. It had seemed like a Zen koan.

She had wanted the baby from the minute she'd known. There was no question of abortion. She had not considered it.

Jane goes into the pizza parlour and orders a slice, and the smell of baking dough and tomato and oregano makes her very hungry. She thinks she can smell oregano on the hands of the man who gives her the change from her twenty. It is oregano or the smell of dirty silver coins. She can smell his sweat too, from being near the heat of the ovens. The smell of his sweat mingled with the smell of his deodorant, which is fruity, and for some reason he smells good.

The walls of the narrow pizza shop are mirrored and the lone customer leans into his pizza slice, and as he bends forward his image splits where the mirrors meet in the corner and there he is, an infinite number of times, his woollen coat and plaid scarf, pulling a piece of pizza away from his mouth, thousands of him, an indefatigable army of the same man having to lean forward after his food, the strings of cheese stretching long, and he leans back again and the infinite reflections fold together and disappear.

She and John are going to meet. John has a business dinner tomorrow and then he will fly to Toronto on the last plane and get a taxi from the airport to the hotel. He has booked himself a separate room. They would meet for lunch, he said. After a pause he said: I'm looking forward to seeing you.

· · · · ·

John's Job Interview, 2005

I'VE WORKED INSIDE petroleum tanks, John said.

Mr. McPherson touched the knot of his tie. It was a crazy, distracting tie. John felt his eyeballs stretching towards it against his will.

Shoreline Group had invited John for a job interview. He'd heard he was going to get a call and a few days later they called. The money was spectacular.

John told Mr. McPherson about his employment history, a job he'd had in his twenties. When he had started with the oil industry.

You crawled in there with equipment, Mr. McPherson said.

I did that job, yes.

Checking for fissures.

Fissures and cracks, John said. Anything that's going to—

Cost, Mr. McPherson said.

Leak, John said.

They'd tie ropes around John's ankles and when he was done he'd knock on the side of the tank and they would haul him out. If he got stuck they would pull him through. Climbing into oil tanks, checking them with ultrasound equipment—this was a job he'd learned in Fort Mac. You needed to be a certain size for that kind of job, and John was a compact man who watched his carbs. He worked on his chest and arms and he ran 10K three times a week, but he could fit through a pipe. He was what they called health conscious. But during this interview he was suffering a serious case of heartbreak. He had a physical ache from it that could make him short of breath.

John had heard there would be a substantial salary. The trick, he gathered, was to look unmoved when the interviewer quoted a figure.

Memorial University, School of Engineering, Mr. McPherson said. He had a Southern drawl and he was scowling at John's resumé.

A half-hour earlier John had knocked and heard, Come in. He had expected a secretary but there was no secretary. There was a view of the harbour in St. John's, right out through the Narrows. And a large man facing the wall of glass. There was a long beat before the man turned from the window. A theatrical pause. John and the man had taken each other's measure by their reflections in the window. The office floated over the landscape outside the glass. The blue water cooler hanging in the blue sky and the wall of framed diplomas checkering the waterfront. A car coming down the curving road of Signal Hill seemed to beetle across Mr. McPherson's white shirt, and then it disappeared.

Ronnie McPherson, the man had said. He turned and put his hand out. And John shook it. McPherson had a too-tight grip that bespoke the motivational speaker circuit. There was a dull zeal in the handshake that would require an unnatural amount of eye contact.

Ronnie, John said. Stifling the urge to say *sir*.

Red.

Pardon, John said. Sir?

Call me Red.

John had started in the oil industry with sonar imaging, crawling into tanks. Anything went wrong, they hauled him out by the ankles. Then he'd done engineering at MUN. He'd gone out on the rigs, starting as a roustabout and working up to toolpusher.

Ronnie McPherson had black hair, longish for his age, streaked silver, curling over the collar of his shirt. There was nothing red about him. There must have been a pause before he put on that tie, John thought.

Shoreline Group specialized in risk assessment, organizational restructuring. They specialized in all the touchy-feely stuff from the 1980s: lateral thinking, creativity in the workplace, psychological support during downsizing or natural disaster, pink slips, sweater-vests and distressed denim, a bold new self-generating speak that boiled over and reduced to a single, perfect word: *efficiency*.

John had read up. Thirty-two was getting too old for the rigs. In his twenties he had spent his summers crawling into pipes, and the air in there — it can't be good for you. He didn't want to be selling drill bits all his life, either. He'd had a stint at selling. At Shoreline there would no doubt be weekend retreats, role-playing, diagrams, sharing, massages. Flip charts identifying personal goals and company goals, with asterisks where they intersected. The unions were getting to be a pain in the ass, according to Red McPherson.

Some pipes John had crawled through, he'd had to work one shoulder forward, then the other. Keep his chin tucked in. That was not a job for you if you were claustrophobic. There were pipes so narrow he'd had to develop a kind of shimmy with his hips. He'd had to put his head down and take short breaths. If you had a fear of being buried alive, you wouldn't go in for the job he'd done when he was younger. Any kind of tank that held petroleum. Once he'd been in a tank from a place that produced gummi bears.

There would be travel with Shoreline, and John loved travel. He wanted to see everything.

Someone intimate who held a serious grudge must have advised McPherson on his tie, John thought. The tie had pineapples wearing sneakers and riding skateboards through white clouds lit with silver lightning.

Crawling through petroleum tanks, you had an added advantage: you were doing something for the environment. John had started in the industry that way. Wanting to make a difference. He might have stayed on checking for fissures. But a guy can't do that forever.

John was smarter than a guy with ultrasound equipment hanging off his hip, but it was Sophie who had pushed him. Sophie said, Do something else. Sophie told him to go back to university. She nagged and insisted. Sophie was his ex. She was the cause of his heartache while he was being interviewed for the job with Shoreline.

Engineering, Red McPherson said. He rubbed his jaw. He was glaring at John's resumé with an eyebrow cocked, as if a degree might be an impediment they'd have to work around.

It's a good idea to have a piece of paper in your back pocket, John's mother had said all his life. She was big on a degree.

Pineapple upside-down cake. John's mother would whip the cake batter by hand and lecture him on the merits of a good education, saying about that piece of paper.

The advantages, she'd say. She'd put the bowl of batter down and make fists and then spread her fingers wide. The world just opens up, she'd say.

John's mother had made one cake her whole life, and it was a pineapple upside-down. The chief advantage of this cake was that you mixed it in the pan you cooked it in. He could see her laying the rings of canned pineapple in the frying pan and pouring the batter on top. It was as if John's own mother had come into the room during his job interview. The cake had come from a recipe she'd found in *Good Housekeeping*, a recipe that promised to take no more than fifteen minutes, start to finish, designed so you could make it over a campfire or on the engine of a car if you had to, and for the years John was growing up it had been his mother's crowning culinary achievement. It was a cake that, if you had to, you could make in a bomb shelter.

His mother had said: If you have that piece of paper you'll be all set.

Or she'd say, A degree is something to fall back on.

She'd be sewing under a single lamp in the living room. The sewing machine rat-a-tatting, full of short-lived spite. John would switch on the overhead light and his mother would press her finger and thumb against her eyes.

Then she'd say, I have been thinking about your education, John.

Back then his sister Cathy was working at the first A&W in town, the one on Topsail Road, and she had the orange hat and the brown polyester suit and she carried the trays out — you latched them onto the window — and if the mugs got stolen the company took it out of your wages. Cathy running down Topsail Road after some car full of boys, yelling, Give me back those mugs, you bastards, I know you got them.

John had gone into all kinds of oil tanks and they were completely dark and any kind of a bang had echoed in his skull. The walls were bubbled and pocked and unfinished, and the flashlight just showed how very black it was in there. There was a crunch underfoot or it was slippery.

When he graduated with an engineering degree, his mother was in the front row of a bank of folding chairs on the grass outside the Arts and Culture Centre. His mother put her arm around him on the lawn. His hat with the silky tassel got knocked crooked, and his Aunt Louise aimed a camera at them and said, Closer.

All over the lawn: young men and women in caps and gowns, and their mothers and grey-haired fathers, and the dandelions. The sun a long, narrow disc across the centre of the dark duck pond. The first in his family with a university degree. He had gone to university because Sophie forced him to go. His mother spoke through a camera smile, Hurry up, Louise.

Say *sex*, Louise shouted.

You've got your piece of paper, his mother said. The flash went off in their faces.

Then they had a big family meal, with John and his sisters doing the cooking.

She never said education to us, Lulu said.

When she said education to us, she meant secretarial school, Cathy said.

She meant get your typing, Lulu said.

That is not true, his mother said.

What she said to us was, Get a trade. She said nursing. She liked the idea of a white uniform.

And she wouldn't let John in the kitchen, Cathy said.

Or retail, Lulu said. She saw Cathy and me in retail. She saw us married is what she saw.

I said education, his mother said. I said it to Cathy and I said it to Lulu and I said it to Gabrielle and I said it to John. I said education to all my children.

Mr. McPherson's chair swivelled and squeaked. The part of Mr. McPherson's leg that showed between his pants and the thin black sock was hairless and had coins of opalescent scarring. Had he been shot in the shin by something with scatter action?

Climbing into a petroleum tank was a feat of contortion, John said. The comment caused Red McPherson to smooth his tie. He put John's resumé down on the desk and laid just the tips of his fingers on it, as if it were a Ouija board. Then he opened a drawer and took out a manila file.

And John knew he had the job. The trick was to look blasé about the money when McPherson made the offer.

Crawling through tanks had been a bad job but it had kept John off the bloody water for a while. Maybe it had integrity, reporting to watch groups, taking soil samples, telling it like it is, but he'd been in that job because he wanted to stay off the water.

He was afraid of the water.

His experience: everybody is afraid of something. Find out what everybody else is afraid of and go into that.

Then you went into sales, Mr. McPherson said.

I sold drill bits, John said.

I'm not going to fool with you here, Red McPherson said. He had been reading the manila file.

Thank you, Red, John said.

I like being straight, the man said. He was lost in a column of figures and he spoke as if in a dream. All the tension had left his face. The wince he'd worn, examining John's resumé, was gone and his eyelids drooped sensuously. How old is he, John wondered.

We're talking a million, a million-point-five a day to keep a rig operating, Mr. McPherson said. We need men with skills. Smart men.

John had a photographic memory, which was something he didn't say. He skimmed a page once and he could recall it word for word. He had to close his eyes to do it and he saw the page and could read it out as if it were a thought that had just occurred to him. This wasn't smart, exactly, but it could pass for smart.

Smart was about intuition, and John had that too. Smart was: you didn't exert effort but you knew the answer anyway. You thought about it, yes, but the answer came via a different route. Smart was: you always had access to that different route. The answer came in the back door while you were cooking or even while you slept.

You grow up with a mother whose specialty is pineapple upside-down cake and you learn to cook. He had a two-hundred-dollar bottle of truffles in his kitchen. He'd ordered the truffles from Montreal. Stinky things, dank and ripe; a lewd smell had puffed out as soon as he'd unscrewed the cap.

This was something he'd bought when Sophie was still with him. John liked to try things. He had that kind of intelligence and a photographic memory and the small gift of knowing that if you went at something long enough, hard enough, you got it. That was called certainty. Sophie had said she wanted a baby. I'm not certain, John had said, that I want children.

Red McPherson closed the manila file. I was told about you, he said. You're the kind of guy who is given a person's name just once and you remember it for the rest of your life.

That is absolutely true, John said. Mr. McPherson, sir. A person enjoys hearing his own name. Red.

But a guy, people also say, who keeps his cards close, Red McPherson said.

John's job selling drill bits, the job that came after inspecting tanks, had required that he go all over. Alberta was different from Newfoundland. John could tell you that, no question. He knew some people who'd had knives held to their throats on a rig off the coast of Nigeria. He knew that in Iceland people buried fish in the ground and ate it crawling with maggots. They were into alternative energy in Iceland. They had hydro buses and hot springs. The place stank of sulphur and the people glowed. In Alberta people were macho. Texas, you got a steak the size of your head. You didn't find a lot of women on the oil patch.

Newfoundland, you did your job and kept your mouth shut. There was a culture in Newfoundland: Shut up out of it. What you said could come back and bite your arse.

Then he'd got the call from Shoreline Group. They were an efficiency agency and there was room for movement, they'd said. Shell was a customer, and Mobil. They were all customers.

We're an independent arm, Mr. McPherson said. John tried to think what an independent arm might be. It occurred to him that the situation was not full of the sort of legitimacy he had imagined, and for which he had hoped.

Impartial, Mr. McPherson said. John felt the interview had turned before he'd had the chance to speak. They wanted him.

You came recommended, Mr. McPherson said. The man swivelled towards the window and joined his fingers as if in prayer and touched them against his lips.

John thought of Sophie and how she was probably still in bed. He thought of her back, of how he had sometimes slept with his hand on the small of her back. And of how the hair at the nape of her neck was a little damp and warm and tangled.

John was a lucid dreamer and once Sophie had found him struggling to get the big window on the third floor open. He'd turned and said, I'm going to have to go out there. Sophie had led him back to bed.

You had a father on the *Ocean Ranger*, Mr. McPherson said. What was distracting was the guy's tie. John knew the oil industry inside out. Ontario, they might wear a tie like that. Or somewhere in Texas. A man who was colour blind.

We are impressed, Mr. McPherson said, with your degree.

Oil was like the military—they trained their own, and they wanted you to learn their way. On the rig, if you had a degree they thought you were full of yourself. A degree, and you had better prove something. You had to lose a finger or crack a collarbone, and John had cracked a collarbone, and finally here was a company who nodded when he said engineering degree. Here was a company that could appreciate.

The chair squeaked when Red McPherson swivelled back. There was an orange light blinking on McPherson's phone. John thought of a hotel room in Edmonton where there had been messages on the phone from everyone who had ever called in to the room. For some reason the messages had never been erased, and one night he had listened to perhaps two hundred messages, some of them in foreign languages.

He had just broken up with Sophie for good. All of the messages were full of the kind of voice people use when they are talking to a machine: dislocated longing, tentative, mildly regretful. Children called to talk to their dads. Girlfriends said ordinary things in sexy voices. Or they said profane things in ordinary voices. Someone had to pick up an entertainment centre at Sears. A man named Tony had to use a go-forward strategy. A very young child said, Nightynight. Someone's father had stabilized for the evening. Someone's plane was delayed. John had pressed his forehead to the cold glass, looking down at the cars fifteen floors below, and watched the fat snowflakes fall from a grey sky, and he missed his mother and he missed his sisters and he was in love with Sophie, but it had taken breaking up with her to find that out.

We want someone like you, Mr. McPherson said. There was a sheet of hard plastic under his chair and one of the castors had edged off it and the man was slightly tilted. He took hold of the edge of the desk and rocked the castor back onto the plastic sheet, wincing with the strain.

Someone who can hold sway, McPherson said. Shoreline Group was a company that went on the rigs and checked out routines, and there was a culture of safety, Mr. McPherson told John, that was detrimental to efficiency. That's what we want to trim.

Trim, John repeated.

Absolutely, Mr. McPherson said.

John had sold a shitload of drill bits, and the line his company gave was all about penetration. The terminology was sexual and violent: The bits were hard and the sea floor was wet and it resisted and finally gave, and there was nothing a good bit couldn't penetrate.

Shoreline Group, on the other hand, worked to eliminate redundant safety procedures. They offered a cost-benefit analysis of the safety procedures in place and drafted modification plans, Mr. McPherson said, that impacted directly on waste and redundancy, and the general good for communities at large, and profit margins, and there were stakeholders to consider. There were safety procedures that did nothing but tie the hands of people looking to make things run smoothly out there. Shoreline Group wanted men who could think for themselves. Mr. McPherson wrote a figure on a piece of paper and folded it twice and pushed it across the desk to John.

Yes, my father died on the *Ocean Ranger*, John said.

They'd found his father's glasses tucked away in his shirt pocket. John's father had taken off the glasses and put them in his pocket. He couldn't see a thing without his glasses. He must have stood on the deck as the rig was tipping, removed his glasses and put them in his shirt pocket, and then he probably jumped. His father would have had all his bones broken if he'd jumped from that height. But he might still have been alive when he hit, John thinks. John imagines he was alive. He has always imagined it that way.

My father knew they were going down, John said.

This is what you'd start with, Mr. McPherson said.

John opened the paper and it was more than he'd imagined and he kept a neutral expression.

. . . . .

Helen Making Wedding Dresses

HELEN HAD TRIED yoga and she had taken up running and when she was in her thirties she had started teaching a water-fitness program for women over fifty at the Aquarena, youth being her only qualification. She had worked those old ladies hard and she had learned how aqua-fitness was like everything else, dragging your limbs through all that water, jogging on the spot through a massive weight.

In the 1990s she had developed a hobby making wedding dresses, evening gowns, prom dresses, a hobby that became something of a business. She had nearly lost the house after Cal died; it took a long time for the settlement. She'd almost lost everything. The bank had threatened, but she had kept the house.

The family went without, certainly. But children don't need much, Helen thinks. She had raised her kids on nothing. They had not been spoiled. She could certainly say that about them. She'd shopped at the Sally Ann. Children needed food, yes. They needed a warm bed. She and her kids had got through.

My girls are unscarred, Helen thinks. My girls are frugal and shrewd, but they know how to have fun. When her girls were young, Helen had an idea she wanted them to be free of guilt. It was not an idea she had been able to put into words. But it was what she had wanted for her girls.

John could brood. He spent every cent he got his hands on. The girls had been wild until they'd had children of their own, and then they'd become serious. They read parenting books and nodded at the wisdom and told their children, You were not bad, your *behaviour* was bad. I think you need a *time-out*.

Helen had called her own children *little Christers* and told them she would lash their arses or skin their hides if they gave her any sauce, or she'd threaten to horsewhip them. She had flicked her slipper at them when they were rude and, she reminds her daughters, it had worked well enough for them.

A good swift kick in the arse, she would tell them. They were going to get a clout.

Now Helen babysits the grandchildren and makes her daughters go out and get drunk. She bought the babies pacifiers when the girls were dead set against pacifiers, and said, Who's a saucy baby? She smiled until the babies smiled back. A baby can smile back a couple of hours after she's born. It's not gas, like the books say; what bloody nonsense.

She fed her grandchildren ice cream for the first time when they were five months old and watched their little faces. She watched as they smacked their lips and thought about the cold and got their first real hit of sugar, and how gleefully they went after the spoon. Oh-da-dear.

Helen spoils her grandchildren as best she can. *We don't need to mention this to Mommy.*

Maybe it is true that John was her favourite. He didn't fit in when he was a kid. He was always hugging someone or wrestling someone to the ground. Johnny was a little scrapper. How many times have I told you? When will you learn? He shouted out in his sleep, a deep ongoing argument. If Johnny cried he'd claim something had got in his eyes and he'd rub them hard with his fists.

Dust from the stupid carpet, he'd say, and kick the old rug with his sneaker.

Cal had bought him Jesus boots one afternoon at a yard sale. Cal couldn't swim but he coached John from the wharf. Come on, Johnny, you can do it. Two Styrofoam pontoons, one for each foot. The squeak when Johnny worked his feet into the holes. It had gone through her.

You never saw a father so proud of his kids. Helen could say that about Cal. Cal told Johnny that with these boots on, he could walk on water. The white pontoons kept Johnny upright for a few strides before his legs scissored out and he splashed down and went under, coming up laughing and gasping and punching the surface with his fists, swimming after the freed pontoons sailing on their way with the wind.

But after his father died, Johnny was afraid of water. Wouldn't put his face under the shower head if he could avoid it.

And John has no children. John is capable of hard work, and when he drinks, he really drinks. He forgets to call. He travels when he feels like it, or he goes away on business.

Sometimes he is remote. He can lie easily when it suits him. He is, Helen thinks, clutching the phone somewhere in New York right now, talking with a near stranger, the woman who will be mother of his child.

. . . . .

Helen and Louise Are Lucky, August 2008

AND THERE WAS Louise striding across the beach, and I said, Louise, I said, you're fifty-eight years old and you have a bad heart. I said, If you attempt to rescue those children you won't come back and I can bloody well guarantee it.

This poor young mother was racing up and down the beach screaming for help. She had two small children — what were they, Louise? Eight and six years old maybe, and they were on an air mattress and the undertow had carried them out, and there was Louise.

They were out there so fast, Louise said.

We go to Topsail Beach every weekend when it's nice during the summer, Helen said. Bring a picnic, have a few swallies.

These youngsters screaming for help and the mother gone cracked, Louise said.

Nobody else could swim, Helen said. So next thing, there's Louise striding across the beach and into the water and she's giving it to her, batting the jellyfish out of her way.

I didn't care about the jellyfish, said Louise.

You know what that water is like, Helen said.

I didn't mind the cold, Louise said. And people were standing up on the beach saying, Who's the old lady. Look at the old lady go.

Louise was in the paper for saving the children on the air mattress. Her white hair smoothed down and the zebra towel and a big smile.

We had seen what was going on and Louise stood up, and I said about her heart. I said to her, Louise, let someone else do it. She just stood up and ran down the beach and dove right in. And then the crawl. Which we'd learned as children. Head down in the water and turning to the side for breath and the arms straight and the fingers straight, and each wave passing over Louise. She just kept going and there was a flare on the ocean and Louise was almost a silhouette, and I could see the heads of the children but I couldn't hear them, whatever way the wind was blowing. And when Louise got there, she hung on to the edge of the air mattress and she must have been trying to calm the children, or just catching her breath. Everybody on the beach up to their knees in the water.

She's too tired, someone said. The old lady is tired. The old lady won't make it.

This is my sister they were talking about. And I'm going, She better Jesus make it! Then a speedboat came around the spit of land from the next bay, and not a second too soon I'd say, and the boat was upon them in a minute and turned a hard turn, throwing up a wave of water, and they cut the engine.

And everyone was pulled into the boat, first the children, and then Louise.

. . . . .

Minor Redemptions, October 2008

BARRY'S CELLPHONE RANG and he unsnapped a tiny leather case on his tool belt and the thing was invisible in his hand.

There was a kind of carpenter who cleaned up after himself, and Helen gathered Barry was that kind. He'd worked big sites but he could do the small jobs too. He had built a boat alongside his father and he mentioned this while looking at the sky one evening, and Helen found it very Old World and romantic. But this was not the old world. Or, they still lived in the old world but it was not romantic.

We all learned that way, Barry said. He was steady, neither fast nor slow, and sometimes he stood holding his forehead, working out the math of an angle. She had noticed a small tremble in his pinkie finger when he stood that way.

He kept a pencil behind his ear. It was solitary work and he sized up everything he did. He knelt on one knee, and placed the spirit level, and drew the pencil over the wood, and put the pencil back behind his ear. His work required physical strength, and that wouldn't last forever.

Helen could guess that Barry had not saved; he had the face of someone who worked hard and spent what he earned.

It was a wrinkled and tanned face. And the eyes. They were the kind of eyes people would remark on, and they were hard to get used to.

Helen listened when Barry's cellphone rang. The ring was a theme song from a TV show, but she could not place the tune. Something from the early eighties, something the kids had watched back then.

She guessed that Barry was Catholic. They knew each other, the Catholics did. She could tell without asking. It was in his posture and the way he spoke. He was from the Southern Shore. His stories had to do with sacrifices that paid off, and minor redemptions. There was a self-deprecating humour to his stories, and he was willing to let a silence stand. There was respect for privacy and a belief that pleasure required mystery and that there was mystery behind every bald and ordinary fact.

Helen could picture Barry in his twenties with a sink full of dishes and cans of Vienna sausages stacked in the cupboard. She could see the apartment. The people who would have visited and slept on the couch for months, and the women who would have hung around, halfway lost or on the way to somewhere else. Maybe he had been hard on women.

Barry was a self-taught carpenter, and his was a kind of knowledge that accepted how fast everything else was and it refused to be that fast.

Finicky, he said. You want to take your time. Helen had hired him to cut two arches from the living room to the dining room and to expose the fireplace and put down hardwood floors, and he would also do the painting. She wanted two bookshelves moved. And she wanted big windows in the kitchen.

The sills are rotten, she said. She ran her fingernail over the wood and the paint crackled up in pieces.

I'm not a painter, Barry told her. Helen would have to wait before he committed to the painting. He would have to see.

There are other guys will paint for you, he said. He squinted at the ceiling, his hands on his hips.

If need be, he said.

Helen had seen that his work was in demand. You won't be available, she asked.

I'm pretty steady on, Barry said, up until June. Then I can't be had for love nor money. He winked at her. She saw he was reliable even though he could have afforded to be sloppy. There's only a few master carpenters in town, he said.

In October he put down the sub-floor and she stayed out of his way. It rained most of the time and there was fog. It was cold and she felt it in her wrists. If her friends visited, she introduced them to Barry and he nodded or he touched his cap, but he was absorbed.

The hammer was methodical and from the third floor, where Helen was, it sounded as though it were full of thought and knew how to drive an argument home. Not insistent, but declarative and certain.

She would be in her study sewing and would forget, for long stretches, all about the hammer.

Sometimes Barry would call out that he was going for coffee. Or that he was packing it in for the day.

I'll leave these tools, he'd say.

He would tell her it was a nice evening. He would call out to her about the sky.

You should see this, Helen, he would say. There's a bloody big red sun. That was Catholic. That was a Catholic thing to say.

There was a strain of loyalty in him that Helen could almost smell. Of course he didn't go to mass or take communion. None of them practised any more, her generation. They'd gone to confession as children and been cowed by the idea of original sin, and they had been confirmed, and they still prayed.

None of them really believed, but they had been led to think that whatever existed was out there, whether they believed or not.

Barry stood up straight when he answered his cellphone and looked out the window. There was a bird feeder attached to the glass with clear suction cups, but the birds never came to it.

He said: What time should I pick you up? When he hung up, he whistled a part of the cellphone tune.

He has someone living with him, Helen realized. Someone he drives places, someone depending on him. He was not available.

· · · · ·

The Portal

THERE WAS A smashed portal, and that is key. But everybody knows this already; there is always a key, there is always a portal. A wave of ice hit the window and it smashed. The metal lid had not been drawn shut over the glass, as it should have been, and the window smashed and water got over the electrical panel and short-circuited it. The men had to operate the ballast doors manually and they didn't know how. But everybody knows that; so let's just take a moment. Just slow down.

Imagine instead a man with his feet up — for the sake of argument — and a cup of coffee cradled near his crotch, and maybe he's reading the manual. For the sake of argument: he has a manual open on his lap, and he's going to place a call later to his wife, and he's also got a book. It's a long shift. Later on he will read the book.

Do we know what they had on the rig for supper that night? Helen does not know. She is imagining pork chops with applesauce and she is imagining big steel pans of mashed potato on the steam table, dusted with paprika, smoothed over, decorated with parsley. The men won't eat the parsley. The Newfoundland men won't. Cal wouldn't.

The rolls were good. The rolls had butter melted over the top of them and they were salty, and there were stainless steel bowls of ice with smaller bowls in the middle full of pats of butter, and each pat is between two squares of waxed paper...but we should think about the manual. We should think about the portal.

It wouldn't be a cup of coffee, it would be tea. And this guy has been on duty in the ballast room for about forty-five minutes and he's leafing through the manual. If it's coffee, it's instant coffee. This is the part of the evening Helen likes to think about best — when the man in the ballast control room is having his instant coffee.

Imagine his surprise when the ocean forms itself into a fist and flies across the ballast room through that portal. The ocean burst through the window sometime between 7:45 and 8 p.m. So there is time for the man to have his coffee after supper.

We can imagine that in a moment.

First there's the idea of ballast.

But first there is this: The ballast operators learned on the job or they learned through private study. Which means they leafed through the manual. They read it through.

There was a manual and they read it; or they did not read it.

Where's the bloody manual?

The ballast control operators had been promoted from the drilling floor. They had marine experience or they had drilling experience, or they didn't have very much experience in anything. They had no experience.

But they were in charge of maintaining stability. The company liked you to learn on the job because that way you learned the way the company wanted you to learn. They wanted you to learn a certain way, and that way can loosely be called, or referred to, or otherwise spoken of as *their way*. You learned their way. The company's way. Which was: Don't answer back. Which was: Do you want a job or not? Which was: All you have to do is read the manual. There will be long hours in the ballast room while you are on duty and that'll be a good time to peruse the manual. Later on you might get a few courses, but it's all in the manual.

There was a policy concerning who got promoted to the ballast control room, but the company didn't follow it. One fellow didn't have any drilling or marine experience at all.

But he had a good attitude. It helped if you had a bit of university education. Or an education went against you. It was all about whether you wanted to learn. If you expressed interest. It depended on your attitude.

The portal and the fist of water, a piston driving itself through that portal, a fist of ice with stone knuckles; the ocean has become part monster, part machine, driving its paw-piston through that plate of unbreakable glass or whatever the hell and smashing it to smithereens . . . but forget the portal.

It's still quiet in the ballast room.

Very quiet.

We know what's going to happen so it's hard to appreciate the quiet, but let's just take a moment to do that.

Let the man have his instant coffee. Helen likes to imagine the time before things started to go wrong. When things start to go wrong it gets spotty. She's easily confused. She tries to run down the corridors, she tries to find out where Cal is, what he's doing, but she gets lost. He's in his bunk but he won't stay there. She doesn't want him in his bunk. She wants him playing cards. She wants him with the other men. They would have been anxious, but they had faith in the rig. They had faith in that monstrous-large hulking mass of metal. It's easier if there are a few men sitting around a card table and Cal is one of them. It's easier if he's playing a hand of 120s. As far as she knows, Cal never played a game of poker in his life, and if he bet it was with quarters. She gives him a pocket of change. She lets him win a little. She can see his hand cupping a little mountain of coin and dragging it towards him. She sees the way he lays down a heart he's been hoarding.

Inside the control room there's also a panel with brass rods that allows the ballast control operators to control ballast manually, and here's the thing.

Here's the thing.

Helen has a hard time with this part. Why would this part choke her up? Why do her eyes smart when she thinks of this part? There's worse to come, but the brass rods are what get to her.

Those brass rods. Nobody knew how to use the brass rods. If they'd known, the rig wouldn't have sunk. She has learned. Helen has read the reports; she has studied the diagrams; she knows where the rods go and why and how. Because those men didn't know and they didn't know, they didn't know, and it could happen to any one of us.

You might get attacked by a fist through a window and you can bet Helen is ready. She wakes up in the middle of the night knowing where each rod goes, and she will never forget. Brass rod, appropriate solenoid valve located under the mimic panel.

The man in the control room has got the cup of instant coffee and he's reading the manual, but here's the thing: the manual didn't say how to control the ballast if there was an electrical malfunction.

So he can read the manual all he wants.

He can read it backwards if he wants. Or he can read it in Japanese. It's never going to tell him what to do.

And so the water from the broken portal hits the electrical panel and short-circuits it. The men do not know if the ballast doors are open or closed, but they think they are open so they try to close them. Or the other way around. The rig starts to list very badly. And Helen is desperate to find Cal now. Where is he? She is racing through the corridors, she is running down hallways, and she passes a card game and there's an empty chair at the table and the men have no faces but they're Cal, and she's running and there's a lot of noise now, down the corridors, and she's banging on doors.

She can't imagine where he is. She can't even imagine.

· · · · ·

Her Profile, 2006

AND YES, OF course, Helen had let the girls talk her into online dating. Yes, she had.

You're not a dinosaur, Lulu said. Lulu was putting makeup on her mother. Brushing a cinnamon shimmer onto her eyelids. Lulu was a beauty technician. She had won awards at home and abroad. Lulu worked hard, hours on her feet, and her joints ached and her knees were shot, and she had no medical and no pension, but she had her own business.

Lulu dated men, most of them younger than her, and danced in big stadium-like bars and drank hard. She cut hair and did manicures and pedicures, and she did things with body mudpacks and a sensory deprivation tank that were pseudo-spiritual, and she intimated in all that she did and all that she said that if you took care of your image it would improve your soul.

She could do things to you, Lulu's advertising claimed, that would provoke self-discovery. What Lulu did to you would provoke a profound and unrelenting interest from the opposite sex. Or the same sex. She sold organic vitamins and wizened mushrooms and certain tinctures and resins that Helen was convinced were mildly poisonous. Perimenopausal women all over the city swore by her chakra massages and cactus juice. There was a chakra point smack dab in the middle of the vagina, as far as Helen could tell from looking at a diagram featured on one of Lulu's pamphlets, and Helen did not allow herself to think about it.

Lulu visited Helen to raid her mother's fridge. She visited not so much to talk but to draw all the curtains and get drowsy on the sofa while her mother cooked macaroni and cheese. Lulu cleaned out Helen's liquor cabinet and cooked up limp vegetables and ate Helen's peanut butter with a spoon. Helen waited on her hand and foot. Lulu was a waif. She was sexy and petite and lazy as a cut cat.

Mrs. McLaughlin is an example, Lulu stage-whispered as she applied Helen's eyeliner. She stood back with her arms crossed over her chest to survey her work.

And Mrs. Buchanan, she said. Remember Mrs. Buchanan, she taught grade four? They are both Internet dating.

Lulu had a sponge and she was touching Helen's cheeks. You are still a beautiful woman, she said. And she dabbed Helen on the nose.

The girls had said a computer. The girls had said online dating. And Helen had tried it. Sometimes now she woke up in bed in the middle of the night zinging with humiliation.

She had written online with candour. What a fool. She had been earnest. She did not put her picture up; the girls said, Don't send a photo. The girls said: There's plenty of time for photos later.

Helen had struggled to define herself and what she wanted in a man. It seemed important to know what was true about herself. How to put into words the tumult of pleasure her life had been; how to say she had lost something big and was left with a hole in the middle of her chest and the wind whistling through. How to tell the pride she took in her work. That she had friends. How to explain that her friends were celebrating anniversaries, the twenty-fifth, the fortieth, and they were smug in their marriages, smug in their happiness, rude about it, and it was a smugness that seemed designed to exclude. They didn't even know they were smug, and Helen had forgiven all of that. She wanted to mention that she didn't begrudge her friends that happiness. She wanted to mention that she was the kind of woman who had kept her heart open and it had been a struggle.

There were other questions. How old, how young. What interests. What she could offer; what she could share. She wanted to say: I am so bloody lonely it doesn't matter who you are or what you are, I am capable of loving you. She wanted to say: I will make love in such a way that you will be thankful for the rest of your days. She wanted to say: I am capable of giving that kind of pleasure. I am capable of experiencing it.

What she wanted was to talk. She wanted to have sex but she didn't write that, she wrote that she wanted to talk. She wanted to cook for someone, or (this is the most humiliating part) to hold hands. Or (this is the most humiliating part of all) she wanted to discuss books. She wrote that she liked candlelight. She wrote that she expected kindness and a sense of humour.

There was no humour evident in what she had written. No humour at all. It was morosely serious. And completely dishonest.

If she had been honest she would have asked: Could you be my dead husband for an afternoon. Could you put on his clothes, I still have them. Will you wear the cologne he wore. Will you smoke Export As, just for an afternoon. Will you drink India beer and burn the steaks on the barbecue, will you be funny and tell jokes and leave groceries for the family down the road who have no groceries. Could you be Cal? Could you smile like Cal, a soft, lopsided smile, and raise a family like Cal, and be brave and courteous and charming with my women friends, and beloved by all who know you, and could you be as smart and awake as Cal, and can you make me come over and over and over again?

Helen and Cal had never held hands. It was one of the many things she regretted. They both saw the importance of keeping some distance. They were the kind of lovers who could have fallen into each other, been swallowed completely, and they had to guard against it. They did not hold hands; they did not eat off each other's plates. But Helen had served him. She had made Cal coffee and put his wool mitts on the heater at night. And had thought about him when he was on the rig.

The trouble is, you get used to it, Helen thought. You get used to being alone. You use the end of a fork to dig the packed-tight coffee grounds from the espresso maker your children gave you for Christmas. There is the smell of cold coffee, of Ethiopia or Somalia, at five in the morning, hitting the plastic bag in the garbage bucket. And how hard-edged and real the garbage looks, how it smells (potato peels, a lump of wet dog food, the coffee). There was a snowstorm raging, the wind was loud, and the house was cold. It was the high ceilings in these old downtown houses. These houses were never warm. This was the trouble, how comfortable she had become with solitude.

· · · · ·

The Night the Rig Went Down, February 1982

HERE'S THE FUNNY thing. Helen had left the burner on. There was a giant pot on the back burner because she was going to make soup, and she had dropped in the chicken carcass and a few onions, and the funny thing was, she went off to sleep on the couch with her book.

She'd already put the kids to bed and she was reading *The Grapes of Wrath* and she woke up because of a kink in her neck. The house was cold and all the lights still on. The cold brightness.

Helen went into the kitchen and turned on the taps so the pipes wouldn't freeze. She felt stupid, thinking about it. She had not dreamt, but the book had been in her hands and she had fought to keep her eyes open. Stupidity was a knotted muscle in the centre of her forehead.

She ran a thin thread of water. If the pipes froze she'd have to be down in the basement with the hair dryer. The pot was boiling furiously but she didn't notice the pot, and all she could think later was that she must still have been asleep.

She switched off all the lights as she went. The girls had the heat on blast in their rooms, and there were clothes and Dinkys and dolls all over their floors. Lulu was snoring and Helen stood and listened to her for a moment and then Lulu flopped onto her side and was abruptly quiet.

The bedsheets were cold, and she got in the bed with her sweatshirt on and her track pants. She began to read her book again but she noticed that her eyes were closed. They had closed by themselves and she tried to open them but she couldn't. She couldn't see the words but she was generating the story herself so she would not have to open her eyes. In the novel someone told her to turn off the light and get some rest, so she did.

But then she was awake. And she heard Cal in the bathroom. She heard the water running and she heard the tap turn off with its particular *squeak*, and she could hear him brushing his teeth and she heard him spit. She heard the drawer open under the sink and he was rummaging through all the cosmetics and she heard, eventually, a length of dental floss being drawn from its plastic case, and the *ping* of the dental floss as he worked it through his teeth. Then the water ran again and was turned off. She heard Cal close the drawer. She wanted to cuddle into him; she wanted his heat. She was strangely chilled. It was from falling asleep on the couch. She was shivering in the bed.

The lid to the wastebasket in the bathroom banged off the wall and fell back down.

Come and look out the window, Cal told her.

Helen got out of bed and put her glasses on and went to the window. It was four in the morning. She knows because she looked at the clock on the vanity table. The ugly brown clock-radio with dust in all the grooves over the speaker and the big red digital numerals, and none of the radio stations worked. The alarm didn't work either. Or they always set it wrong. They would set it for six in the morning and they would hear its tiny *scritch-scritch* noise, what was left of the alarm, at six in the evening. For days after setting it, if they were on the way to the bathroom or putting the laundry away, and especially if the children were outdoors or if she and Cal were making love, the alarm would startle them.

Helen was surprised that it was so late, she remembers quite vividly, thinking how surprising it was, because she felt as if she had not slept at all. And now the day would begin. The window was covered in ferns of frost, elaborate curling tendrils, etched and opaque or transparent. And the wind was banging against the house. She saw the lid of a tin garbage can fly down the street and catch in the branches of a tree.

But then a plow came down over the hill and it was bleating and the revolving light on the top of the cab struck the frosted window and Helen could see thousands of crackles and crystals and grey shimmer burning as white as a flashbulb, violet-white, just for an instant, burning so fiercely it hurt somewhere behind her eyes.

It hurt somewhere deep in her skull. It felt as though the light had pierced her, gone through, and the mad design of the frost, infinitely curling in on itself, had been printed on her retina.

It felt like a puncture. A rapture. It was the pregnancy, she realized much later. It was the pregnancy that had made her so profoundly sleepy, as if drugged, and she was faint or the hormones had created some kind of mild hallucinogenic effect or the light hitting the frost at that second had refracted, each minute crystal a hall of mirrors, so that the intensity was hugely magnified.

The pot on the stove. She blinked and a spot floated down behind her eyelid in the shape of the light from the plow, and it was white in the centre with a violet aureole. She did not exactly remember the pot on the stove; rather, she was jolted and suddenly knew. The pot had been left on the stove. Or perhaps she had smelled the smoke, and in an instant of panic some synaptic misfire had made her experience the stink as a blinding light.

The water had boiled down and the bones of the carcass were black and the inside of the pot was black and the kitchen was full of smoke. The smoke hugged the ceiling and filled half the room like cotton batting, and it was a dense grey, and she held her breath. She flung open the back door and the snowdrift was up to the door handle and she grabbed the oven mitts and took up the pot, threw it into the snowbank on the back deck. It sank out of sight.

It was four in the morning. She opened all the kitchen windows and she left the back door open and the wind howled through. The snow whirled down from the uppermost reaches of the universe, it spun and swarmed the naked bulb of the back-porch light, and it sparkled near the bulb; each snowflake shot through with pinks or blues or greens. The sound the pot made when it hit the snow was a reptilian *hiss*.

It was weeks later, or months, that she remembered Cal had not been in the bathroom; she had only dreamt him. But she had known, unequivocally, that there was reason to be afraid. She had known he was dead.

A NEW DAY

A Lesson, November 2008

HELEN IS AT her morning yoga class and everyone is absolutely still on their separate mats, inward-searching. The first orange rays of the sun are coming through the big frosted windows, stretching in long rippled rectangles over the tiled floor. Flinching concentration. They are a class of shiny, flinching women, except for the gay high school boy, who wears a spandex headband and has dyed blue hair.

Lulu said yoga, so Helen has been doing yoga. The smell of feet and floor polish and the scrudge-squeak, now and then, of a naked foot on the royal blue gym mats that unfold with a slap and send up the smell of dust and sweat.

Sweep your arms out and turn the palms towards the sky, the instructor says, so you can receive the breath. You're going to offer your hearts, she tells them. Helen feels the thump of her heart and tries to look like she is offering it. She glances around. There are expressions on some of the women's faces; they seem to be sincerely offering their hearts.

And reach, reach for the sky, they are told. The instructor breathes in audibly, and then the class breathes in. The instructor exhales. They all exhale.

Consider all you have learned, the instructor says. And let's practise gratitude while we stretch. They practice gratitude silently.

Bring your left foot in, the instructor says, when she figures they've been grateful enough for the moment. And come back to the centre. A muscle in Helen's ass has clenched. It happens every time.

Turn your heart, the instructor says, towards the sky. Helen holds the pose. They are required to think philosophically about their lives while they stretch. Stretching is not enough for the yoga instructor. They are supposed to summon the wisdom they have achieved thus far. And hold. Yoga has a spiritual side, Lulu had explained to Helen. And Helen thinks: a slippery, yeasty-smelling religion having to do with church basements and community halls, ache and release.

Easy pose, with a twist, the instructor says. Look over your left shoulder. They all turn at once to the left and glance back.

This is what Helen has learned: it is possible to be so tired you cannot reach for the sky, you cannot breathe. You can't even talk. You can't pick up the phone. You can't do a dish or dance or cook or do up your own zipper. The children make such a racket. They slam around. They play music on bust or they lie on the couch watching soap operas. They fight and smash things and lose their virginity or they lose their way. They need money and they need to borrow the car. One shoe is always missing. You go through the bookbags, you go through the closet; always one shoe. Gone.

Easy pose, with a twist, look in the other direction, the instructor says. Helen lets the pain invade her other thigh and it is a sonorous voice. There is a voice in her thigh full of recrimination, rising in volume. An April afternoon, she thinks, that was so cold the dog's water bowl had a film of ice and the kids found a sheet of bubble wrap in the church-yard and tied it to their arms — Lulu and Cathy — and they flapped like damaged birds all afternoon. They made potions with mustard pickles and dish soap and dried grass in Mason jars. Their noses ran and the sky looked like it would snow and then it did snow.

Cat-cow pose, the instructor says. As you're opening your chest and your heart, ask yourself, Am I grateful?

They get on their hands and knees and stretch their chins to the ceiling. They stick their bums high in the air and then they arch their backs. The bums in the row in front of Helen are all very different. Shiny and squeezed into Lycra, the bums in the front row look scrawny and forged, or as dim-pled and shapeless as beanbags. She is grateful for these women and their earnest, hard-working bums. Helen is grateful that she has more or less kept in shape.

She is grateful that her children made it through. Her daughters got drunk; they got stoned. There was always a priest who had something to say. There was a teacher. And later there were people who said *coke*, who said *promiscuity*.

But that was all grossly exaggerated. Next I'm supposed to achieve balance, Helen thinks.

And balance table, the instructor says. The foundation of yoga is balance.

And I am grateful, Helen thinks, for the blockbusters at the mall in the summers. All the loud soundtracks, things blowing up and busting apart and all the pieces flying upwards, end over end, into the sky. She had liked the slow tumble of wood and metal, the flame and smoke that covered the big screen. She had liked the roaring music and buckets of popcorn and how it was still bright out when she left the theatre. Helen took the children to the movies on the bus, and they ran up and down the aisle of the bus and swung on the chrome poles. She took any neighbourhood kids who wanted to come so long as they had their own money. It was an hour and a half together in the dark and she and the children felt united, lined up in the seats when the lights dimmed. She was grateful for all the brief escapes.

And balance table the other side, the instructor says. And they extend one arm and one leg. Helen's left buttock bunches tight, all knotted and achy. Her arm begins to tremble. The high school boy is whistling softly. Just part of a phrase, something she actually recognizes, from Nirvana.

Keep your tongue pressed to your palate, breathe through your nose, open your chest and offer your heart, the instructor says. You're going to offer your heart.

Helen is grateful for every one of her children. But she is most grateful, at this moment, for Gabrielle. Her youngest daughter is coming home for Christmas. If John buys the ticket. They sell out, those tickets. She had been after him. Remember to get your sister her ticket.

And Helen thinks of the crib. She'd had to put a crib together — Gabrielle's crib — and she was alone and had jammed the skin between her thumb and index finger in the sliding metal thing that allowed you to lower the side, and she could not turn off the mobile that played "Twinkle, Twinkle, Little Star." Something had caught in the winding mechanism of the mobile so it played on and on.

The crib would not go together — the piece labelled A did not attach to the corresponding latch that was also labelled A — and she took a hammer to it and bent the metal slot just slightly and then she kicked the shit out of it.

She kicked until she was certain she had broken a toe, and then she leaned the railing against the door frame and jumped on it so two wooden bars splintered, and then she threw the mobile at the wall and this somehow slowed "Twinkle, Twinkle, Little Star" so that each note came out sluggishly.

It was the father's job to put the crib together, it was Cal's job, and now she didn't have a crib. She was on her knees, bashing the thing with her fists, screaming at it, Cal's job! She threw the hammer at the wall and it made a hole in the gyproc. She learned not to throw a hammer at the wall. It was one of the things she had learned and was grateful to know.

She stood in the corner of the bedroom looking at the broken crib with she didn't know what kind of expression. Perhaps the same expression she wears now, the twisted silent yowl of stretched stomach muscles.

Helen is grateful her girls are honest with her. Her daughters tell her everything. They tell her because she does not judge. Helen has always let them do what they like. She doesn't want them to be careful, but they are careful. It is the sinister calmness they can muster when they are all in the kitchen together that causes Helen to doubt herself. They worry over her and she does not like it.

Spread your fingers, the instructor says, so you have a strong foundation. We are going to move on to the warrior poses. For those of you not ready for the warrior poses, just follow as far as you can.

I am ready, Helen thinks, for the warrior poses.

Keep your back long, the instructor says. Lulu and Cathy are taller than Helen and they took jobs during high school without her telling them to do so and gave her money for rent. They waitressed or they babysat. They worked at the Newfoundland Hotel. They had uniforms and made excellent wages and it was their own business what they did with the rest of their money. They went to university. They had developed pragmatism about higher education; it would get them places. They hadn't needed to know what they wanted to do; they were willing to do what everybody else was doing, but they kept an inner eye on a kind of anarchic wildness.

When Cathy was in high school, a policeman had knocked on Helen's door and there was Cathy, so drunk she could hardly stand. A young cop holding Cathy up, and the cherry sending out streaks of red and blue for all the neighbours to see. And all Helen could think: Thank God. Thank God. Thank God. Thank God. Four in the morning and she had walked every street, going into the bars, wearing a cardigan that drooped below her ski jacket and sweatpants, seeing the crowds, everybody young and drunk and sexed up and sullen looking, and she had felt as though she were wearing a sandwich board that said *Somebody's Mother.* But Cathy was not among them. Helen had made phone calls and walked in the bitter cold, and the stars were out and it was snowing.

And then the police car, and Helen was certain...because she'd had news before and it had felt like this, the gelid air, the brightness of the fluorescent light in the kitchen, the vaulting horror...but Cathy got out of the back of the patrol car more or less on her own; she was drunk and the knee was torn out of her jeans but she was alive.

She was asleep in a snowbank down by the harbour, the cop said. Helen held Cathy up by the shoulders of her jean jacket: her daughter's pale skin, her black hair, her torn jeans, how comical it all seemed now that she was safe.

Thank you, Officer, I am certainly grateful, Helen said. The bloodied knee, streaks of mascara on her fifteen-year-old daughter's pale freckled face. This was the daughter with the bluest eyes and an uncanny aptitude for math. A fierce intelligence she could mislay like an earring or a key.

The event flooded with its own ending. It was over. Cathy was safe. It was already mawkish and laced with the spice of a near miss, already converted into a story they would tell later on, chuckling: And that poor young police officer, the look on his face. And your mother, then, walking into that bar, Helen imagined herself saying later on. Down the road she could hear herself saying at a family dinner, referring to herself in the third person: And your mother, then, going into the bar in her sweatpants all in a panic, frightened out of her wits, and next thing there were the cops and all the neighbours up to the windows, getting a gawk.

Let's get my little girl to bed, Helen thought. Cathy's forehead hit Helen's collarbone. They were swaying gently. Or the ceiling light, which hung on a chain, was swaying. Cathy raised her head and there were those eyes, and Helen knew before Cathy spoke.

I'm pregnant, Cathy said. And Helen slapped her face. The print of her hand.

The girls left hair on the sink and in the drain, and they shaved their legs and left a ring of grey scum around the bathtub, and they talked on the phone, and the parties they threw, the cold smell of cigarette smoke in the morning and beer and all the windows open, the freezing air coming in.

And they fought with each other, her girls; they bickered. A hairbrush hit the wall, someone borrowed someone's something or other without asking. Where's my new sweater? She took my sweater.

But just let someone outside the family make a disparaging remark. Just let some outsider say something about one or the other of the girls and see how they flew together, ready to defend. They took care of one another. There was the worry of them driving with drunk boys, the worry of illness or no date for the prom, or they wanted expensive things for Christmas or their birthdays, or there was some injustice with a teacher, some threat of expulsion, or they wanted a job or someone wanted to marry them. And then, without warning, they were gone. They had all grown into their own lives, and it was very quiet. Helen had thought she would have to claw her way out of that quiet, and then, very soon after, she was grateful for it.

Bring your awareness to your abdomen, the instructor says. Relax the lower ribs. Slowly curl your tailbone. Inhale and arch up. This exercise is designed to unite the mind and body and spirit. It encourages deep relaxation. Remember to offer your heart on the exhale. This pose is about a vital force rather than a brute force. It is a key that can unlock who you are and make you grateful for all you have, with the added advantage of strengthened abs. And breathe.

· · · · ·

Broken Glass, 1987

HELEN GOT A call from the hospital when John was fourteen, and they asked was she John O'Mara's mother and she said she was. They said it was the Janeway Hospital calling, and John was fine but he'd suffered some cuts and the doctor was just stitching him up.

Quite a few stitches, the nurse said, huffing after Helen as she half-ran down the hospital corridor. John had been to Zellers on Topsail Road with his buddies Neal Yetman and

John Noseworthy, and they had decided to steal some cassette tapes, which they'd put in the hoods of their jackets, and John, her John, was stealing little chocolate Easter bunnies. He'd stuck them into his socks and a security guard was on him in a second, and he ran down the aisle and turned the corner. There was a security alarm pealing out through the store and security guards coming from all sides, three or four of them, and at the very last second they were shouting in a different way, their voices sounded different, or they were saying something different, but John didn't catch it. He was going so fast and full of thrill, and he ran right through a plate-glass door.

He just bashed through, and triangles of glass burst into the sky and somersaulted all around him, and they caught the sun and flashed and bounced on the pavement on their sharp points, and then each giant jagged piece split a thousand times more and John had terrible gashes under his arm and on his legs but it looked worse than it was, the nurse said, just a few scratches really, the nurse charging after Helen as she flew down the corridor—It looks a hell of a lot worse than it is—but his face was okay, thanks be to God. He had passed through that plate of glass and had not done any damage to his face.

After that John mowed lawns. Helen made him mow. And he painted fences. He mowed every lawn she could think of.

The girls didn't give her any trouble and they covered for John when they could. The girls lied for him and lent him money, and they snuck out at night to bring him home if he was drunk, so Helen wouldn't have to worry, and they cleaned the house if John had a party, and they did his homework for him, and still John never gave Helen a moment's peace.

. . . . .

Visitor, June 2008

IF YOU LOOK at it, Helen heard John say. He was home between trips and he was reaching for a puff pastry. There are safety protocols designed, John said, so the men don't think. They don't have to think.

John, Cathy said. This was a party at Helen's place, to celebrate her granddaughter Claire's high school prom.

It was just yesterday, John had said earlier. He had showed Claire how big she was the day she was born, with his hands held apart like you'd measure a trout.

No bigger than a minute, he'd said.

Get in the picture, Cathy said to John. She kicked John and hip-nudged him until she knocked him off the kitchen chair. There was a big spread in the dining room. John had done the cooking. Puff pastry with caramelized onions and apple and Brie. He had the fattest scallops he could get his hands on wrapped in prosciutto. He'd cut miniature beets in half and put ricotta in the middle. He'd wanted to do rabbit but his sisters wouldn't have rabbit, so he'd let Helen do the turkey.

Someone was talking about sodium in the diet of the average Newfoundlander.

I'm just saying, Cathy said. Look at John going with the salt.

Boiled vegetables without salt, Cathy said. She rolled her eyes. They were all crowded in the kitchen because Claire was going to come down in her prom dress. Cathy's daughter Claire, graduating from high school already.

Timmy and Patience were out playing street hockey and the front door kept opening and slamming and there was the smell of fresh air.

Helen pinched the rubber bulb on the baster and drew up the bubbling fat and squirted it out over the turkey. Her glasses were steamed. She shoved the roaster back into the oven and lifted the screeching oven door with her foot.

I've got a carpenter coming, she said. To do the floors, and I'm getting the place painted.

Mom, Lulu said. That's fabulous.

Helen smacked the rims of the pots with the stainless steel spoon after she stirred, and she turned to face her children, navy and silver oven mitts on her hands. I want something called Sail White for the trim, and for the dining room a colour they call Latte, she said.

The thinking has changed, Claire said, on salt. There she was, in the doorway. She was wearing pink with a shiny bodice, and the skirt was full of layers and sheaths of different pinks, and there was glitter. She was unsteady on the new heels. Helen gripped her hands together, still in the oven mitts, to stop herself from clapping.

I'm not liking the lipstick, Claire said. She twisted her mouth up.

Oh, you have to wear lipstick, Cathy said. Wear it for me.

I don't want to.

Finishes it off, Cathy said. A little touch of colour.

You're beautiful, Helen said.

Isn't she something, John said.

Cathy slapped her hand over her mouth. How did this happen, she wailed. How did you grow up so fast?

I'll wear the lipstick, Claire said. For some reason Mom's gone all apeshit about lipstick.

Cathy started to cry and hustled out of the room with her head down, hunched and trotting. They heard the bathroom door upstairs slam. The door opened and Cathy screamed down to them, I just want her to look nice. Is that a crime? And the door slammed again.

I'll wear the lipstick, Claire yelled at the ceiling. A toilet flushed and it sounded doleful. They were quiet in the kitchen. Helen had turned off the pots on the stove and even the sound of boiling water had gone quiet, and they could hear some kind of bird chirping in the backyard.

Cathy came back into the room and drained the potatoes and started with the masher. She pounded the vegetables. Lulu handed her a foil-wrapped stick of butter.

I'm just so proud of her, Cathy said. Her grade average.

I know, Lulu said.

She graduated with honours.

You told us.

I don't know where she gets it.

I know where she gets it, Helen said.

I don't care, Cathy said, about the Jesus lipstick.

I'm wearing the lipstick, Claire said. Mom? See? I'm wearing the lipstick.

There was a thump of silence while they took in the seventeen-year-old, while they allowed her beauty to radiate through the room. They all took in the moment and they could feel how it was portentous. And in the swollen beat John brought it up again about the oil patch.

What I was saying, John said, is that the trouble now is a guy doesn't have to think any more. And this can be a danger. It's not good for the industry, the culture that has developed around safety. They're like a crowd of old women.

He would not shut up about the rigs and protocols and things none of them wanted to hear.

Safety is a good thing, Helen said.

Nobody spoke. Claire was fiddling with her corsage and a pin dropped on the table.

Did you hear that pin drop, Claire said.

I don't want to start something, Helen said.

Then don't start something, Mom, Cathy said. John knows safety is important.

I was just saying, John said.

Shut up about it, John, Cathy said.

What I was saying—

Why don't you shut up?

Okay, champagne, John said. Can I say champagne?

It was spring and still cold outside, but there was sun, and Claire had been at a beauty salon and she smelled of product.

Let's get one with your grandmother, Cathy said. Helen put her arm around the girl and drew her in.

Don't wrinkle me, Claire said.

The champagne cork shot up, hit the ceiling, and fell on the table. A white twirl of foam spewed out of the bottle and

Cathy held out a glass, but John put his mouth over the bottle opening and his cheeks bulged out.

The doorbell rang.

He's here, Claire said. She flapped her hands in front of her face as if she were overheated, and her eyes watered. Her eyes turned, under the glaze of tears, from blue to ultramarine, and the bell rang again. She instantly became matter-of-fact. Somebody answer the door, she said. She put the champagne glass to her lips and crinkled her nose because of the fizz.

Don't ruin your makeup, Cathy said. She's ruining her makeup. Tell her not to ruin the makeup.

Don't ruin your makeup, honey, Helen said.

I'm not ruining my makeup. And they turned, all of them, to greet Claire's date. But it was Mrs. Conway from down the street.

I came to get a look at you, Mrs. Conway said. The date had not arrived. The conversation juddered back up to a loud volume. Helen looked at the clock on the stove. On the way to the bathroom Helen checked out the front door and stood there, watching the kids playing street hockey.

Her grandson Timmy in the net. Patience getting ready to shoot. The puck flew up hard and hit Timmy, and he bent over it and dropped to his knees and didn't move. Everybody on the street stood still. Timmy put his hand to his helmet as if his head was too heavy for his neck. Then they were both kneeling, Timmy and Patience. She had her hand on his shoulder, her head bent close to his. They spoke, like that, on their knees. A car came up behind them, headlights in the dusk. They were lit and solemn and lost in something intimate and full of childish innocence.

Then Timmy stood and raised his stick as if he were going to bring it down on Patience's head and bash her brains out. He raised that stick so fast that Helen caught her breath: Two hands, over his head. Helen cracked the door open to shout, but Patience leapt out of the way and doubled over with laughter and the stick came down on the asphalt with a slap and cracked in two. The kids moved the nets to the side and the car went past, and they moved the nets back.

In the kitchen behind Helen the talk kept getting louder and brighter; there was more laughter. Mrs. Conway told about a case of gout. She'd come down with a case of gout, she literally couldn't walk, and then she'd thrown out the opposite hip. They all laughed.

The foot and then the hip, Mrs. Conway said. They were roaring with laughter. Someone slapped the table.

In the bloody mall, then, Mrs. Conway squawked. Going with the shopping cart. First one thing, then the other, Mrs. Conway said.

Helen saw the street lights pop on. They flickered and popped, mostly all at once. One or two came on after the others. And then a taxi pulled up and the kids moved the nets again and Helen backed away from the window, just a little, and there the young fellow was in the suit and he was paying the taxi, she could see him in the cab light, and he was what? A half-hour late? Not even. Twenty minutes. She saw him look at the piece of paper and look at the house, and she went back into the kitchen and the doorbell rang.

The talk in the kitchen faltered. It dipped to a near whisper while John answered the door.

And then, there he was. He walked into a crowded silent kitchen and saw Claire with a cracker and a cube of cheese raised to her mouth, the other hand cupped to catch crumbs. Claire lowered the cracker. How pink that dress is, Helen thought. It had taken a month and a half to do the beadwork. They were all waiting for him to say how beautiful, but he was taking Claire in, and the crowded kitchen and the cracker with the cube of very orange cheese and the silence.

You look beautiful, he blurted, and everybody laughed, and Mrs. Conway imitated her gout walk — across the kitchen floor, slopping champagne — and Helen told everyone to serve themselves.

This is ready, she said.

. . . . .

John's Survival Training, 1992

LIKE ALL THE other men working on the rigs, John had to get into the simulator. He was wearing the survival suit. He had to strap himself in. There was a small staircase that rose to the shell of a helicopter with chairs strapped to the floor. You punched out a window. You pulled the ribbon and pushed gently with both hands so the helicopter window floated away. That was the idea. You pushed gently or you kicked the shit out of the window.

He broke into a drenching sweat. The survival suit was too warm, the rubber boots too heavy. It was a big suit, with ventilation zippers, but John had zipped everything up. He'd Velcro'ed the polypropylene cuffs. The suit stuck to his calves and his back; it rubbed against his neck. He strapped himself into the helicopter seat.

The instructor's name was Marvin Healey. Marvin tucked his index finger under the safety belt and lifted it away from John's stomach and let it slap back against him. Then he patted John on the shoulder.

You're all strapped in there, Marvin said.

He glanced down at John and must have seen the lines of sweat on his brow and temple. John knew what would follow: they would sink the capsule and water would flood through all the seams, rising in the plastic bubble to cover his feet and legs and groin and chest and neck, and then they would tip it over so John would be upside down, and his face and neck and the rest of him would go all the way under.

It was that covering of the face with how many cubic tons of terror that got him. It closed in on you and pressed and was cloying, and it would be only a number of seconds before it sucked away your life. You had to trust the others to get you out. He had lost consciousness the last time.

Passing out was easy, passing back in was difficult. Passing back in required intuition and faith. Faith cannot be willed. Shame and failure and vomiting were all part of passing back in. You awoke to all that was wrong with you. You were left inside out, all your most private parts showing.

The instructor had introduced himself as Mr. Healey and he had called each man by his last name followed by the first. O'Mara, John. As if he were reading from the clipboard.

Mr. Healey said: I'm looking for a volunteer. O'Mara, John did not volunteer to go first.

Mr. Healey gave a lecture about safety and how it would change your life in ways not necessarily obvious at first, but eventually — Mr. Healey promised — there would be an occasion, such occasions fell into each modern life at least once without warning or fanfare, and then these safety skills would most definitely be required. The men would be grateful, Mr. Healey predicted.

The ordinary survival suit is a man's best friend on the water, Mr. Healey said. It's that simple.

As Mr. Healey lectured, John remembered a nun from elementary school talking about a boy who had died near the water fountain when they were in grade three. John had been standing behind Jimmy Fagan, waiting for his turn at the fountain. Suddenly the boy had held the side of his head and staggered to the staircase and clung to the banister as if they were in a rough sea. John remembered the little spigot, the water that bubbled up when you twisted the handle, and the boy, Jimmy Fagan, with his mouth buried in that wet silver arc.

A simple soul, the nun had said. John remembered that. It was what they were to strive towards: simplicity. As far as he had understood it, simplicity entailed a kind of forgetting. Forget that you matter. Or that anything matters.

The surface of the pool behind Mr. Healey was glaring with ceiling light, weaving and unweaving.

They were to strive towards a forgetting equal to the glacial scraping John had learned about in geography that year. A gouging out of anything that was not simple.

Somebody has to go first, Mr. Healey said. He rose twice on the balls of his feet. He was wearing white sneakers and they were unpleasantly feminine. Marvin Healey worked out and the muscles in his chest were like those of a comic-book avenger, and he had a tan, and his hair was incandescent silver. It was an easy shade of grey to associate with wisdom.

Can I have a volunteer, Mr. Healey asked. Only two of the ten men in the class could swim. These men did not volunteer. They were mute.

O'Mara, John: Marvin Healey said. He was looking down over the names on his clipboard. Mr. Healey had divulged personal information about himself now and then during the classes, sometimes by way of instructive anecdote — he had told the men, for example, about his phobia of birds. One day he'd come out of a gas station in Bay Roberts to find a seagull sitting on the front seat of his convertible. He had gone next door to Mary Brown's and bought a jumbo box of fries to convince the gull to leave the car. He'd called to it and clucked his tongue and stood in the sun, bareheaded, for close to a half-hour, begging the seagull, whispering and praying and tossing fries, and the bird had watched him, thoroughly unmoved. Then Mr. Healey had felt something brush against his pant leg and had looked down to see there were perhaps fifty seagulls at his feet, pressing closer and closer. The lesson, he had told the class, was not to panic.

Mr. Healey gave a little wave to someone in the office and the capsule sank into the pool.

Water has a single imperative. Every drop is hurling itself towards itself always. All water wants is to eat out its own stomach. It flushes through itself and becomes heavier and faster and it plows on, even while remaining still.

There were divers on the floor of the pool, dressed in black rubber, and when viewed from the surface their bodies warbled thin as burnt matchsticks and then ballooned squat and wide.

No man would ever survive the North Atlantic for more than five minutes without a survival suit that fit properly, even if he could swim. And the chances of surviving a helicopter crash, even with the suit, were next to nothing. Every man knew that. They all knew. But each man ever to set foot on an oil rig had to kick his way out of a simulated helicopter crash if he wanted to keep his job.

John and his plastic capsule were dropped into the pool. The water rushed in faster than anything had ever rushed anywhere. It was a property of water — it could move faster than you'd think. It moved all at once. Water came in and John's head was under and he kicked the door.

He remembered to release the straps, which was better than the last time he'd tried, and then he passed out. Which only meant he would have to do it again.

· · · · ·

A Storm, 1980

SOMETIMES HELEN REMEMBERS how that dog went missing a half-hour before the storm started. The rain fell in straight sheets, without a breath of wind. There were hundreds of thousands of separate sheets, one behind the other, and together they made a translucent wall. The trees at the corner of the lawn warped and wobbled behind the wall of water as if they were in gelatin. The shed was wonky. The rain danced off the flagstones. It struck the stones so hard it might have caused sparks. The water in the dog's bowl spilled over. It was getting dark and the dog hated the rain. One of the kids had forgotten to shut the back door.

Cal put on rubber boots and an oilskin he had hanging in the back porch, and he took the flashlight. The pale circle cast by the flashlight jiggled all over the grass. He got in the truck and started the engine. Sometimes the sound of the engine was enough to make the dog come. The headlights came on and the rain in the headlights fell very fast and straight like sewing needles.

Helen couldn't leave the house because the children were asleep. There was lightning and it lit up the bedroom with a stark light that seemed blue-tinged or too white. She went to the window to watch, and the lightning showed the rain outside and it leached the green lawn of colour so that it looked grey and it made the side of the white church, far away on the hill, flash. The ocean went grey and the wild foam on the waves was ultraviolet. It was a spank of unnatural light that lasted too long, and then it fluttered and sucked itself back off the land and the ocean, and everything was darker than before. The thunder rolled a long way. It seemed to roll all the way from Bell Island, across the ocean. It came right up to the lawn. It rolled onto the lawn and boomed there just outside the window. It made the window panes rattle in the old, half-rotted mullions. This was the house they had bought around the bay, and they came out in summer when Cal was off the rig.

Helen had fallen asleep without ever having decided to lie down, and she woke when Cal came back. He leaned against the door frame and wept.

All I can think, he said. He must be trapped or he can't come home. He doesn't like the rain. Helen went to hold Cal but he shook her off.

I'm soaking wet, he said.

They'd fought about the dog. They'd fought about it sleeping on the bed. Cal left forks with wet dog food in the sink and the smell made her gag. He let the dog kiss his face. He fed the dog from the table. Cal held a chunk of barbecued steak in the air above the dog's head and the dog looked up at it and remained very still.

Watch this, watch, Cal said. Don't move, he said softly.

The dog stayed still and then there was a sound that was high-pitched and came from the dog's throat, and the dog lifted one paw and put it down and lifted the other and put it down.

Don't, said Cal. And the dog went still again. Helen could not stand any of this. And then the meat dropped, and the dog's jaw snapped and ripped the meat out of the air and there would be two more wet snaps of the jaw and the meat was gone. This whole show delighted Cal so much he'd push his chair from the table and slap his thighs and the dog would jump up and put his head over Cal's neck and they'd both growl at each other, and Helen would say, Not at the table.

Cal peeled off his wet clothes and he got in bed beside her and his legs were freezing, and his feet. Then he threw the blankets back off with a ripping sound and he was gone again, and Helen heard the back door and the truck and Cal driving off.

He came back at dawn and Helen dressed and went outside to look for the dog herself. She walked for an hour. Her clothes were soaked as soon as she went out. Her jeans stuck to her thighs and calves.

The river was swollen and churning brown, and there were broken trees, and the splintered wood looked very yellow in the dark. The river was rushing faster than she had ever seen, and it had pressed itself out over the banks and it was smooth and thick over the boulder the kids usually jumped off, and it was dangerous. She stopped to smell a wild rose, the petals covered with big drops of rain, and it smelled like cinnamon and a dusky sweetness that was particular to wild roses.

The dog must be dead, she thought. It was crazy how much Cal loved the dog. People said it was a Nova Scotia duck toller, but it was a mutt. Reddish brown with a curling tail, and after several summers they saw a lot of dogs with that tail in their neighbourhood. It was a small pretty dog, but it tore the arm off her when Helen tried to walk with it on a leash. Busting with energy. When it wanted to get out in the backyard the dog barked at the door and leapt up and down, yapping.

When Helen came back to the house the lawn was covered in water and only the very tips of each blade of grass stippled the glassy surface, and the rain had almost stopped. It was still falling, but it fell silently, and there was sun and the clouds and the blue sky reflected in the glassy surface over the lawn. The smell of the wood-stove smoke was very strong. Everything smelled fresh. The kids were up and Cal was cooking scrambled eggs and he didn't turn around when she came in.

I know he must be dead, Cal said. But I can't imagine it.

We'll all get in the car, Helen said.

If he wasn't dead he would be back by now. Cal put the eggs on small plastic saucers with Big Bird on each. He had a plate with the toast in the oven and he took it out, forgetting it was hot, and dropped the plate on top of the stove and flicked his hand hard, holding it at the wrist.

Fucking plate, he said.

He served the eggs and gave everybody toast, and he poured the children juice, and there was coffee and he poured two cups.

Everybody in the truck, Helen said.

Let them eat, Cal said.

Everybody in the truck, she said. The children all got in and Helen climbed up and pulled the door closed and rolled down the window. All of the land was steaming now.

Seat belts, she said. The sun had come out hotter now, and ragged bits of steam drifted over the highway, and there was a low-lying bank of fog drifting across the bay. They all called to the dog along the highway. Cal drove slowly, and then Cathy screamed.

There he is, Cathy screamed.

At first the dog didn't move and it looked like he was dead for sure, but then he lifted his head and Cal pulled over. They ran down the steep bank, and the dog was hurt. He was lying in a puddle of water, and the cold, and his fur was soaked, and he looked like he might die even though they'd found him. His fur had been scraped off his hind leg to the bone, which was yellow-white, and he was shivering violently and hardly able to move, and Cal picked him up and spoke to him.

Cal said, It's okay, we're not going to let you die.

Cal drove them all to the vet, and they drove back home at the end of the day. It had taken a long time to get to the vet in Carbonear and so they left the dog overnight. His back leg was broken but there were no internal injuries and it was going to cost them two hundred dollars.

When they got back to the house it was dark, and Cal turned on the light. He had Lulu asleep in his arms. He and Helen got the children settled. Then the two of them went back downstairs, and the scrambled eggs were still sitting on the yellow Big Bird plates and there was the untouched orange juice in three small glasses. They both stood looking at the table. The overhead light bulb was bare.

The eggs and the Big Bird plates and the juice and the smell that comes after a rain — Helen remembers how all of these things made her think for a moment that she was walking in on a scene in a museum, a tableau from a lost life: Outport Newfoundland, circa 1980.

．．．．．

John's Girlfriend, 2005

JOHN HAD HAD two of the sort of relationships he would call serious. The question of children had come up with both of the women. They had each fallen in love with him not quite believing he couldn't be convinced or tricked into father-hood.

Both times the end had come down to a cauterizing discussion. The end with Sophie took place in her basement apartment; they had just painted the kitchen pale green and the paint was scented. Forever after, the smell of mint reminded him of the late hour, the stark walls, and how Sophie had slid down one of them, leaving a streak in the wet paint. She sat on the floor, her shoulders hunched, elbows together between her knees, her wrists loose so that her hands were hanging limp near her face.

She was shaking with hard sobs but there was very little noise. John tried to pat her, or smooth her hair, but she slapped his hand away. She looked up, her face slicked with tears and snot, pink with ferocity.

You will be alone, she said. A lonely eccentric old man with no one to change your colostomy bag, you won't even have a cat, or you'll have thirty cats shitting on the kitchen floor. You'll stink of loneliness.

He left the apartment without another word. It had got dark outside Sophie's apartment while they'd been painting. The heavens had opened up. The rain was lashing the sidewalks and bouncing back up under the street lights. It ran in little streams near the curb, piling against a pop can and hurtling on, dragging brown leaves. It glassed over the street in overlapping sheets that flared with the reflection of passing headlights. John's socks were soaked inside his shoes. What he didn't feel was regret or sadness. He felt exhilarated.

He had loved Sophie; or he had enjoyed her cooking and the dope she grew in her bedroom closet. A big closet with grow lights. The dense green stink and tickling leaves when you stepped inside. The bushes were almost as tall as she was and half a joint could knock you silly. She had a way of rubbing the leaves and then bringing her fingers to her nose to smell them that he found erotic. There were things she claimed she could tell by smelling the leaves. She spoke as if the plants had an inner life and he didn't question her because he was afraid of what she might say. Sophie knew an esoteric vocabulary of wattage and seed and water and she tended those plants with a feeling that verged on respect.

She sold her weed for reasonable prices; that was important to her. She liked the social aspect of meeting with her customers. She liked the secret lazy hours she'd spend with unemployed people or university professors or retired lawyers. They talked about politics and ways to change the world.

John had admired the way she set a table: chunky and tarnished candelabra, a hand-woven Mexican tablecloth with a stripe of outrageous pink down the middle. She went in for novelty drinks and the sort of gamey meat that was full of tiny bones and that she covered in pastry. Or she went vegetarian for weeks. Sometimes the entire surface of her kitchen table had been covered with drying chanterelles. She frequented poky health-food stores and bought grains and spices John had never heard of, and she spoke about putting together a barbershop quartet. If she had a gift, it was for harmonizing. She was smarter than John and had a way of narrowing her eyes while she waited for him to catch up.

But a baby; the cry for a baby was like a haunting. John had thought they needed a priest or some holy man of another stripe to exorcise it. He felt that he'd been let in on a glimpse of what Sophie would become: hunched and puffy-lidded, ghoulish against the faintly green-tinted fresh paint. This had nothing to do with the nakedness of Sophie's back in her black sequined dress or the sound of her flute in the late afternoon — the things he loved. She was looking for an enslavement that would chain them both. She wanted to put aside all of her elegance for something squalling and blood related. The sight of blood made John faint.

The walk across the lane from her apartment that night drenched him to the skin. He waited for the car to warm up. It smelled of the wet tweed coat he was wearing. It was as if Sophie had been washed away.

And she didn't phone, though he'd expected her to and had made plans to change his number.

He saw her two months later on the street hanging off the arm of a guy with a guitar strapped to his back. She looked overjoyed to see him. There was no sign of fierceness now. She hugged him with one arm, not quite disentangling from the musician. She introduced John, calling him *a really fantastic friend*, and did not provide any identifying information about the musician who was tugging her away.

We're late, Sophie explained to John. She shrugged, as if being late was a little caprice she shared with the musician, a cute quirk to which they had become inexplicably vulnerable as a couple.

After this chance encounter John had been briefly but thoroughly heartbroken. He saw what he had lost: the scratchy scarf she wound around her neck; she was gawky and too tall; she had a camera, was always concocting some kind of memento; once he'd seen her twist the foil from someone's cigarette pack into an origami swan. He was thirty-two at the time; what was wrong with children? He found himself looking at backpacks and Snuglis. It was the fact that children were not portable that frightened him. Not portable enough. He racked his brain but he could not remember the musician's name.

After Sophie, John discovered he enjoyed sleeping with younger women. Five, ten years younger. These young women were not in any hurry to get pregnant; they were militant about protecting against it. He loved their Facebooks and pink cellphones and cotton panties, more athletic and good-humoured than sexy, with half-funny quips scrawled across the ass. He loved the hundreds of pictures they took of themselves with cameras held at arm's length, their Mike's Hard Lemonade and midnight binges of chips, dressing and gravy, and the empty beer bottles on the faded Arborite and chrome tables they picked up at the Sally Ann and frequently threatened to sell on eBay for a fortune. He liked their lip gloss with flavours from childhood (watermelon, bubblegum), and just how fast they were to parse a romance or a brawl.

They were fast/slow at sex, both diffident and indefatigable, petulant only in a sort of parodic way, and above all, generous. Ultimately, it didn't seem to be about them. It was as though they had all read Dale Carnegie and expected to get somewhere by being friendly. He found there was plenty to go around, and he could not get enough.

John's parents, before his father died, had spent time around the bay and eventually bought land near a lake where they spent their weekends. John had liked the saturated intensity of those childhood evenings, his mother and father on the wharf holding plastic glasses or enamel camping cups with rye and ice. His mother's crocheted bikini, her dark tan. His parents would watch him fish and they would drink, sometimes talking to each other, sometimes not. When they spoke to him they spoke quietly, knowing their voices carried over the still surface. He could hear a neighbour's fishing line at the other end of the lake, unfurling, cutting through the air.

His parents had been more together than apart. They had grown together; they had been the same. John did not want that for himself.

. . . . .

Helen Dating, 2006

AND SO, AFTER many emails, Helen had a date. She had said she would be wearing a purple coat and she would be at the bar, and it was awful sitting there alone with her gin and tonic.

Every eye was on her, knowing she was a fraud. Knowing she did not belong in a bar. She was a hunk of meat hanging on a hook, waiting for a buyer. She had been to Halliday's that afternoon and the butcher had opened the door to the walk-in fridge and she'd seen what must have been, at one time, a cow, hanging from a hook.

She had smelled the frost and mineral-laden air. The rusty smell of frozen blood, and she'd seen the skeins of yellow fat. The butcher had come out and smacked his hands together and rubbed them back and forth, and he'd laid a steak on the stainless steel cutting board and turned on the saw, and he'd cubed it for her. Little stiff cubes with frost fibres in the purplish flesh, and this, Helen realizes now, is herself, her own heart, sliding back and forth under the blade.

Her heart was loud in her chest and it would be a lie to say she wasn't exhilarated. None of her friends would have the guts to do this, to stay on this bar stool, to wait. She did not know one person who could do as she was doing.

The poor young waitress behind the bar—she tried so hard to look like there was nothing strange about Helen. She tried to look like she had never in her life heard of loneliness or decay or rot or maggots or something slower and less dignified, this middle-aged need to touch someone. The bartender mentioned the weather and her courses at university, she made small talk, and Helen kept saying, Pardon me? Because she couldn't hold the beginning of a thought together with the end of it; she was too scared.

When customers came into the bar there was a blast of cold and snow because it was snowing hard, and the traffic would be a problem in this kind of weather. Helen sat where she could see the door and she counted seven men who might have been Heathcliff.

The man she was waiting for had called himself Heathcliff and he was an insurance salesman, but somebody somewhere had told him that women like literary types. They like to think you're sensitive, he'd written to Helen.

He had confessed all this to Helen and he was liberal with the emoticons. They had written to each other every day for three months, Helen and Heathcliff.

Nineteen people entered the bar while Helen waited and seven of the nineteen might have been him. There were seven possible Heathcliffs, and they came in and got themselves a drink and left, and none of them looked at her. They sat by themselves without removing their coats and the bartender put drinks down in front of them and they drank hunched over the glass as if they expected someone to grab it.

Or they took off their coats and were joined by someone from the office and they drank one fast beer because the wife was waiting. The wife had supper on. They accepted a glass with their beer but they didn't drink from the glass; they drank directly from the bottle and they put the bottle down with finality and shrugged themselves back into their coats.

One man in a herringbone coat with a wine-coloured cashmere scarf and black gloves leaned into the bar beside Helen, and of course she thought it was him.

Some weather, he said.

Is it getting nasty, she asked. The bartender put down a shot glass in front of the man and he peeled off a bill from a wad of bills and he said to the bartender: I want you to make me a solemn promise. You won't give me another one of these supposing I twist your arm.

The girl rolled her eyes and Helen saw they were flirting, though the man was thirty years older. The girl was happy to flirt. She couldn't have been more than twenty and Helen felt ridiculously warmed by the flirting. It was as if they were including her, and the girl was rolling her eyes for Helen's benefit, and wasn't it funny — the ugly weather and the older man draining the shot glass in one gulp and touching the glass back down deliberately. His cellphone rang and he took it out of his pocket and looked at the number and turned it off and put it back in his pocket.

That's the wife, he said. He gave a little shudder and the girl behind the counter smirked. He was the kind of man who wanted the bartender to know what his usual was. It wasn't Heathcliff because Heathcliff didn't have a wife.

The man exhaled deeply and Helen smelled the Scotch and a mint, and underneath those smells something bad. It was just a whiff of mint and Scotch and a bitter smell, the smell of a long afternoon trapped in an office, trapped in some unsavoury pursuit.

Now, the man said. Give me another one, my love. The girl made a little show of crossing her arms, closing her eyes and tilting her chin up, a show of primness. She was pretending to be unmovable.

Don't make me come over this counter after you, the man said.

The girl sighed a deep stage sigh and poured the drink.

Because I don't mind one bit coming after you, the man said. He was smiling. He was not Heathcliff.

And it occurred to Helen then that Heathcliff had come and gone. She was slow to accept it. She was stunned.

Heathcliff had come and looked at her and didn't find her attractive. It was so far outside the scope of what she knew to be decent human behaviour that she could not fathom it, though some part of her also knew it exactly. She went to the bathroom and got down on her knees in front of the filthy toilet and puked. The floor of the bathroom had slush all over it and the knees of her nylons were soaked; a single tiny stone dug sharply into her knee. What she was vomiting was the belief that getting old didn't matter. Because it did matter. It mattered a lot and there was no stopping it, and everything inside her heaved out that idea.

Helen had read an entire email about the pain of having a plantar wart removed from the sole of Heathcliff's foot. She had commiserated. He had been afraid and she had written right away to find out how the laser treatment had gone.

They had been erotic online. She had confessed certain fantasies. He had said what he liked. She had been flowery and subtle; he was blunt and clichéd.

The bar door slammed with the wind. The wind took the door and it crashed closed.

Heathcliff never wrote her again, and Helen never wrote him. But the grotesque banality and the acute intimacy of the plantar wart email haunted her for months afterwards.

· · · · ·

Back in the Workforce, 1990s

THERE FOLLOWED, AFTER Cal died and the children were older, a job in an office, and Helen had to learn about computers. All the other employees were twenty years younger. The bloody audit, the bloody audit. For ten years she had a boss who called to her through the corridors, Here comes the old bat. Trevor Baxter was American and he was trying to be funny.

Helen hated computers. All she did was work and sleep. She fell asleep in her car, waiting for it to warm up. She fell asleep in a bank lineup, her wallet spilling out of her hand. She was depressed, the doctor said. She was menopausal. He prescribed transcendental meditation. He prescribed confession and the Holy Eucharist. What about a trip, he said.

Trevor Baxter said, Here comes the old bat, five minutes late, I see. Standing in the door of his office, looking at his watch.

The old bat is late again, he'd boom.

Helen would not complain because she knew Trevor Baxter's wife was leaving him and his heart was a canker. He could not boil an egg, he had once told her, weeping at his desk. He could not match his socks when they came out of the dryer. He banged around his empty house by himself; he did not sleep. He hadn't slept in months.

The children are on her side, he told Helen. The children barely spoke to him. His sister-in-law had attacked him in the supermarket, shrill and castigating.

So tight you squeak, the sister-in-law had hissed.

Trevor Baxter had grown up in poverty. He would not have it. All the spending. He knew the value of a dollar. Let her loose with a credit card? he'd snorted. Not in this lifetime.

Trevor had come home one day and the dining room table was gone, and the chairs and half of the cutlery, and there were things missing it took him weeks to notice. His wife had taken the corkscrew. She had taken the oven mitts. The salt shaker that had been passed down in his father's family for four generations. He had been making all the money for both of them; in his mind, it was for them both. And so she had taken half. There was nothing he could do to stop it. She had taken half but he had lost everything. That was the math of it.

Of course Helen pitied him; but beneath the pity was a colossal irritation.

You had someone, she wanted to shout at him. She wanted to hit him. She wanted to punch his face, and with each blow she would have said: You had someone; you had someone.

Back to work, Trevor Baxter said.

Helen pushed the Kleenex box towards him and he took one and blew his grey hairy nose, loudly, wetly, wagging it back and forth in the tissue, wiping from side to side. She saw that he was ugly; the ugliest, most misshapen man she had ever seen, and he would be alone forever, and Helen would be alone forever too.

And later in the morning he opened his door and shouted down the hall: Where is the old bat with my memo?

The girls in the office were young and they thought Helen was fair-minded. Helen could settle disputes with a tilt of her head; she was regal and intuitive about all the small hurts and poverties and flares of temper that ran like grass fires through an office; she collected for the shower gifts. Helen had something they did not have, something they aspired to but could not name. They would have been mortified to learn it was experience. They did not want experience. Helen was sad and the young women didn't understand the sadness but they respected it. A blow had been struck, bull's-eye, without warning, and it had scarred Helen. If such a thing should happen to one of them, they would want to survive it the way Helen had. She was not austere; she did not advise; she would not judge. Helen was what their grandmothers would have called a lady, the girls in the office thought.

These young women had missed feminism by half a decade. They thought of a lady as a woman who had achieved minor spiritual enlightenment, who was accomplished in — but ultimately eschewed — the domestic arts, vaguely romantic and generous. Helen was generous in her every gesture and the young women in the office saw she was not diminished by it. The girls knew Helen's husband had gone down on the *Ocean Ranger* but they did not put it together with the woman who did payroll.

One day Joanne Delaney came into Helen's office and closed the door behind her. Joanne Delaney's eyes were glittering.

We have all decided to walk out, she said. We will walk out together. Every single one of us is willing. We are not going to let him speak to you that way any more, Helen. This is for all of us.

Even as Joanne Delaney spoke Trevor Baxter called out, Where is the old bat? Where is she?

But Helen took the situation in hand. Simmer down, Helen said. I can manage him.

. . . . .

Who's There? *1995*

ARE WE GOING to fight over a salad bowl, Cathy asked. There were two big salad bowls exactly alike. Cathy dug the bowl out from the back of the cupboard and wiped the dust out with a paper towel.

Mom, can I have this?

Why don't you take everything, Helen said. Claire was five and starting kindergarten, and Cathy had a new apartment. They'd all gone over together for a look and it was a bloody shithole. Indoor/outdoor carpet that smelled like feet and you could hear someone on the other side of the wall opening a kitchen drawer and the clatter of cutlery.

You couldn't fart in here, Helen had said. Without the whole world knowing.

Cathy had gone to night school and got her grade eleven, and then she'd registered at MUN. She'd done nursing. Helen said nursing and Cathy did nursing. All those books lying out on the dining room table. Helen would cook supper for them and she'd do the dishes while Cathy studied. Helen would put Claire to bed.

She and Claire read *Goodnight Moon*, and *Thomas the Tank Engine*, and they read Beverly Cleary and Amelia Bedelia and

Five-Minute Mysteries. They read *1001 Knock-Knock Jokes* over and over, the answers printed upside down on the bottom of the page. Orange you glad I didn't say banana. Dwayne the bathtub, I'm dwowning. Cantaloupe, I'm already married.

This had been Helen's approach to parenting: Because I said so.

Parenting. The verb hadn't even existed back when Helen was doing it, as far as she knew.

Helen did not take tranquilizers. Her children would never know it, but this was her approach to parenting: she was there for them. Her doctor had said pills, and she had said no. Helen was there, morning, noon, and night. That was her approach. She had wanted to die. She did not die.

The public health nurse had told pregnant fifteen-year-old Cathy: Adoption. She had said the Catholic Church offered support for girls in her situation. She didn't say *abortion*. The public health nurses didn't say *abortion* back then.

She had been speaking to Cathy, but she was looking at Helen.

The other children had skulked around the house during this time. There was a time when they were quiet in their rooms. They were quiet at the supper table. They were quiet while Cathy was throwing up behind the bathroom door. They could hear her retch and they heard vomit hit the toilet water and then the kettle would start to boil and it would sound like a roar. Gabrielle demanded to know what was going on. It made John stab his green peas. The tines hitting the plate *ping, ping, ping, ping.* And then he dropped the fork with a clatter.

Helen was sewing a wedding gown for Louise's soon-to-be daughter-in-law and John had slouched against the door frame. She let the machine run the whole seam and the needle had cracked, and then she put down her glasses and said, What do you have to say for yourself?

Nothing, John said.

I am doing my best, she said. John pushed himself off the door frame with great effort and went down the hall and the screen door slammed.

Where are you going, she called after him. But he was already gone.

Cathy had raised the child with Helen, and now Cathy had a place of her own. Helen said about the expense, but they both knew it had nothing to do with money. This is the thank you, Helen thought. This is the way they say thanks these days.

Because it's my bowl, that's why, Helen thought. Because if I want two Jesus bowls exactly the same I'll have two Jesus bowls. Because I said. But she did not say this.

I saw the ultrasound by mistake, Cathy had told her before Claire was born. She'd called Helen from the hospital. She was in one of those dark corridors on a smelly pay phone crawling with germs.

I saw it, Cathy said. They weren't supposed to show me but the technician turned the screen.

She hadn't wanted Helen at the birth.

I want to come, Helen had said.

I don't want you to, Mom.

Why not?

Because I said, that's why.

The agitation as the due date approached. Helen wanted to be there but Cathy wouldn't give in.

Why can't we raise it together, John said. Nobody spoke. I'm just asking because isn't this, we're supposed to be a family? Isn't that baby related to us?

Cathy was pouring water into her glass and it went over the top and sopped into the tablecloth and she kept pouring.

Look what you're doing, Helen said. This was parenting: let them do what they have to do.

This is hard enough, Cathy said.

The evening Cathy called from the hospital, Helen was sewing sequins on the wedding dress and there were large bunches of them on the bodice and it was all hand-done. Cathy hadn't come home from school and it was dark. It was snowing, and Pink Floyd was coming from John's room, which she hated. Lulu was at figure skating. Gabrielle was at Brownies. The lamplight hit a sequin and it was like a little fire on the fabric and she had the phone next to her and she could feel it was going to ring just before it rang.

My water broke, Cathy said. I wish you were here.

Me too, Helen said.

I want my mother, Cathy said.

I'm coming.

Don't come, Cathy said. I have to do this by myself.

And Helen hadn't heard anything until seven the next morning. Helen had not said, Please keep the baby. She sat up all night and did not say, Please keep the baby. She had worked on the wedding dress. John came down in the morning and Helen was still in her chair.

She had the baby, Helen said.

What is it, John asked.

It's a little girl, Helen said. John went into the kitchen and she heard him getting down a plate and she heard him push down the toaster, and open the fridge, and then she heard him smash the plate.

Lulu came into the room.

She had the baby? Lulu asked. She was yawning and she had the heel of her hand dug into her eye and she was wearing baby dolls. Is she okay?

She's okay. They're both okay.

After the call in the morning there was no other call and so Helen phoned for a taxi. Cathy might be signing adoption papers. Helen had to get up there. She would intervene. She would convince.

The taxi was outside and the phone rang and Cathy said, Mom, she has Dad's ears.

I'm coming, Helen said.

I'm keeping her, Mom.

Are you, honey?

She has a big head of hair.

Cathy and Claire had lived with Helen, and Helen loved her granddaughter in a leisurely way. She read to her every night. She said to Cathy, Go out. Have fun.

Helen had not disciplined Claire because there was no need. She made Claire dresses with smocking. Her own girls she had dressed like boys. They had to be tough; that must have been what she was thinking. They had to be ready. They had been girls with grass stains on their knees and dirt under their nails.

But for Claire she bought white ankle socks with lace. She made Claire three dresses from the same pattern, pale lemon, pale pink and pale blue, and the smocking took ages and there was a bow at the back and a Peter Pan collar, and she bought patent leather shoes, and one of the worst fights she and Cathy ever had: Helen got Claire's ears pierced when the child was three. Two gold studs.

They must have said. When Claire was five, Helen's grown children must have got together and had a talk. They must have sat Cathy down and given her a good talking-to about moving out. Nobody wanted to be stuck taking care of an old lady. That's what they must have said.

She'll suck the life out of you, Cathy, Lulu must have said. It's okay now, but ten, fifteen years from now, you won't be able to leave.

Get out while you can, John would have said. John must have said for Cathy to get an apartment. John had been giving Cathy money. John was making it possible.

The hurt had been monstrous. The only thing bigger than the hurt was Helen's desire to make sure that her children never guessed it.

I'm sick of picking up after you, she told Cathy. Or: Nice to have the space back.

Helen was afraid of being alone. She went to the doctor because of shortness of breath and the doctor said an inhaler. The doctor said a mild tranquilizer. Sleeping pills. Helen was afraid of being robbed. She was afraid of ghosts. What if she had a medical emergency? Knock, knock. Who's there? Nobody.

But Helen did not say anything to Cathy.

She said, Take the bowl. Yes, you can have the bowl.

We're only two streets away, Cathy said. We're just around the corner.

Helen was down in the basement going through old dishes and Cathy came down and stood beside her. The basement had a damp mineral smell. The walls were stone and there were musty knapsacks they had all taken on trips and a pile of suitcases and boxes of Christmas decorations. They had moved most of Cathy's things earlier in the week, and Helen had been digging in a box for a spatula. She would not have Cathy buy a new spatula when there was an extra one.

That's just a waste, she'd said.

Helen had spent days looking through boxes for the spatula. She had turned up a key chain that had a marijuana leaf encased in clear plastic and a pair of cords Cathy had worn when she was seven — two-tone, purple and wine coloured. Cathy could not believe how small they were. There was a Disney plastic cup with sparkles that floated up and down whenever it tipped, and tiny plastic shoes that floated up and down, and Cinderella in her gown. The spatula sat beside Helen on the cold concrete floor. It was spotted with rust. Helen was on her knees and she had something in her fist and her fist was held against her chest.

She opened her hand. It was a roll of film. She'd found a roll of undeveloped film.

This is from God knows when, she told Cathy.

And afterwards Helen picked up the envelope of photos from the drugstore and sat in the car and she took her time opening it. She just sat there and watched a woman with a toddler in a shopping cart, and all her grocery bags fluttering in the wind, and big drops of rain hitting the windshield. The splats of water big as loonies.

The first two photos were of aspen trees. Just the tops of the trees and a lot of empty, bleached-out sky.

The third picture was Cal at the regatta. He had on a faded blue sweatshirt with a hood and he was wearing the grey corduroy Snugli.

Who was it? Was it John in the Snugli? It must be John. Cal had on black sunglasses and there was a crowd all around him and the sun and the water behind and pink spangles of sunshine from the light hitting the lens at the wrong angle or because the film was so old.

Three spangles of light, one inside the other, pink and yellow and white, floating out of the sun. Cal was holding out a cone of pink cotton candy overexposed along the edges, white as a light bulb.

And of course, Cathy met someone. Mark Hamlin lived in the apartment below. A PhD in musicology, hair down to his shoulder blades. Helen liked him the moment she met him.

. . . . .

Helen and Louise in Florida, 1998

LOUISE PUT FOURTEEN casseroles in the deep freezer for her husband, each labelled with a piece of masking tape that said the date it had to be defrosted. She and Helen went to

Florida. They drank by the side of the pool and they walked the beach and read all day long. They cooked their own meals because they had got a place with a kitchenette, and they knew everybody. All the Newfoundlanders went to St. Pete's in the winter. The Murrays were there when Louise and Helen went, and the O'Driscolls and the Roaches. Meredith Gardiner was there; she'd met a rich widower with a condo. Meredith had them over for supper.

Helen and Louise just lay on the beach, and the water was warm, and they got very brown, and they shopped for the grandchildren. They bought shorts sets and snorkels and masks and clear plastic shoes with red lights in the heels.

One day Louise drove down an off-ramp and screamed: What are these bloody fools doing?

It had got dark and all the headlights coming at them, careering to the side, scraping along the concrete retaining wall, a shower of sparks, horns blaring.

You're going the wrong way, Helen screamed back.

Louise put her feet on the accelerator and the brake at the same time and they spun three or four times and went over the median, the front passenger wheel cracking down hard, and Helen's head hit the windshield, and then the rest of the car bounced or jumped, and the tail end might have hit something. The sound of horns as they zoomed past, and then their car was facing in the right direction. They snaked, and there were more horns, and Helen looked back and saw some cars had hit each other in their wake. Louise kept going; they did not slow down. You can't slow on those highways. They didn't slow down until they pulled into the parking lot of a fast-food outlet — what was it, a McDonald's or Arby's or Wendy's? One of those places, and Helen and Louise just sat, but the car still seemed to be spinning slowly underneath them. Helen put down the visor and checked her face in the mirror and there was blood dripping down her forehead from her hair and she looked very white.

For several months after, Helen would wake to feel her bed turning like a slow carousel in an empty park with just a bit of wind. She remembered the feeling from childhood of hanging on to the carousel with both arms and letting her head drop back so the treetops moved in a lazy wheel, with all the clouds in the centre.

· · · · ·

Another Lesson, 1998

WHAT YOU WANT to do, the instructor said, is ease in.

I'm easing, said Helen. This is me, easing.

The instructor said, You're going to want to indicate.

Helen's shirt was soaked under the arms and it stuck to her back. The other cars were very bright in the sunshine. The sun spanked on their red hoods and blue hoods and on the chrome.

That's it, said Jim Picco, the driving instructor. It's very easy. When you're a mature student.

Helen lurched forward and the seat belt cut her and she bounced back.

That was... Jim said. I had to use my brake because we were headed for the telephone pole. Pull over.

I can't do this, Helen said.

You were drifting into the other lane.

I'm too old.

You can't drift.

You have no bloody idea, Helen said.

Jim lifted his pelvis slightly and tugged at the ironed creases in his pants so they were straight. He touched the cuffs of his shirt, snagging one down from inside his jacket. Then he worked a kink in his neck and clamped his hands on his knees. Mrs. O'Mara, you're going to take a moment, he said. Then you're going to indicate and check your blind spot and check your rearview. Then you're going to ease into traffic.

Jim Picco had hard grey bristles on his chin and Helen had the feeling fright had made them stand up, because she had not noticed them before. He moved his hands up and down his thighs vigorously.

I'm ready, he said. Are you ready?

Helen put on the indicator like Jim said. She put the car in gear. Jim turned and looked behind and sat forward and rolled his shoulders, and then he said she could go, and she put her foot on the accelerator, but she hit it too hard and she'd had the car in reverse, not drive, and they slammed backwards, burning rubber, and lurched to a stop, and she bounced against the seat belt hard, and so, she saw, did Mr. Picco.

Mrs. O'Mara, he said. Can I call you Helen?

Yes, she said.

Helen, we have to go forward.

．．．．．

Tug-of-War, 1978

CAL WAS ON the other team. The parents picked up the heavy rope from the grass and joked and sidled in next to each other and watched out for elbows and where they placed their feet. Don't step on me.

Helen was behind Felix Brown's dad. The school secretary, who had a child in grade one with cerebral palsy, was behind Helen. The secretary was all muscle. Then there was Monique LeBlanc, who affected a helpless girlishness, and Maggie Ferguson, and Maggie's husband, Brad. The Ferguson twins standing on the sidelines to watch their parents. The twins had cans of pop and special plastic drinking straws that wiggled out of the cans and formed eyeglasses that hooked over their ears and came down below the jawline into the corners of their mouths. They sucked in unison and orange pop zoomed up the clear tubing and circled one eye, then the other, and disappeared. The parents chattered and giggled and their shoulders knocked and jostled.

The sky was pristine blue mottled with cloud, and the buttercups in the shade at the edges of the field were yellow and shiny, as if they had been lacquered. The sun baked the tops of the parents' heads and blotched the field emerald and lime, and under the trees it was a dark, dark green. Almost black. It was the first warm day they'd had. A whiff of boiling wieners and soggy buns.

There was an experimental pull from the other side and Helen's side stumbled forward, a step or two, and pulled back. She couldn't believe Cal was on the other team.

Hey, what are you doing over there, she shouted to him. Why is my husband on the other side? But Cal didn't hear her.

There was a shrill whistle. Parents, wait for the flag, please, the gym teacher said. Quiet, please. She said it sardonically, and the children loved to see the parents scolded in this way and they doubled over in giggles.

John's first Sports Day. He was in kindergarten and had already won a ribbon for the three-legged race.

Earlier that morning it had looked like everything would be cancelled. It had been cold and overcast for days. Fog like wet concrete crawling down Signal Hill.

But the radio had said that Sports Day events all over the city were going ahead and had rattled off all the schools and warned about sun hats and snacks.

Clearing mid-morning, the radio had said. Sunny and twenty degrees all afternoon.

Helen had hung some laundry in the garden very early, and the scent of the lilacs had been strong and she had felt the wind change. The leaves on the maple trees had suddenly brightened. Things change instantly, she thought. Things can change for no apparent reason.

That night when Helen put John to bed, he asked, Do you still dream when you're dead?

She was reading him a story and she put the book down on her chest and closed her eyes. She had hurt her neck and she knew exactly how. The whistle had cut shrilly through the hazy air and she'd been startled by how hard the other side had pulled. They were pulling as hard as they could, and it knocked her off balance. She decided to pull back. Helen put her whole self into it. She scudded her heels into the grass and the mud beneath the grass. She gritted her teeth and tugged hard and didn't give up.

Her team started to lean back, and there was a knot in the middle of the rope they had to pull over the tip of a pylon, and the knot was inching towards their side.

Helen and the other parents on her side were leaning all the way back, knees bent, their bums close to the ground, and it suddenly struck her as funny that Cal was on the other side. What was he doing over there? How had they become separated? She leaned out slightly and saw his face. His eyes were screwed shut and his upper lip was wrenched back and all his teeth showed. It was the way his head was thrown back; she was convulsed with kinks of laughter. The kinks worked themselves all through her body and she gave up. She gave up pulling because she was weak with spasms of silent laughter and somehow she'd hurt her neck.

Helen had not cared. She and her team were eased back and tipped over, and the children cheered and hopped up and down and screamed Mommy or screamed Daddy. Her team were eased back up and tipped the other way and the knot inched back over the pylon in the other direction. The whistle burst through the air and the orange flag fluttered down. When Helen let go the rope, her hands tingled. She had to clench and unclench.

Helen's eyes were closed and the storybook was open on her chest, and she said to John: When you're dead, you're dead. There's nothing else. Absolutely nothing.

She forgot she was speaking to a child of five. She didn't realize she'd spoken out loud.

Nothing, repeated John. His astonishment filled up the bedroom. It was as if the day, with all its glaring sun and bright, riffling leaves and nasty yellow buttercups and ribbons and thrill had come into the room on a scouring wind, and blown past them. John sat up on one elbow and stared forward into the empty dark.

. . . . .

The Standard, November 2008

LULU HAD MADE her buy a standard because you get a rebate and they're good on gas.

The environment, Mom!

Helen is driving home from her yoga class, she's on the top of Long's Hill at the red light, and there's a bus up her arse. She doesn't give a good goddamn about the bloody environment. Green. The light is green. She slams her foot, the engine cuts out and the car rolls back, and the bus blares its horn. It blares and blares. She starts the car and slams her foot. Lets up on the clutch, and there's a screech of metal, and she burns rubber, and the engine cuts out and the car rolls back. Hand-brake, Jesus hand-brake, and is that bus going to give her any space? It inches up as close as it can get and there's the horn again.

Helen lurches, something catches, pig-squealing parts. Second, she remembers second. Go, you son of a bitch, go. Hand-brake! Release the Jesus. Two bunny hops and then she's moving. She's fine. Helen guns it through the next red light.

Last night on the news there was a story about two women who ran out of the Magic Wok without paying, and the waitress chased them down. The women told the TV camera they felt no remorse.

I don't regret nothing, one woman said. Coming out of court in cuffs. Hard as nails. Helen had the sewing machine going but she stopped to watch. And then on to the end of the seam, a zigzag stitch.

Someone put Iceland on eBay. Markets crashing, Harper and Dion, Obama and McCain, they're talking Afghanistan, they're talking Gaza. The reign of the Emerald Tiger is on the wane.

Helen regrets the bloody standard is what she regrets. A silver Yaris. Brand new.

Last night watching television, Helen bit the thread with her teeth and lifted a tiny velvet dress to the ironing board to press the seam. Patience's eldest sister Elizabeth had had a baby and Helen was making the baby a red velvet dress for Christmas. White lacy petticoat. A matching bonnet. Three days old, and the baby with a full head of black fuzzy hair and pink fingernails. Elizabeth had put the baby in Helen's arms. Oh my. Who-da-dear? Who-da-saucy-baby? She would run across the street with the present for the baby when she finished the hem.

A matter of practice, Lulu had said. Standards are fun.

Helen thinks of Lulu coming home at sixteen, up the stairs and quietly closing the bathroom door. Who was that drip of a boyfriend? Aaron somebody. Or Andrew. Helen had not liked him one bit. Some snotty remark he'd made. Helen knocked on the bathroom door and waited. She rested her forehead on the door and said Lulu's name. It had been a remark about processed cheese. Andrew Somebody, who had mentioned casually that his family never ate processed cheese.

It's all celluloid and wood chips, he'd said. Just as Helen plunked the economy-sized no-name container of Parmesan in the centre of the table. Cathy grabbed it up, tipped it over her spaghetti, knocked the bottom with the flat of her hand, several hard taps. Cathy hadn't liked Aaron — or Andrew — either.

Helen touched her hand against the bathroom door as if to feel her daughter's mood through the wood. Then she turned the knob and went in. Lulu was applying the wet edge of a face cloth to her lower eyelid, removing black eyeliner, and she was stinking drunk. She pulled the eye until it was a slit.

Did Aaron walk you home, Helen asked.

Andrew.

Did Andrew walk you home?

Andrew had walked somebody else home that night. Not Lulu, with her white nail polish, white lipstick, and dark hair dyed a flat, shineless black. The ring in her nose, a tattoo of a tarantula on her shoulder. Or, later, she had shaved her head like a scored ham, each square a different colour, and she'd put safety pins through everything, and for a time she had a bra she wore outside of her clothes, spray-painted stiff and metallic, studded with big plastic jewels like a comic-book hero.

Lulu had been loaded that night and not willing to admit it. This was a stubbornness that came down from Cal's side. The last thing rubbed away, the refusal to surrender to an obliterating drunk. It kept Lulu from slurring. She dragged her lower eyelid down trying to get the makeup off, and her eye was bloodshot and glazed over, and the underlid fiercely red. And what could Helen do, you had to let them experiment with alcohol, get their hearts trampled and spit on and ground into the dirt; they had to learn.

But had Lulu been safe out there?

The eye roved over to Helen's face reflected in the mirror, and had Lulu ever looked sad and stoic, deciding she would appear as sober as she could; the water was crashing in the basin.

Did you have fun, Helen said.

And the eye looked back at itself (the other one pinched shut) and Lulu put down the face cloth and blinked. When she spoke it was mostly to herself, both consoling and demanding: Yes, I had a good time. And I will be okay.

And she had been. Mom, let up on the clutch. Feel the shimmy? It shimmies when you have to let up.

Lulu's punk look had turned overnight. Now she wears stilettos and tweeds, Helen thinks, shifting gears in the bloody Yaris; Lulu works out in the gym and cracks gum.

Everything she does is emphatic and sure. She had taken an evening course in dry-walling.

There are things you can learn only by doing, Lulu had told her mother. Things you can't know without losing a thumbnail or being honest when a lie is called for. She had been through a string of boyfriends and long stretches with no relationships at all.

Lulu has a facial expression—brow furrowed, lips pressed tight—that means she is working something out having to do with money. She does hair because she loves doing hair, but managing the spa is where she makes all her profit. She goes on buying trips and comes back with cases of mud and loofah sponges and lotions that are painted on the most delicate parts and peeled away. She does things with hot wax that she will not explain to Helen. Mom. You don't want to know.

Massage is her area of expertise. Lulu believes every tender hurt and sorrow collects in the flesh and can be worked out with warm baby oil and a good spanking. Fast, merciless karate chops to the grey buttocks and thighs and calves of men and women who acquiesce to middle-aged stiffness. Lulu's thumbs have a name around town. What she can do with her thumbs. Victims of whiplash swear by her. Athletes with esoteric sprains, new divorcees who weep uncontrollably. Lulu kneads the tight flesh of broad angry shoulders and makes them relax. She has three tanning beds, and the tops come down over her naked customers like coffin lids. Everyone leaves the spa golden and pumiced, bitter cares and dead cells sloughed off, smelling of spruce.

Gabrielle and Cathy complain that Lulu's flamboyance turns obnoxious when she drinks; Lulu is opinionated and acutely sincere. For all Lulu's hard edges, her sisters can lie to her easily because she never expects it. Lulu expects the best of people. She expects them to be generous and to tell the truth and to work hard.

Her sisters tolerate Lulu's temper tantrums and minor spite storms because she gives them money and advice and she makes it her business to order them around so they get the very best of everything for themselves. Helen's daughters have in common that when it comes to rules they are unbending. Helen's daughters prevail. And John...John is on his way home for Christmas.

I'm going to have a little one like you pretty soon, Helen tells the gown for Elizabeth's new infant. I'm going to have a brand-new grandchild.

. . . . .

Business Luncheon in New York, November 2008

THE ONE WOMAN at the table full of men, her mouth full, raises her escargot prong, a wet grey slug hanging from the end. She has a slug in her mouth and her lips are glossy with slug juice. John is surprised to discover he finds this erotic. Butter. It is garlic butter that makes the woman's chin greasy, and she is trying to say something but her mouth is full. She waves a slug on a little fork, trying to get the men to shut up. This is Natalie Bateman from Neoline Inc., and she is presenting an advertising campaign to promote offshore drilling development on a global scale. John's company had asked for tenders and Neoline Inc. came out on top.

Butter and the sweat of a boiled organism, all muscle. John tries to think of a muscle in the human body that is the same size as a slug. Natalie is bobbing in her seat and waving the little fork. The men wait. One by one, they fall into an agitated silence.

John thinks about the Heimlich manoeuvre. He once cracked a seventy-six-year-old woman's rib because he thought she was choking. Winnipeg. That was in Winnipeg. She'd just been laughing, her sixty-year-old daughter said.

That was laughter, you great stupid idiot of a man, the daughter shouted.

John had tipped over a chair, and the tablecloth came with him, and all the waiters watching and plates falling, and he was in there, doing the Heimlich, because he was witnessing a choking. Death had its fist around this scrawny old woman's neck and John was there to intervene.

Thug! the battle-axe of a daughter shouted.

The woman's black orthopedic shoes knocking listlessly against his shins. She could not have weighed more than seventy pounds. A man nearby with his napkin tucked into his collar, and his fork and knife upright in his fists. The picture of indignation, standing by with his mouth agape, paralyzed with sour awe. Later this same man would offer John his card. A lawyer and a witness, he said. It was not a napkin in the man's collar; it was a cravat.

The daughter had threatened to sue. John had assaulted a seventy-six-year-old woman. A bungled effort forged out of the sincere wish to do something good. Laughter. The sound had been laughter: ugly wheezing squawks of joy had snagged like beef sinew in the woman's throat.

Natalie Bateman puts her fingers over her mouth and chews and chews and rolls her eyes comically because this is a table of men held up by a miniature fork. Her eyes water and she takes a gulp of champagne and John sees she is beautiful. She reminds him of somebody. Somebody he cares about.

Natalie says, We're planning a series of ads from all over the world, specifically indigenous, acutely indigenous, showing high-powered cocktail parties, parties on rooftops, beach parties. We're looking at Bondi Beach, and subtitles, just very, very international, speaking to that thing, that ethnic thing, that thing, connectedness. Zoom, we're in Thailand; zoom, we're in Alaska; zoom, Nigeria. Do you know what I'm saying, zoom, zoom, zoom, the camera flits all over the world in an instant, this is everybody partying together, yada, yada, it's gritty, it's arty, and we end with a sunset shot. Natalie pops the slug into her mouth and she clamps her lips shut and she is wagging the little prong with one hand and covering her mouth with the other. Wait, wait, wait, she continues: The thingies, the derricks or whatever, the rigs on the ocean fade to silhouette, music of course. Something Wagnerian.

It has been a long day and John is hungover and, he realizes, the woman at the other end of the table with the snail prong — Natalie — reminds him of someone. He watches her wrinkle her nose when she drinks from the champagne glass. The bubbles are tickling her and now he knows who it is: Natalie reminds him of a nun who taught him in high school. Natalie has some kind of goodness, he thinks, despite the advertising crap. Goodness.

What John remembers from high school: a nun with chalk dust all over her blue polyester habit. It came to the knee, that habit—a crisp white blouse underneath, and a short veil on the nun's head. He could see her hands on the desk, leaning into him, because she had tried everything else with him.

She had been writing on the board and her dress had jiggled all of a piece, her sturdy shoes and stockings. She had written out the path to the answer, and to John it was like waterskiing. She was dragging him behind her, and every muscle in his head hurt, and the skis hit the hard ruts in the water and it was easier to let go; or there was no choice, and he sank, and the nun kept on. Then she turned and saw that she had lost him. She put her hands flat on the desk and leaned in.

Pythagorean geometry. John understood that there were infinite theoretical planes and that they could be labelled A and B. The nun had a few stiff white hairs on her chin. She was mannish and kind. She could not teach him math: John was impermeable. But in her he saw how kindness was generated. That is what she had blasted through his skull. She had blasted the will to be good, to take care of his sisters, his mother, the dog.

She leaned into him and her eyes held his eyes. The school's corridors were almost empty; the echo of a slammed locker rang out.

And then it struck him, the answer. He would retain the answer only long enough to write the exam. It was sunny outside and the trees were full of small new leaves, an innocent green that would get darker as the summer wore on.

The summer started bright and many things were going to happen because high school would be over, but they had not happened yet. John and his classmates were in a queue. Waiting for things to happen.

The old hag still came to John in his sleep, but less often, and he accepted it. There was monstrous sadness in the world, and you had to look it in the eye.

Natalie Bateman sips her champagne and her eyes close. She has an earnest way of tucking her hair behind her ears that makes her look truthful. It was as though that nun back in high school, John thinks — unconsciously letting his own mouth open as Natalie tugs another snail off the prong with her teeth, and closing his mouth as she closes hers, her lips full and wet — it was as if that nun had opened his forehead and put a chestnut of geometry and kindness behind the bone. He had felt bruised by the power and intent of her stare. She taught math, but John had seen it was not math. It was religion. She wrote on the board and covered herself in white dust, the residue of answers. John could see that the answers were spectral but had certain physical properties, and the answers had blasted through the nun and she was covered in their pure white residue.

And John thought: she should not be allowed to do this, just move the hard nut of love into his head. He might explode. But he had asked for it. He had asked for mercy. And the nun had leaned in and said, Aw, honey. Which was what she always said to students who had made an effort to follow but could not follow. And she made the decision, and John saw her make it. He saw it in her eyes, and then he knew.

The knowledge fell out of his brain onto the exam paper, and when he stood up from the exam it was gone.

Natalie Bateman passes a package to everyone at the table, a glossy black envelope that folds out ingeniously, with pockets and inserts — glossy eight-by-tens of locations and the bios of key personnel, designers, actors, directors, location scouts. There is a breakdown of the deliverables, sample budgets and storyboards.

The sun is going down and John glances at his watch. He will be on a plane to Toronto by 9 p.m. There are things he has to do. He has seen a white T-shirt in a shop window, no bigger than his hand. *I Heart New York.*

HOME

Helen Invisible, November 2008

HELEN IS AT Value Village with the cellphone and it buzzes against her hip. Louise is calling to say the police are doing riot training in the parking lot near her house.

They're getting ready for riots, Louise says. They do this every year. The nurses might go on strike. Half the cops are married to nurses. They've got their shields and helmets with the visors and they advance together. If the nurses get out of hand they'll hit the nurses over the head with those batons they have. I'm here in my car just to watch. Those horses, Helen, what lovely animals.

Louise's son is a cop. Sean, Louise's son, is a long-distance runner with silver hair who cleans the house and makes his wife coffee every morning and brings it to her in bed. Sherry Aucoin. And he takes care of his mother without complaint. Sean shovels for Louise in winter and gets her medication and sets up her computer. He does her plumbing and fixes the motion-sensitive light over the back door and puts down salt on her walk.

What they do, Helen. They bang, Louise says.

I'm looking at a cashmere sweater, Helen says.

They hit the batons against the shields, a drumming effect, and it's very intimidating, Louise says. Very exciting.

These minutes cost me, Helen says. She turns to the side to get rid of the static. I have this phone for emergencies.

Are we going to look at kitchen counters today, Louise says. Helen has discovered a hitch under the arm of the sweater. The sweater is beaded and pink and very soft. She puts her face in it and there is a smell of perfume. Somebody wore this sweater, she thinks.

I'm not wasting any more minutes, Louise, Helen says. Meet me at the hardware store in an hour. And she hangs up.

There is a tall, hunched woman a little ways down the aisle with permed black hair so sparse her white scalp shows through. The woman is trying on a coat. She is looking down the length of herself, smoothing the fur with one hand, the other hand clutching the collar closed at the neck.

Very nice, Helen says. The woman gives the coat a little swish. She strikes a pose. Then she lets her arms drop.

We had eight die out our way since September, the woman says. I'm in Flower's Cove up on the Northern Peninsula. That's a lot of people for a small community. I'm here with my friend Alice, and I said to myself, this is a nice coat. She flicks her hand through the fur again.

It looks very warm, Helen says.

Do we buy these things to make ourselves feel better, the woman asks. She comes up close to Helen then. Her watery eyes sink loosely into soft pouches of skin, veined with fine wine-coloured threads. One tooth is outlined in gold and her breath smells of spearmint gum.

In Flower's Cove I'm guessing you need a warm coat, Helen says. She has the sleeve of the pink sweater bunched up in her fist.

The priest was the last, the woman whispers. She turns to the rack and begins sliding the steel hangers over the bar quickly, stopping at something flaring red. Took a heart attack at the door of the church. He was from town. Originally.

Did he? Awful, Helen says.

If I were small like you, the woman says. She nods at the sweater in Helen's hand. I would treat myself. She flicks through several more hangers and pauses at something silver that catches the light with a flash.

Because life is short, she says. Life is very, very. She draws the silver shirt out and puts it in her cart.

Helen thinks of Louise saying: I am not wowed. Louise had not been wowed about a shade of taupe Helen showed her at the hardware store last week. They were looking at the samples and they had winnowed the pile, and Helen said she wanted something fresh and clean. She held out the paint sample at arm's length.

Louise lifted her bifocals from the string around her neck and put them on. They both glanced at the ceiling to determine what kind of light was shining on the sample. Then Louise shook her head and removed her glasses.

I am not wowed, she said.

Helen thinks of her granddaughter Claire, coming for a visit a few days ago. Claire had rung the bell and then she'd stood looking down the street, the sunlight in her hair, and then she'd turned and put her face to the glass of Helen's front door and blocked the light with her cupped hands, her nose pressed flat and white. She had been looking straight at Helen and could not see her.

Helen was invisible. Claire was looking straight at her and not seeing anything at all.

And Helen thinks of Barry, who is working right now in her living room. *I am wowed*, Helen thinks. She feels a clutch of surprise. As if a fist has closed on her heart. She feels lust. But also something more layered and dangerous than lust. Something deeper.

Companionship, she thinks. A longing for it.

Treat yourself, the woman says, nodding at the sweater in Helen's hand.

Oh, I can't, Helen says. She puts the sweater back on the rack.

· · · · ·

Seance, November 2008

JOHN HAS LEFT the boozy business meeting and is walking several blocks in the direction of his hotel. Outside a novelty shop there are four inflated George Bush punching bags, weighted with sand, bowing and tottering and bouncing off each other in the wind. It has begun to snow. John is supposed to buy an airline ticket for Gabrielle but he needs a coffee. He needs, always, a pause before parting with money.

John needs a pause to think about the baby.

It is very, very cold in New York.

He ducks into a coffee shop where the staff wear ear-pieces and peaked caps. They marshal the line so it moves along, pointing to a clerk behind the counter and saying: Inez is ready for you now. Or: Jasmine, at the end, is ready.

A woman asks if she can sit with John because the coffee shop is crowded. She unzips her jacket and sighs so deeply she falls into herself like a cake.

They are getting ready for Christmas in New York and there is a fashion window across the street with mannequins in red evening gowns and a gold fireplace and a pyramid of gold boxes. The reflections of yellow cabs float in the glass like giant carp.

The woman sitting across from John in the café says she channels spirits for a living. It's draining work, she says. She glances over at the counter that holds the cream and milk, and says she needs sugar and she's going to get some. But instead she narrows her eyes and stays very still.

I feel a vibe, she says to John. Coming from you.

Let me get the sugar for you, John says. What do you want? Sugar?

I believe you've lost someone, the woman says. She stands up. She is about to pronounce upon John and all that he is; but an ambulance tears down the street and she is distracted. The siren screams and the red light from the cherry washes over the woman, once, twice, gone.

John thinks of the men and women who had been sleeping on the plane from Singapore, the red sun spilling in their windows. People with their mouths hanging open; the concentrated, hard-won abandon on their faces. Was that just yesterday? The world below had seemed like a dream they were conjuring together.

I'll just get the sugar, the woman says. She is wearing, John notices, faded black jogging pants and cracked plastic sandals with white sports socks and a lilac down jacket with grime around the cuffs. She comes back to the table wagging a packet of sugar between her finger and thumb.

You commune with the dead you were saying, John says.

The woman pours the sugar and jerks her teabag by the string. Spirits come to me, she says. She smiles at John and rubs her hands together over the steam of the tea.

So, with candles, he asks. He is thinking about Jane Downey at the Hyatt in Toronto. John has booked her a suite and he has a reservation for himself. A separate room. Would they sleep together? He has never had sex with a pregnant woman. Jane Downey said he would be able to feel the baby move.

You just have to put your hand on my tummy, she said.

I don't need candles, the woman in the café tells John. He can smell her raspberry tea.

You hear voices, John says.

Spirits show themselves, the woman says.

And you hold seances.

Seance is an old-fashioned word, the woman says. We say channelling now.

And it costs, John says.

The woman pulls the teabag out of the cup and drops it onto a pile of napkins. A red stain spreads at once. I have to charge, she says.

John takes a bank card out of his wallet and turns it end over end on the table and picks his teeth with it; then he realizes what he is doing and puts it away. All he can really think about is the baby. He is having crazy thoughts. He is thinking: Why not marry Jane. Or: Just don't show up and it will all go away.

He is thinking about the way it had been light for twenty-four hours that week in Iceland with Jane, and he has a crazy notion that the light made her pregnant. The light had done something to them both. Befuddled them. They had hiked and eaten a lamb dinner with wine, and there had been orange light on the broken up, glittering pieces of hardened lava, and the stories of berserkers that Jane wrote about in her notebook while the tour guide talked.

I'm just curious about how it works, John says to the woman in the coffee shop.

Everything's on the surface with you, she says. I'm seeing things already. Things from your past. Things in your future.

What things, John says.

The woman shrugs. Shapes, she says. Colours. I see sadness and loss. That's without even trying.

That's pretty good, John says. Without trying.

She glances up from her cup and her eyes, John sees, are green. She has an intense, theatrical glare. Her skin is milky and her eyebrows thick and arching. She must have been beautiful when she was younger.

Something is coming, the woman says. John takes a twenty out of his wallet and slides it across the table to the psychic.

What's coming, he says. Jane had an infinite capacity for generosity, that's what he remembers. Or he is mixing her up with all women everywhere. He and Jane had a week together. Jane was angular. Lean. Cinnamon-coloured hair, wild curls.

John has avoided being a father all his adult life. It has taken stealth and some underhandedness. It has taken clarity of purpose when the moment called for dreamy abandon. He has practised withdrawal. He has kept what he wants, what he *actually* wants for his life, in the centre of his thoughts even while in the throes of orgasm. He's kept a tight fist on the reins of himself.

I'll tell you what the future holds for you, the psychic says. She has not touched the money. The bill is sitting in the middle of the table. When the door opens, the bill lifts a little and moves sideways.

Maybe, John thinks, he doesn't want to know what's in the future. He has given a lot of thought to the nature of time and how a life can be over much too quickly, if you're not careful. The present is always dissolving into the past, he realized long ago. The present dissolves. It gets used up. The past is virulent and ravenous and everything can be devoured in a matter of seconds.

That's the enigma of the present. The past has already infiltrated it; the past has set up camp, deployed soldiers with toothbrushes to scrub away all of the *now*, and the more you think about it, the faster everything dissolves. There is no present. There was no present. Or, another way to think about it: your life could go on without you.

John had enjoyed making love to a gorgeous woman in Reykjavik. That is true. There was sunshine all day and all night. He hadn't stopped to think about it.

Looking back, it seems to John as though he'd been in the present with Jane. The whole week had happened in the present tense. Maybe that is love. These are the kinds of crazy thoughts he is entertaining.

He and Jane had gone to the Blue Lagoon and put white mud on their faces because they were told it would heal them. They'd laughed at that because they felt there was nothing to heal. They both claimed they'd never felt better.

Stay in my apartment, John had said to Jane. Be my guest. Because it was fun and the sunlight lasted, waning only slightly at about four in the morning, and there wasn't a whole lot else to do. He'd watched the waterfall splash down over Jane's head and onto her hands as she held them up, and the water fell in a glossy sheen over her face, and her mouth was open, and her hair was plastered down and shiny. Her nipples in the glossy red bathing suit. The curve of her hip. He had seen the shadow of her belly button. The hard ropes of waterfall had washed the white mud off her face in rivulets.

Steam had risen up thick and torn apart, and there was the stink of sulphur that you could forget for a moment before the breeze brought it back twice as strong.

Anthropology, Jane said.

He said, Remind me.

The study of humanity, Jane said. Ritual, symbolism, magico-religious practices, class, genre, kinship, taboo. The way we move and talk, she said. What we eat and drink and dream and what we do with our shit. How we fuck and raise the children. All that.

It's Jane, she had said on the phone. As if he would remember.

You've lost someone in the past, the psychic says. Then she grabs John's hand. Her fingernails are digging into his wrist, hard enough to break the skin. It's as if she's having a mini-seizure. Her eyes have rolled back in her head and the eyelids quiver. The whites of her eyes. It lasts maybe twenty seconds. Then the muscles in her face go slack. John sees a bit of drool in the corner of her mouth. Her pupils are dilated.

The psychic presses her thumb and fingers against her eyes and bows her head. When she finally looks up, she is disoriented. Or you are going to lose someone in the future, she says.

She sees that she is holding John's wrist, and drops it.

. . . . .

Wedding Dresses, November 2008

HELEN HAS A commission to be completed by the new year. Each dress is one of a kind. They are simple and flattering dresses. Her clientele are mostly in their late forties or fifties and they do not want virginal and they do not want foolish. Nor do they want the stiff suits they have worn to boardrooms for the past twenty years. Her clientele are radiologists or engineers or surgeons, or they are at the university.

Lace scares the hell out of them. Lace or anything soft, it makes them feel young again and pretty. This is a tremendous risk. They would have to remember they were giving in to love; they would have to lay down their scalpels and gavels and chain mail.

Weddings have become expensive. The flowers are tropical, waxy, swollen and vaguely anthropomorphic. The videographers are young men who have gone to art school in Montreal or Nova Scotia, young men with longish hair. Helen gets the impression they listen to softer, more lyrical forms of punk. The kind of young men who are always nodding just slightly out of sync with what you're saying to them. Nodding absently, just before you make your point, like they want you to hurry up with it.

Helen's clients are mostly friends of friends, and often she goes to the weddings. She has a feeling about the wedding dresses she makes; they are sacred. They matter to Helen. Not the prom dresses, although she loves the emeralds and magentas and reds and cobalts that came in this year. The prom dresses are all cleavage and puffed skirts. The prom dresses are boisterous, innocent and sluttish in equal parts, almost ironic.

But the wedding dresses matter. Every stitch. Off-white or coral or pearl grey, nothing shiny, dresses that move and are comfortable to wear and durably built, covering more than they expose.

Today as Helen sews in the kitchen, Barry is working on the floor in the living room. For a while in the beginning she had offered Barry whatever she was having for lunch but he said he didn't like to stop.

I don't eat until I'm done for the day, he had said.

Barry had an ethic about working until the job was done. He liked the idea of toughing it out during the lunch hour.

I'm stubborn, he'd said.

He presses a line of caulking into a crack in the door frame and he smoothes it down with his thumb. She sits at her sewing machine and watches his thumb move over the crack. Someone calls him on his cellphone, she thinks, who needs a ride. Someone feels free to demand of him, to ask. It must be a lover or a wife.

She watches Barry's thumb press the caulking into the crack and she thinks again the thing every adult woman thinks of herself—that she is still her sixteen-year-old self.

It is not a thought. Helen becomes sixteen; she *is* sixteen: the shyness and wonder. It comes over her briefly. And then it is gone. She is forty-nine, fifty, she is fifty-two. Fifty-six. The world has betrayed her, arthritis in her wrists.

How deeply she craves to be touched. Because what follows not being touched, Helen has discovered, is more of the same — not being touched. And what follows a lack of touching is the dirtiest secret of all, the most profane: forgetting to want it.

You forget, she thinks. You forget so deeply, desire is obliterated. A profound and altering chill befalls.

The only cure is to chant: I want, I want.

She is sixteen and she notices Barry's worn belt and his jeans bespattered with plaster, and his hair is more silver than grey and there is still some black and it is longish, and he is not speaking. An old hippy. He has already let on that he enjoys the odd draw. He is not a drinker, or he has been a drinker and left it behind. She senses he has left many things behind, and in this way they have something in common.

They are too old for love. It is laughable. For an instant she sees them fucking: grey pubic hair, puckered skin, creaking joints. It is a grotesque comedy, this hunger. She is starving for physical tenderness—the shock of it buckles her knees, there at her sewing machine, and she pauses over her stitch, holding the fabric, the shock of it dizzying her; she is dizzy with lust.

But she and Barry are not too old for carpentry, for making a living, for sewing dresses, for snowstorms and night sweats and threats from the bank and children and crying grandchildren. They are called upon. They are expected to participate. Maybe it should be over but it is not over. It is not over.

And here is the blunt truth of it: Helen would like to sleep with him. She doesn't care what she looks like (she actually looks not too bad in some lights), she does not care about anything except that she wants to maybe have sex with this man, who is a stranger, who smokes, who answers the phone. And how dangerous, how dangerous: I want, I want.

She and Barry have been together like this in the empty house for weeks. Tim Hortons for coffee mid-morning, and again in the afternoon. Barry doesn't come up to the second floor; he doesn't use her bathroom. Helen guesses there is a secret carpenter code about these things: don't encroach. He smokes on the back deck. And Helen has found herself watching him from the third-floor window. The top of his black and white baseball cap.

She is sewing pleats into a waistband and pricks her finger. Her realization: she has been satisfied just to watch him smoke.

. . . . .

Helen Sunbathing, 2007

THE CHILDREN HAD bought Helen an airline ticket for Mother's Day.

Mom, you've got to see Europe, Cathy said.

Enough of Florida, Lulu said.

And so there she was on a beach in Greece with Louise. She watched a young man sailing a catamaran, the belly of the sail almost touching the water, his body leaning out on the other side, leaning, just the bottoms of his feet on the boat, tugging hard on the sail.

Isn't he too far out, she said to Louise. But Louise was asleep.

There was a fishing boat anchored just beyond the catamaran. The fishing boat bobbed up and down, working vigorously against the slapping waves. Every time the bow rose up a sheet of water fell off the rope that anchored it.

The beach wasn't crowded but there was a couple a little farther down. A man and a woman, about Helen's age. They lay side by side, absolutely still.

Finally the man rolled over and reached into his knapsack and pulled out a bottle of water. Helen could hear the plastic bottle dent and crinkle as he drank.

The catamaran slapped down hard and turned, and the sail flew out the other way, and the man ducked fast under the boom.

I just don't think he has control of that thing, Helen said. But Louise didn't move.

Then the woman down the beach sat up next to the man and took the bottle of water from him and drank and passed it back. She had short hair dyed a brassy blonde, and the wind blew it off her face and the dark roots showed around her forehead and she squinted into the wind. Her face was darkly tanned. She looked as though she had been on vacation for a long time. Helen watched the catamaran fly towards the beach. It bounced hard on the waves.

The woman had an apple and a paring knife, and she turned the apple and a ribbon of peel flapped in the wind. She cut the apple in half. The man removed his navy baseball cap and smoothed his hand over his head and put the cap back on. The woman handed him half the apple and she ate the other half, leaning forward, squinting into the wind.

And the catamaran hit the beach and skidded up out of the surf, and the man jumped off and trotted beside it and dragged it hard onto the shore.

The couple sitting down the beach from them might have been her and Cal, Helen thought. She and Cal might have turned out that way, not having to speak until the apple was gone, drifting off to sleep on a beach, and waking, one after the other, and then talking, taking up where they had left off hours ago.

The couple had talked and come to some kind of agreement, Helen thought. They had said something about one of their children, or a neighbour back home, or some banking matter or something to do with their car. The wife had finished some story she'd started hours ago, picking up mid-sentence. Then they stood and shook out their towels. The towels snapped noisily. They put everything in their bags and walked off down the beach. The woman stopped and put on one sandal and then the other one, and after a few steps bent and fixed her strap over her heel. The man waited for her.

If Cal were here on the beach with her, Helen thought, he would be thirty-one. He was thirty-one when he died. And she would be as she was now, the skin on her chest wrinkly like old tissue paper, and tanned and freckled with age spots, and the flab of her underarms, and her arthritic hands and the deep lines at the corners of her eyes. Thin etched lines over her mouth.

Helen would feel a profound embarrassment about how old she was and she would marvel at Cal's beauty.

We have grown apart, she thought. She'd gone on without him. She would have sat next to him and peeled the apple and she would have felt like his mother. The dead are not individuals, she thought. They are all the same. That's what made it so very hard to stay in love with them. Like men who enter prison and are stripped of their worldly possessions, clothes, jewellery, the dead were stripped of who they were. Nothing ever happened to them, they did not change or grow, but they didn't stay the same either. They are not the same as they were when they were alive, Helen thought.

The act of being dead, if you could call it an act, made them very hard to love. They'd lost the capacity to surprise. You needed a strong memory to love the dead, and it was not her fault that she was failing. She was trying. But no memory was that strong. This was what she knew now: no memory was that strong.

What are you doing, she said. Louise was taking off her bikini top. Her breasts flopped out white as potatoes, the dark liver-coloured nipples hard as stones.

When will these tits ever see the sun if I don't do it now, Louise said. She lay back down, nudging her shoulders into the sand under her towel.

The youngsters came, bang, bang, bang, just like that, Helen thought.

Get the diapers out of the way, her mother-in-law had said. Have them all at once. And it was like the snap of a finger. The whole thing was over. At first it had seemed to last forever. Then it was over in a snap.

. . . . .

The Kite, 1977

LET GO, CAL shouted. Let go, let go. He was out on the lawn with four-year-old John and the child let go of the kite when he was told, and the kite leapt up in the air and cut through the sky, this way and that, over his head. John put his arms over his face.

When the kite met the air it sounded like a sharp intake of breath — surprise or fear or elation. Then the *snap* and ripple of the plastic. The kite sliced the air again, and this time it rose higher, and with another leap, higher, and then it was very high.

Cal yanked the line, flinging his arm behind him. He gave hard little tugs or he yanked with his whole body, bending back as if doing the limbo.

The kite dipped down, and then, out of spite, cut up even higher.

It dipped and rippled.

Cal tied the string to the clothesline and he went around the corner of the house. Helen could hear the *chink* of his shovel hitting stone. For a while the kite line was slack, but then it went straight and the kite was nothing more than a speck. The lawn was big and dew-soaked and sparkle-riven, and there was fireweed swaying in the back of the garden. The seeds floated across the lawn.

Their house in Salmon Cove. Helen has a picture of John from that time. A royal blue T-shirt and red shorts and his blonde ringlets, and the stain from a purple Popsicle on his lips.

Cal had taken the children down to the beach to give Helen some peace. He'd found a plastic Barbie Doll kite stuck between the rocks, torn and faded. It was pink and showed Barbie's blonde hair and white smile.

Lulu was on Cal's shoulders, and Cal had John and Cathy in a wooden cart he was pulling, and he had the broken kite in his hand, coming up over the dusty gravel road.

This is the kind of thing Helen remembers, bits of afternoons that sharpen in focus until they are too bright. Just moments. Tatters. How the kids climbed on Cal. Flung themselves. How they clambered over him. He tickled them. Gave them horseback rides. Told stories. He did the airplane. Lying on his back, his legs in the air, their little rib cages resting on his grey wool socks. Soaring.

Cal repaired the kite in the garden with duct tape and John was watching Cal intently and Cal was talking to him all about fixing a kite, aerodynamics, and maybe the strangeness of Barbie and her brilliant, bleak smile.

Helen was in the kitchen window looking at the ocean with the binoculars. She could see Bell Island, a smudged, smoky blue across the bay, a few windows along the coast flashing like mica. Then the loud glitter of the ocean. She thought she could hear whales and she was trying to find them. The binoculars were heavy and smelled new, like the expensive leather case they had been kept in. When she looked through and twisted the wheel in the centre, the fuzzy burrs of light on each wave sharpened, every sparkle hard as a diamond, and after a long time she finally saw the whales. The tail of the mother slapped the water. It was a blue-black tail and shiny, and the water fell off it in a clear sheet, and the whale blew up spray and beside the mother was the baby whale, a small black blur under the skim of water, born a few days before, a fisherman had told them.

Helen lowered the binoculars in time to see the rip of pink. The kite was shooting down, a vicious and calculated dive. The plastic rattled and it was like an arrow hurtling towards John's head.

It flapped down and banged into John's shoulder and covered his face, and John cried out in fright. He shut his eyes and his fists were clenched at his sides and he screamed a piercing scream for his father.

Cal came around the corner and he picked John up in his arms. He put his hand on the back of John's head and pressed the boy's face into his chest. Cal swayed with him. The whole thing was over in a minute and forgotten. John wriggled out of Cal's arms and was off around the corner. The whole thing was forgotten just as if it had never happened. Let go, let go.

· · · · ·

Helen in Greece, 2007

ON THEIR WAY home, Helen and Louise had nearly missed their flight from Heraklion Airport in Greece to Stanstead in England. They had discovered they were at the wrong gate and they'd had to run. Louise was told to leave her water bottle at security or she could drink it on the spot, and she slammed down her bag and screwed off the cap and put the bottle to her lips, and tipping her head way back she drank for a long time, water dripping from the side of her mouth and the *glug glug* of it audible and the security guards watching her. Big bubbles went up in the plastic bottle, and finally

Louise lowered it and screwed the top back on and dropped it in the garbage bucket, and wiped her mouth with the back of her wrist. The men said, Is okay. Is okay. Go, go, go.

But Louise set the buzzers off and had to turn back and remove her shoes and then sit and put her shoes back on.

They were the last people on the plane and then it was delayed on the tarmac for two hours and they only had three hours in a Best Western Hotel in Stanstead before catching a bus to Heathrow. They'd been given a room with a double bed and Louise showered and Helen just fell asleep with her clothes on and woke every twenty minutes terrified they'd overslept. She leapt out of the bed at 4 a.m. when the phone rang and grabbed the receiver afraid someone had died, but there was just a buzzing on the other end and then music, and it was the wake-up call.

We were in an outdoor hot tub with snow falling on our hair, a woman told the driver on the bus to Heathrow. She and her friend had got on the bus after Helen and Louise, and one of them had two walking canes. She was florid with exertion and panting hard from climbing the three steps up from the sidewalk and she told the whole bus, Don't mind me sticks. She gripped the chrome pole and waved one of the canes and started down to her seat.

The driver pulled a lever and his chair sank with a pneumatic wheeze, and he took up a clipboard and crossed off a few lines with a pen. He put the clipboard away and spoke into a hand mike. Settle down, ladies, he said.

They pulled out of the bus terminal and after a while the driver spoke again on the hand mike and he said they would arrive at Heathrow Airport in an hour and fifteen minutes. He said the bus had a bathroom in the back and smoking was prohibited and in England seat belts were mandatory on buses, and he asked them all to belt up. This bus will be going sixty miles an hour, he said. Sometimes the wheels will leave the ground.

Louise had fallen in love. She did not say *love*. She hadn't said anything to Helen. But Helen knew.

On their last night in Greece, Helen and Louise had eaten in a restaurant attached to the hotel. It had been recommended by the guidebook. They had ordered Greek salad, and Louise had asked for the octopus and was surprised when it came that it looked so much like octopus. The tiny suction cups and purple tendrils unfurling on the plate.

I'm going to try things, Louise said, I've never tried before. She decided to start with the sardines.

The fisherman just brought, the waiter said. He flicked his pen towards the ocean to show how fresh. Just now, he said. He made a frown and nodded, showing how judicious Louise's choice of sardines would prove to be.

Helen had never used a guidebook before and she was astonished to find the restaurant right where the book said it would be. She and Louise were surprised to find the *affable* twin brothers that the guidebook said were the owners, right behind the bar, looking exactly like each other except one wore a pink shirt and the other a white shirt.

There was outdoor seating under a thatched roof, and the evening sun shot down spears through the weave. The locals sat at wooden tables on the sidewalks on both sides of the narrow cobblestone road. They were drinking something amber and smoky-looking from shot glasses. The few passing cars nearly brushed their knees. Men with sunburned faces and broad cheeks and pitted, spongy noses that drooped over their upper lips. Stout old women who wore all black and black kerchiefs and leaned on wooden walking canes. The old women walked down the middle of the street and the traffic idled behind them and the smell of exhaust hung in the air, and there were geraniums against the white stucco and cobalt shutters.

The man in the pink shirt served Helen and Louise. He had pouches under his eyes and a pen and pad, and he listened as Louise read out from the menu what they both wanted even though his cellphone was ringing in his pants pocket. It kept ringing, so Louise stopped and waited, and the man sighed and closed his eyes and took the phone out, and his brow furrowed, and he spoke and listened and began to get angry, and listened and wandered away from their table and didn't come back for a long time.

The other waiter brought a basket of bread and two beers they hadn't ordered, and there was olive oil and vinegar on the table to pour over everything.

Finally the first waiter returned and licked his finger and fluttered the pages of his little pad, and he asked Louise if she wanted her fish fried or baked.

I think fried, he said, without giving her a chance to answer.

My sister, you know, the waiter said to Louise. She phones, what can I do?

I know what you mean, Louise said. There was a cat with white and caramel and black patches and green eyes at

Helen's feet. It had pressed its back against the chair rungs and the black patch of fur over one shoulder blade rose and fell as it turned and walked away, a scrawny stilted strut. Then the cat stopped so it could whack at fleas with its hind leg. Thumping the flagstones with a kind of soft violence.

The ocean was dark except for a line of white foam that ran almost the length of the shore and moved in and out, erased itself and returned, erased itself and returned. The waiter kept bringing Louise and Helen beer, and the street got more crowded, and there were Dutch tourists and some old Brits in knee socks, and Louise laid her hand on her chest and put her other hand out flat so Helen would shut up. Louise's eyes watered and she coughed and knocked her chest with her fist.

What?

A bone. Louise coughed and coughed and drank down Helen's glass of water. Then she got up and went around the corner.

You're not supposed to do that, Helen said.

I'll be right back, she wheezed. And she came back with tears running freely, and the waiter in pink came back and he had more bread and he drew up a chair and rubbed Louise's back.

He said, A fish bone and you eat bread.

She ate.

Gone, she said.

See, the waiter said. I told you. The restaurant was nearly empty and the air was starting to feel cold. But the waiter stayed where he was, telling Louise all about his sister, her controlling interest in the restaurant, and his mother whom

· 254 ·

he remembered saying, all his childhood: A fishbone, you eat bread. He tapped his temple.

This I remember, he said.

I think I'll head up, Helen said.

You go, Louise said. The waiter jumped up and came back with two shot glasses and a small jug.

You are married, he asked.

My husband died two years ago, Louise said. He was a dear, dear man. We loved each other very much.

Strong water, he said. He poured one for Louise and one for himself.

I'll be up, Louise said to Helen. In a little while.

But she and the waiter in the pink shirt had ended up in the room next to Helen, and in the morning Helen was out on her balcony and they were out on his.

There was a white stucco wall dividing them, and the blue sky above and the ocean in front of Helen, and all the white roofs, and some men were mixing cement on the street in a tumbling drum and the wet clay sloshed over, and Helen saw that her shadow was very blue on the white wall. She could see the curls in her hair and the edge of her sunglasses and even her water glass with the water's parabola of light shimmering on the wall's surface. It was a hard-edged shadow. Then she heard the wooden doors open to the balcony next door and it was Louise. Helen could hear Louise and the waiter talk.

She could not hear what they were saying but she heard them remark on the sun. She had the feeling Louise was talking about the glorious light. Louise could be theatrical. I could just drink in this light, Louise was probably saying.

Helen heard their cutlery and dishes. The waiter lived in the hotel, it seemed, and he had cutlery and a hot plate. Or they had ordered up.

Helen heard Louise shake a packet of sugar. She couldn't hear what they were saying but she heard the packet flicking back and forth between Louise's finger and thumb and the granules bouncing. And her sister was fifty-eight, if Helen was counting correctly. She heard Louise tear the sugar packet. Helen didn't move; it would look like she had been listening.

Now Louise made her way down the aisle of the bus holding on to the backs of the seats as she passed, and the driver watched her in the rearview. England looked like England rolling past the tinted windows. It was lush and green and there was a field of sheep. It was as if Thomas Hardy and D.H. Lawrence had written down exactly what they'd seen and it had all stayed that way, or as if everybody here had read those books and made the landscape look like it was in the novels. There were trees and hedges and stone walls and sheep. The sheep, scattered here and there on the green hills, were an authentic touch.

Louise had gone to the bathroom and she was in there a long time, and then there was shouting at the back of the bus. Louise was shrieking and kicking the bathroom door, and Helen leapt up, and the driver was pulling over, and everybody turned in their seats, looking towards the back. The bathroom door slammed open and bounced shut, and Helen was screaming, Louise, Louise, Louise.

The door flew open and it was raining hard inside the small cubicle and Louise was shrieking. Her pale blouse was plastered to her chest and the lacy texture of her bra was visible, and when she pulled the blouse away it sucked itself back onto her skin, and there were little pockets of trapped air inside her blouse, and her hair was plastered down and her mascara ran down her cheeks.

Jesus Christ, Helen said. She had her sister by the arms and she was looking into her face. She was looking for blood or a bullet wound or some kind of gash, but there was nothing. Louise was soaking wet. And the rain kept pouring down in the cubicle and it ran out of the bathroom in widening rivulets and people in the back began lifting their luggage off the floor and mincing their shoes to the side. Little mincing steps to the side.

The driver spoke into the hand mike and his voice was relaxed. Later on Louise and Helen would describe it as a bedroom tone. A voice full of sarcasm and mirth.

There will be no smoking in the bathroom, the voice said.

Briefly the driver and Louise were standing out on the side of the road. Louise had her arms crossed and she was tapping her foot. She was nodding. The driver was pointing at the bus and pointing down the road and he had some ideas, it seemed, about duty and proper behaviour and the evils of smoking in general. He believed in punitive action, and he had some well-hammered-out thoughts about clean air and second-hand smoke and the importance of following rules on public transportation while visiting the United Kingdom.

Louise looked as if she were taking these views into consideration for the very first time. She looked as if she had never heard of them before.

People behind Helen were tutting and sucking their teeth and lifting themselves up in their seats to watch and dropping back down, and someone said loudly, for Helen's benefit, that she had a plane to catch.

Louise came back on to the bus and grabbed her things; she gathered her purse and luggage and her little jacket.

You go on, Helen, Louise said. I'll meet you there.

I'm staying with you, Helen said.

Helen, stay on the bus, Louise said. Do you hear me? We won't give that bastard the satisfaction of throwing us both off.

They left Louise on the side of the road. Helen watched Louise pull the little retractable handle out of the luggage, and she watched Louise set the bag on its wheels and tilt it up, and she watched the bag bounce around behind Louise on the crushed gravel. The bus pulled away and two big plumes of dust rolled up and Louise was gone.

Hours later, Helen was in the departure lounge of Heathrow Airport and she dropped down into a chair and opposite her there was a young Indian man—he looked Indian—clutching a briefcase, and he was fast asleep.

He had a knapsack beside him and his cheek rested on a corner of the briefcase, and his mouth was open and a thread of saliva hung from his top lip to the bottom one, and it shivered with each breath he took, and his hold on the briefcase was fierce but his glasses were askew. One arm of the glasses stuck off his face at an odd angle and one lens of the glasses was up by his eyebrow.

It was a committed sleep and it made him vulnerable and Helen felt a ridiculous wash of love for him. Or it was for someone else and she couldn't quite think who. And then she remembered Louise covered in the roiling clouds of dust from the bus pulling away.

The noise in the waiting area washed in and out, and there were cash registers, and babies crying, and couples flung over each other in sleep, and gentle-voiced reminders about watching your baggage, and gate announcements. It washed in and out and Helen could not pay attention, and the young Indian man's glasses were in danger of falling off his face.

A woman in a fluorescent lemon-coloured vest came along with a long pole with a claw that she manipulated with a squeeze-lever in the handle. The words *Cleaning Operative* were written on the back of the woman's vest, and she reached the claw under the seat of the sleeping Indian man and snagged a crumpled napkin and drew it out without touching the man's pant leg, and she dropped the napkin in the garbage trolley she was pulling behind her. Helen had the idea that the cleaning operative had reached into the man's dreams and taken out a plot turn. She had surgically removed the key, the turning point upon which everything hinged, from the man's dream. Or it was her own dream. The napkin had been like a plug and all the world on this side would swirl down the drain in a great spiral into a parallel universe, and Helen either had that idea or she dreamt it. She felt herself dropping off.

The soiled napkin had held everything in place, exactly so, and without it, all that came before and all that followed would be misaligned, and forget it, she would never get home, and she jerked awake, and when she did the Indian man was gone and in his seat, directly across from Helen, with a cup of coffee, was Louise.

I hitchhiked, Louise said.

. . . . .

Helen's Paint, November 2008

BARRY SAID RED was an unforgiving colour. He hoped she wasn't thinking red.

The number of coats, he said. He'd had a lady in Cowan Heights wanted to cover up a red living room and it had taken ten coats.

Barry had agreed to stay on and do the painting after all.

Not a word of a lie, Barry said. He looked at the spackled walls and he had a stainless steel ruler he tapped against his leg while he spoke.

Lately there's a lot of dark brown around, he said. There were pauses when he and Helen spoke. They took the time to imagine brown walls. They could do this because they weren't in a hurry, because everything, every utterance, could be turned on its head and mean more than one thing.

Chocolate, they call it, he said.

I'm thinking light, Helen said. Barry nodded.

Eggshell, she said.

He had worked on the mainland, Barry said. He'd had a guy ask him to build a mansion in the country by a lake, and he had laid down black marble floors. This was back when he was a kid.

That house, he said. He shook his head as if he could not believe his own capabilities. Marble floors, he repeated. He could get loquacious during the breaks. He liked to view his work and then he would tell bits of his story. They were all stories about construction. They were about taking a ripsaw to something, or a hammer or a crowbar.

He was thinking of Toronto in the seventies when he said money. What opportunity. He had worked sometimes two or three months at a stretch without taking a day off. The money.

Like picking it off the trees, he said. He had a way of squinting into the distance when he spoke. His eyes were a grey Helen had not seen before and she had to admit she found him to be good-looking. She did not tell Louise. She did not tell her daughters. Barry's eyes were grey and they did not change in outdoor light. They weren't sometimes blue or sometimes hazel.

Today she made him a sandwich and put carrot sticks and olives on the plate. She wanted to make the plate attractive. He has someone who calls on his cell and asks for things, interrupts his work, and when he hangs up he is utterly lost in the exchange. He sings quietly to himself.

Barry Kielly loves whoever it is on the phone. It is a calming, peaceful love and Helen is shocked by how territorial and disappointed she feels in the face of it. She has, on occasion, sat down in the middle of the staircase and listened. Or she has stopped sewing and listened. Today she stops with the squeaky Windex and listens. Unaware she is listening; straining to hear.

She made him a sandwich because she was making one for herself, but she found herself peeling carrots too. Garnish. She was making a garnish for the plates, and when you live alone you are a stranger to the idea of garnish. You are a stranger to any flourishes at all. Because you do not exist: there is the TV and your sister Louise and the wedding dresses and the grandchildren; there is the worry of John. There is Christmas. But Helen does not put a garnish on a plate.

Both Helen and Barry are taken up with their work and the precision it demands. And Helen listens to Barry. She draws patterns and cuts the brown tissue paper and pins it to the fabric and uses the expensive shears and hangs the pieces over the backs of the furniture. There are stacks of *Vogue* and *Bride* and *Cosmo*. She draws with graphite or she draws with a charcoal pencil. She has a tomato pincushion and a wicker sewing basket with compartments within compartments and needles and satin lining, and it looks like it comes from another age.

People like the idea of a hand-sewn wedding dress because it is a kind of talisman.

Lately some of her brides are lesbians and they are married on boats in the harbour or on windswept cliffs, and they do not go in for flounces and bows, but they want to be beautiful just the same and not in an ironic way.

My son was after buying us the plane tickets, Barry had said. Come on, Dad, we'll go up to Toronto for a game. His mother was a contrary woman. I don't pretend to understand women. We got up there and one afternoon I said to him, I said, Let's look for the house. I must have drove for four or five hours and do you think I could find that house? Thousands of houses, and all of them exactly alike. We never did find it.

Now it is dusk, and Helen is standing in front of the mirror in the bathroom holding a sodden ball of paper towel. She was a young woman, she thinks. When Cal died.

And at first you think you will not be alone forever. You think the future is infinite. Childhood seems to have been infinite. Downstairs, the saw revs and Helen hears a stick of wood fall to the floor. And so will the future be infinite, and it cannot be spent alone.

But, she has learned, it is possible: not to meet someone. The past yields, it gives way, it goes on forever. The future is unyielding. It is possible that the past has cracked off, the past has clattered to the floor, and what remains is the future and there is not very much of that. The future is the short end of the stick.

· · · · ·

A Blessing, November 2008

JANE WALKS IN the dusk through dropping temperatures, and it has started to snow. Christmas garlands swooping across Spadina Avenue. Everything lit up. She has already passed two Salvation Army Santas with hand bells and plastic globes full of crumpled bills.

A while ago she passed a choir of at least thirty men and women singing in Latin on the steps of the stone church at Bloor and Avenue Road. They were dressed in red and white gowns, and clouds of breath hung in the air. The conductor pinched her fingers together and pulled them apart as if pulling an invisible thread taut, and the music snagged. A sudden breathless silence. The conductor nodded, once, twice, and flung her hands up and the voices boomed again at twice the volume.

Jane kept walking because her feet were cold, but she had an eye out for a taxi. She will see John in the morning and she is full of dread. Why did she call him? She is afraid of what he will say. She is thrilled.

A man wrapped in a voluminous patchwork quilt stops Jane and waves a sheaf of papers. It's a novel I wrote in a course I done to help me achieve employment, the man says. He gives the papers a little shake.

This is a book about redemption, the man says. The glorious light that come into the world with the baby Jesus.

Jane opens her purse and takes out a fistful of change. The man turns his head and coughs hard. His chest is full of phlegm. Jane can hear it. The man has dreadlocks, rust and grey and whitish and hanging over his shoulders, and a veil of snow covers his head.

I just need a break, the man says. He is gaunt, and the thinness makes him look regal, and one lens in his black-framed glasses shows a white, burning star from the streetlight.

The shops are all closing and Jane sees the traffic is thinning out. The man has been crouched in the doorway of a deli and there is a line of very yellow chickens hanging upside down inside the window, and on a bed of AstroTurf there are silver trays full of crushed ice, showing dark steaks marbled with skeins of fat, and a stainless steel bowl of pig hearts.

The Christ Child, the man says quietly, looking past Jane's shoulder down the street. Came into a world of darkness and eternal damnation and he brought the light.

Jane smoothes out the pages of the man's novel on her thigh. She sees that the handwriting is regimented and full of hard points that dig into the lined paper. The novel is about Rastafarianism.

The man has reached under the quilt and is fiddling with something below. Jane can hear his breathing go ragged, but she doesn't care what he's fiddling with. Maybe it is the cold or her hormones, or it's because she will soon be a mother, or it is the choir bellowing out in the dark in a dead language— she doesn't know what it is, but she feels compassion for this man. She will deal with John when he shows up. Jane will tell him: this is how it is.

Last week, the man wheezes. Last week I accepted the spirit of the Holy Ghost into my heart. He draws out from under the quilt an inhaler and puts it in his mouth and presses the button and draws a deep breath. His eyes bulge.

Jane skims a few pages of the man's novel, tilting the paper under the street light. She brushes away a few snowflakes.

Do not eat anything with a face, the man's novel says. There is mention of good and evil and a pure light that will break the hearts of men, grind them to dust, and the dust will blow away. She reads a line that says: *Unto your children and your children's children, and unto them will be born a child, and that child will be the light of the world.* Jane's baby somersaults, a kick in the belly, a kick in the spine.

I am only asking for enough to get these few pages photocopied, the man says. So I can get a start in the world of publishing. I just need a start. Just last week I was born again.

Jane opens her purse and gives the man a twenty. He scrunches it up in his fist and draws the fist back under the quilt. Jane thinks he must have put the money in his pocket, because now he puts his hand back out for the pages of his novel.

Bless you, he says.

. . . . .

John's Cornish Hen, November 2008

JOHN IS EATING snails in a restaurant and they are doused in garlic butter and parsley and he has a little prong to dig them out of the shells but the prong keeps bending like boiled spaghetti and his high school math teacher is at the other end of the table. Then he notices one of the snails has crawled out of its shell and left a slimy trail on the white rim of the plate, and it is moving, very slowly, clinging to the edge of the rim.

He puts the snail in his pocket and forgets about it, but then he's in a taxi going through the streets of New York and there is something big and wet jammed in his pocket, and it has soaked the leg of his pants and he has to work hard to get it out of the tight pocket, and it's a Cornish hen. It is plucked and cold, as if it has come from the freezer.

John knows intuitively that the hen can think. He feels a gushing love for it. A geyser of love and the need to protect it. He knows it hasn't acquired language yet but it is something he can love with his whole heart, and though it is deformed in some way and therefore it is wrong, very wrong, to hope for it, he does hope. He hopes that maybe it will someday speak and love him back.

It occurs to him now that he might be dreaming, and he remembers to put his lucid dreaming techniques into practice. If he tries to read in a dream all print will appear as gibberish. Then he will know unequivocally that he is asleep. There is a physical ache of sadness radiating through his chest, a love so deep and piercing and lonely it is paralyzing him.

He can feel himself beginning to drool. He sees the taxi driver's identification paper on the dash, and he tries to read it but it's in Arabic, and since he cannot read Arabic he has no idea if the writing is gibberish or not. No idea if he is dreaming.

Then he is running through a building, an abandoned school. He finds the hen trembling in the corner of an empty classroom. It has been attacked by a cat. It has several puncture wounds and is bleeding. He runs his hand over the hen's cold, blue-white, bumpy skin. Here and there he can feel little prickles where the very ends of feathers were left in the animal when it was plucked. He tries to cuddle it in his arms and he is weeping. He sticks his finger in one of the wounds the cat has made. He sticks his finger deep into the puncture and it is warm and wet inside, and when he pulls his finger out his fingernail is rimmed in blood, under the nail and along the cuticle.

He jerks awake: the plane to Toronto, through the night sky. He is scared and exhilarated. He wants to get there. He wants to arrive.

. . . . .

The Phone, February 1982

THE PHONE RANG and woke Helen. Telling her to turn on the radio.

Do you have the radio on?

That's the way the families were informed: It's on the radio. Turn on the radio.

Nobody from the oil company called.

What must have happened was this: the men had not been dead an hour and the company had public relations on it. They had lawyers. Helen can imagine the meeting in the boardroom. Or maybe it all happened on the phone. She can imagine the kind of language employed.

Or there was horror. Of course there was horror and it had numbed them. When did words like *situation* enter the vocabulary? Because Helen believes they thought of it that way. She believes they all wanted to *manage the situation*.

And the fury of the storm outside the boardroom window. The veils of snow erasing everything outside and then everything bleeding back through. The wind roared and the Basilica was gone in a blast of snow and came back. The edge of the building showed through the white in a lull of the wind and then the rest of the building came through. Gower Street was gone and came back with a new howling gust. The wind was an eraser working backwards, erasing all the white, leaving the buildings grainy and soft-edged and smudged.

If they had met in a boardroom there would have been a coat tree in the corner. Helen needs to picture this part. There will be a jug of water. Do they really have a jug of water? Has someone gone to the kitchenette down the hall and filled the jug? Is there a mini-fridge with ice cubes and Tupperware containers with names and dates taped to the lids? Do the ice cubes crack and pop in the plastic tray and spill into the mouth of the jug? Forget the jug. And now they must speak. Helen wants to see it. She wants to hear it.

Or it was a series of phone calls. She does not know. How did they decide not to tell the families?

But Helen can get no further. Because how did they get to the idea *Let's not phone the families.*

How did they come up with that?

And further: How was such an idea spoken aloud, given form, enunciated?

The company was formulating spin. They may not have known about spin back then, Helen thinks, but they were thinking spin. Making it up as they went along (later, much later, someone would say: We should have done some things differently; but that was also spin).

Or, nobody knew how to tell the families. They were not managing the situation. They were in shock. On her better days Helen can believe they didn't know what they were doing.

And so the families heard on the radio that their loved ones were dead. And they didn't believe it because surely the company would have called.

Helen had phoned Louise and was incoherent. She had screamed, Cal is dead, Louise. Cal is dead. Cal is dead. And she had slammed down the phone.

Tim Brophy had come over from next door. Helen saw him through the kitchen window, making his way through the drifts.

The snow was lifting off the drifts in transparent glittering sheets that twisted and flapped and folded together at the corners and folded again, and she could hear someone's tires squealing on the road. The tires were burning and squealing and the engine was growling and it was such a magnificent morning and her knees gave. The trees were encased in ice and the sun shot sparks down the length of the branches. The sun like an old nickel in the sky, tarnished, dull, behind all that flying snow. Helen's knees would not hold her. The whole world floods you, bursts you open; the world is bigger than expected, and brighter.

It was not that she was closed off to the beauty, because she wasn't. The beauty flooded her pupils and nose and ears and all of her cells, and there was the belief that what was happening couldn't be happening, and she hung on to that.

The Brophys had heard and Maureen Brophy had sent Tim over is what was happening. Tim wading through, his cap scrunched up in his fist. He hadn't done up his jacket. He was rushing, Helen saw.

Maureen couldn't face her, Helen thought. She must have been standing at the sink washing the dishes, or feeding the baby in the high chair, and she must have said, You go, Tim.

Tim would have started to protest, and Maureen would have spun around, pointing at the back door like you might to a child or a dog, and there would have been no arguing with her.

Maureen would then have straightened herself up because a tragedy requires some people to be normal. Someone has to bake a casserole for the recently widowed. Maureen was thinking of baking Helen a casserole.

This was going on all over the island because the news was on the radio. At the university there were students who had fathers on the rig and brothers on the rig, and some of the teachers brought televisions into the classroom from the audio-video department so they could watch when a story came on the news. People were calling relatives on the mainland; people were arranging airline tickets. The idea of men drowning in that cold darkness was staggering and nightmarish, and the company had said the bloody thing would never sink no matter what.

Maureen had no intention of going over to Helen's.

Once he'd left his own kitchen Tim was in a hurry to get to Helen, and the blanket of white was aglitter out there. Magnificent and frigid and light-spangled. As long as she lives Helen will never forget how beautiful the snow was, and the sky, and how it flooded her and she couldn't tell the beauty apart from the panic. She decided then, and still believes, that beauty and panic are one and the same.

She forgot the children; the children were asleep. She had been knocked back to a time before the children. Before anything except when she'd met Cal and, though it sounds silly and made up, though it sounds completely untrue, she'd decided to marry him the very first time she slept with him. This is mine, is what she thought. Let's keep doing this.

Panic and beauty are inside each other, all the time, copulating in an effort to create more beauty and panic, and everybody gets down on his or her knees in the face of it. It is a demonic, angelic coupling.

Everybody who had listened to the radio in the morning knew by then that the men were dead, and they had tried to imagine the deaths and could not. Tim Brophy was sitting in Helen's kitchen with his coat still on, his boots dripping over the linoleum.

He answered the phone when it rang, and it was Louise calling back. Louise was phoning back because Helen had hung up on her. Helen didn't know what she was doing.

Later Helen would say: I didn't even know I'd called you.

Louise called back and Tim answered, and Louise thought Tim was Cal. It was a weird mistake because Tim sounded nothing like Cal.

Louise said: Cal, I think Helen is losing her mind; she said you were dead.

Louise was forgetting that Cal was out on the rig.

And Tim Brophy said: It's Tim Brophy from next door. The *Ocean Ranger* went down and it looks like no survivors. The whole bloody thing went under.

The men on the *Seaforth Highlander* saw the men in the water. One is always haunted by something, and that is what haunts Helen. The men on the *Seaforth Highlander* had been close enough to see some of the men in the waves. Close enough to talk. The men were shouting out before they died. Calling out for help. Calling out to God or calling for mercy or confessing their sins. Or just mentioning they were cold. Or they were just screaming. Noises.

The ropes are frozen, the men on board the *Highlander* were telling the men in the water. The men on the *Highlander* were compelled to narrate all their efforts so that the dying men would know unequivocally that they had not been abandoned. And the *Highlander* crew were in danger of being washed over themselves but they stayed out there in the gale on the slippery deck and took the waves in their faces and tried to cling on and did not give in to fear. They stayed out there because you don't give up while men are in the water, even if it means you might die yourself.

We're cutting the ropes.

Have you got the ropes cut?

Bastard is all iced over.

Hurry up.

And there must have come a moment, Helen thinks, when all this shouting back and forth was no longer about turning the event around, because everybody on both sides knew there would be no turning it around. The men in the water knew they would die and the men on board knew the men in the water would die. But they kept trying anyway.

And then all the shouting was just for company. Because who wants to watch a man being swallowed by a raging ocean without yelling out to him. They had shouted to the men in the water. They had tried to reach the men with grappling hooks. They saw them and then they did not see them. It was as simple as that.

· · · · ·

John in the Dining Room, November 2008

IN THE LATE morning light John brushes his teeth and stands for a minute looking at his reflection. It was midnight last night before he made it through the revolving door and checked into his hotel in Toronto. He doesn't like his shirt and he doesn't have time to change it. But he wriggles out of it fast and a button comes off and pings against the counter. He pulls on a cashmere sweater. His mother gave him a black cashmere sweater for Christmas last year.

John runs his hand over his face and stands still like that, his eyes closed, full of excitement and jet lag. He's nauseated. Then he pats all his pockets, and his wallet in his back pocket and the swipe key in his wallet, and he's out the door and waiting for the elevator and down two floors, and three girls get in and the smell of shampoo and the damn thing goes up two floors and the girls get out, and then it goes down to the lobby.

He's greeted at the entrance of the restaurant and he takes in all the tables. Jane isn't here yet. He's glad she isn't here. He wants to see her walk in. An hour later he has read the paper or tried to read it. Obama gaining in North Virginia. Change. The time has come for change. Yes we can.

John orders poached eggs and they come with grilled asparagus, two pieces crossed like an X on the white plate, and a broiled tomato that he doesn't touch. The asparagus stinks. He hates that smell. It smells of an overripeness that sickens him. He cuts the egg with the side of his fork and the yellow spills all over the white plate and he puts down his fork. The burst yellow eye of the egg stares up at him. He's not hungry. A minute ago he was ravenous and now he can't touch the food.

A woman is standing next to him as big as a house and he nearly tips over the chair standing up and his napkin falls to the carpet.

I fell asleep, Jane says. I'm sorry. I fall asleep all the time. Sitting up in a chair sometimes. Hours and hours. Yesterday I fell asleep in the lotus position. I have no control. Out like a light. The alarm was ringing when I woke up.

You're so big, John says.

Anyway, I'm late, she says. I'm sorry.

Beautiful, I mean, John says. But he is not at all sure. He knows there is a baby coming but he has not imagined Jane's body. He has not imagined this beach ball that gives her a waddle, and the softness in her face. He leans over to pick up his napkin and Jane must think he is going to kiss her and moves in and they bang foreheads. Then he tries to make it look that way, like he was going to kiss her, but it's too late. Two women in business suits at the next table stare at him.

Then Jane looks as if she hears something. She looks distracted and absorbed.

Oh, she says. Oh. She grabs his wrist and puts his hand on her belly.

John feels a ripple, a soft bump.

Did you feel anything, Jane asks. She is lit up. She shifts his hand an inch or so. Do you feel it?

· · · · ·

Free Fall, December 2008

HELEN PUTS IN the other earring. She is going to a concert. There will be Christmas carols and a trapeze artist and men dressed as toy soldiers, and fifty teenage girls in spandex Santa suits cut to show the cheeks of their bums.

She straightens her rhinestone necklace and catches herself in the mirror. She touches the skin under one eye with the tip of her finger. How did this happen? Decades have passed. Centuries.

Sleet rattles the bedroom window; she squirts perfume on her wrist, touches her wrists together.

I've got to pick up my grandson, Barry said this afternoon. So, it was his grandson. It was not a wife or girlfriend. It was not a lover. She felt elated. The cellphone rang and he said, I'll be there, Henry.

My grandson, he said to Helen. He closed the phone with a little flick of his wrist and went suddenly very still. There, in the bird feeder on the window: a blue jay. Where had it come from? How blue. And it flew away.

He let her know, just as if it were any of her business. Not another woman; a grandson.

Tonight a girl of twenty-two, a trapeze artist, will climb two flowing strips of white fabric suspended from the theatre ceiling. Some sort of fabric with sway and give. Hand over hand the girl will climb, until she is suspended in a spotlight. Helen will cover her eyes and squirm in her seat. It is too high. The rhinestone necklace from her fifth wedding anniversary; she looks haggard in the mirror.

Life barrels through; it is gone. Something rushes through. The front door slams and then a door slams in the back; something burns on the stove; birthdays, brides and caskets; babies, bankruptcy, huge strokes of luck, the trees full of ice; gone. She touches her necklace. All gone. She grips the arm of her chair. Switches off the lamp and watches a car come down the hill. The headlights burn through the lace curtain. Pattern on the wall. A pause for the stop sign, then the car turns the corner and the shadow of the curtain moves around the whole room: her dresser, her cardigan on the hook, the mirror, and Helen's face and arms.

The Christmas show is a fundraiser for the families of soldiers in Afghanistan and her grandson is an angel in the second act. Timmy is an angel.

At the show, Helen spots Patience in the front row, in front of Timmy. Helen bought wings for them at the dollar store. The children sing and twirl and patter off.

Then there is a meaningful hush. The audience anticipates. Two white strips of fabric unfurl from the ceiling. A fog machine switches on and the ballet dancers move on tiptoe across the stage into the wings. The aurora borealis is on the scrim, and stars descend from the rafters, and there is no net, ladies and gentlemen. Please note. There is no net.

The girl in white, in flaring sequins, has climbed the streaming bands of fabric. She is too high. The girl has wrapped herself in the fabric and she does not hold on. She swings her arms in an arc over her head.

The applause comes in bursts and it climbs a ladder and climbs back down and quiets itself.

If I were to ask Barry to stay for dinner, Helen thinks. She has her hand over her eyes; she cannot watch this young girl thirty feet above them. Instead, Helen sees herself putting down a candle on the dinner table. She sees the good silverware.

She cannot ask him.

The girl swings one leg so the fabric circles her thigh, once, twice. She swings the other leg so that leg is wrapped in fabric too.

I could not use candles, Helen thinks. How formal it would seem, and full of expectation. She is abashed. Candles? Candles are romantic and intimate, and she will not use candles, she'll put the dimmer up as far as it will go. She'll light the meal like a shopping mall.

Would Barry take off the baseball cap?

He said the room was shaping up. What do you think, he said. They were standing together in the empty room.

I'm almost done, Helen, he said.

It looks pretty good.

I have to say, he agreed. He nodded at the ceiling.

The girl falls all at once, the girl is tumbling to the stage, tumbling and unwrapping, tipping, somersaulting towards the stage, and there is no net and the audience cries out, and she snags halfway down. Helen flings out an arm in terror and hits Louise in the seat next to her. A smack on the chest.

The girl dangles in mid air, triumphant. Wild clapping that breaks like waves.

Louise grips Helen's wrist. It's part of the show, Louise whispers.

Helen will ask Barry for supper. She will risk candles. What the hell. She will risk candles if she bloody well feels like candles.

THE NEW YEAR

Fireworks, January 2009

THE FIREWORKS WERE moved from the harbour to Quidi Vidi Lake because it occurred to someone to be careful of the oil tanks over on the South Side. Barry said they could park the truck up in the White Hills.

I'll come get you, he said.

That sounds nice, said Helen.

You know, there by the school, the building, whatever it is they have up there.

The building up there, Helen said.

There's a good view, Barry said.

I'd say that'd be the spot, all right, Helen said.

Around eleven thirty, then.

Barry had finished the renovations three weeks before. He'd left his tools and said he'd be back to get them. A few days later his stuff was gone and Helen's house key glittered on the bristly welcome mat.

Imagine if a spark from them fireworks landed on those oil tanks, Barry said. Helen was talking on the phone and looking out her bedroom window. The South Side Hills had long, dangerous icicles all over their craggy cliffs. Snow streaked the smooth bare rock farther up. The five white tanks, fat and implacable against the blue sky.

What if I cooked supper for us, Helen said. She had not meant to say it. She heard something crunch. It must have been an empty pop can. Barry had crunched a pop can in his fist.

I don't want you to go to any trouble, he said.

If you're too busy, she said.

What time, he asked.

Everybody in town had the same idea. Helen and Barry couldn't get near the White Hills because of the traffic. They parked, and it was snowing lightly and the ground crunched and squeaked with new snow. They walked down to the lake. There were long lines of traffic and the snow fell between the crawling cars and shone in the soft fans of the yellow headlights.

There were teenagers hanging out of a van in the Employment and Immigration parking lot. The doors of the van were open and music was thumping into the cold air. The kids had fake ice cubes in their drinks that crackled with light. The girls were shrill. One swaying blonde in a rabbit-fur bomber jacket yelled Happy New Year to Helen and raised her glass so beer slopped over the side and sizzles of light from the fake ice cubes shot out through her fingers.

Earlier, Helen had answered the door after the bell rang and she was dressed up and Barry was not dressed up. He wore jeans speckled with paint and a plaid shirt. They'd sat down to eat almost at once because there was nothing to say. The risotto had been gluey and cold. The beef was grey.

Helen had just finished serving herself and she pushed out her chair and it screeched over the hardwood. Barry glanced up, startled and guilty looking. He was wiping his empty plate clean with a chunk of bread before she had even started.

There had been a hole in the centre of the dining room and all the things a man and woman could say to each other had dropped into the hole, and it had closed over, and the new hardwood floor gleamed shiny and mute. It was a silence full of what they expected, and what they expected was turned up on bust, and it was sexual and full of need and too much to expect. Helen had the dryer going at the back of the house and she and Barry listened to the clothes tumbling around. Something with snaps scraped and was muffled and scraped again, over and over.

Then Barry brought up the subject of his ex-wife. He glossed over the subject. He put his hand against the edge of the table and pushed his chair out and ran his other hand down the front of his shirt, and bread crumbs bounced onto the floor, and then he just casually mentioned his ex-wife.

She took up with my best friend, he said. Old story. This was long ago. They collect meteors in Nevada.

Helen's plate was full of food and she didn't want to touch it but she couldn't leave it there. The gravy had congealed with a crackled sheen over the cold risotto.

You mean, like comet tails, she said. She stabbed a limp shred of colourless broccoli, then shook it off her fork.

Worth their weight in gold, Barry said. Chunks as big as your head. The two of them out there, shovelling sand. They got a house built almost entirely of glass. That's not what they do for a living, he said. That's what they do for fun.

And this was the wistful closing statement about the ex-wife. The mother of his son. He did not begrudge his ex-wife falling stars.

Helen suddenly remembered to put on music. Something perverse or decadent made her choose Frank Zappa. Barry poured them a second glass of wine.

I'm not kidding, Helen, he said. This is a fine meal.

Helen's mouth was full. She chewed and swallowed and flapped at the kitchen with her white napkin.

Go, she said. Help yourself.

Do you mind, he said.

She laid her hand flat on her chest and swallowed and gulped wine. Be my guest, she said.

Barry came back with his plate heaped up and he was saying about the journalist who'd thrown a shoe at Bush. Did you see that on the Net? Then he said about the mayor who had thrown up in her purse years ago. He'd done her floors too. She was a ticket, Barry said. And then the new mayor had demanded that a councillor bring him DDT in a cereal bowl with a spoon and he'd eat the whole goddamn thing for breakfast. Because there was nothing wrong with it. DDT wouldn't hurt a fly, that mayor had told the TV cameras.

Helen said, Shut up. Stop. She was laughing. Barry had worked his hand into his pocket and then he took out a lighter and lit the candles. He walked over to the wall switch and dimmed the lights while he was talking.

Helen raised her hand, clutching her napkin, and lifted one finger to make him stop. I have to show you, she said.

What?

She was already up the stairs and he was following two at a time.

You have to see, she said. Helen stumbled forward in the dark and turned on the gooseneck lamp on her dresser. The wedding dress she'd been working on lay over the arm of a chair. It was finished.

That's really something, Barry said.

And the girl who is going to wear it, Helen said.

That's a beautiful thing, Barry said.

Helen had a hundred-watt bulb in that lamp and it hit the white satin and the dress was blazing white. Pearls and sequins sparking, light spilling along the folds, beading up like mercury and spreading in all directions.

Then it struck Helen that they were in her bedroom, and the wine hit too. Her bed was appalling. The pillows were appalling and the personal things on her dresser were appalling: her deodorant; a pair of nylons that still held the shape of the ball of her foot, shiny with dirt, and the rest like a crumpled reptile skin, faintly shiny and lewd; a black patent-leather evening purse with a broken strap. She had come into her bedroom forgetting it was her bedroom. She had come in by accident. She turned off the light to make the bed go away, and Barry said her name.

Then they were in the dark. Just standing in the dark, and Barry was not sure what to do. Helen fumbled around for the light and turned it back on. It was an uncompromising light. Barry looked at his watch.

It's time to get down to the lake, he said. Or we'll miss the fireworks.

And now Helen and Barry were in a crowd at the lake. A *bang* clapped against the low hills and they both turned. The explosion of light seemed to reach through the darkness towards them. It was coming at them fast. Silence followed the *bang*, deepened and became fathomless. The light flew into their faces as silent as something at the bottom of the ocean. Helen stepped back. The snow crunching under her boots. Then the booms overlapped. The fireworks looked like underwater plants. Starfish, phosphorescent flowers with stamens and petals and seeds. They pushed up out of the dark and were extinguished by it before they could touch or come anywhere near her.

A family of ducks on a pan of ice tried to flee, all huddled together in a pack, waddling fast and then stopping. Staying still. They waited, and with the next bang the ducks turned together and waddled in the other direction. Helen was close enough to hear the ducks, but they didn't make any noise at all. A red spurting fountain shot up a geyser of white spirals. More flowers over their heads dropping petals.

A girl a few yards behind them was counting down with her boyfriend. Five, four, three, two, one. And then the girl yelled Happy New Year, hopping up and down. *Boom, crack, boom crack, boom*, and Barry drew Helen into his arms and his mouth was on her mouth and they pressed hard together, and his tongue and the firm strength of his body and his hand under her jacket on the back of her cashmere sweater. They kissed for a long time.

When they drew apart, the dark sky had clouds of smoke and the crowd had started back up over the hill, and Helen said, Do you want to come back for coffee or a whisky or something. And Barry said, Yes I do.

In the kitchen, Helen screwed the espresso maker together and put it on the stove. She had whipped cream in the fridge and a bottle of Baileys, and she set those things out. Barry was on the couch in the living room and Helen went out and flopped down beside him, and it was ordinary. They were friends and it was well past midnight and her thighs were cold.

Then his hand was on her crotch, moving, and she lifted her hips towards his hand. He was looking into her eyes. It wasn't ordinary. She was mistaken. His thumb on the seam of her jeans, rubbing intently. The reflection of his watch face, a disc of light, was jiggling on the faded pink floral fabric of the couch. It was a frenetic, crazed jiggling.

The espresso maker on the kitchen stove began to bubble. Helen hadn't screwed down the top canister tightly enough. Steam was escaping through a groove that hadn't been threaded properly. The metal canister was whistling, high-pitched, and then chugging like an engine. Then it was screamingly high again. Helen pressed hard against Barry's hand and turned her face into the sofa.

I am going to come, she said. She was not speaking to Barry, and he didn't answer. The jiggling oval from his watch fluttered over a printed flower on the couch near her mouth. Helen pushed her face into the cushion so he could not watch her. She put out her tongue to touch the disc of light. She could feel the texture of the Scotchgarded couch. It tasted of sawdust.

Then Barry was tearing her jeans down. He was a little rough. Helen held his ass with her hands and their feet hooked together. He was wearing slippery nylon socks. He grimaced during orgasm the way she had once seen him grimace while lifting a sheet of plywood into place, holding it with his shoulder while digging for a nail in his carpenter's apron. And he grunted. It was a sound so unselfconscious and from so deep inside him that it thrilled her. He said, God almighty. A thrill ran the length of her body like a spill of icy water. Then he said, Goddamn. Goddamn. He closed his eyes and drew in a deep breath and he kissed her collarbone.

Somebody should turn off the coffee, Helen said. But the espresso maker kept whistling. Finally Barry stood and pulled up his jeans and fastened the leather belt. He walked to the window and parted the curtains. People were walking up from downtown. A cop car went past with the lights on and a few whoops of the siren.

Helen walked into the kitchen and the bottom of the espresso maker was glowing orange as if it were about to melt.

· · · · ·

What Did He Say

THERE WERE A lot of men in the water. There wasn't very much time, Helen. We were trying to get to them.

What did Cal say? Did he say anything? Helen wanted to hear that Cal had said her name. She wanted to hear that he knew she loved him. She wanted to hear: tell Helen this or that.

It didn't have to be love.

It didn't have to be her name.

Just some shout to show that he knew what he was leaving behind. Some shout to acknowledge that she would have to raise four children by herself now. That she would have to get through without love. That she was pregnant. She would like to think some part of him knew, or had intuited, or that some paranormal force had let him know, there was a baby coming.

Helen would like to know that Cal understood how dark the rest of the winter would be, and how the fetus in her womb was kicking and making her throw up, and how the baby would have the cord wrapped around her neck and would be blue, bluish, as none of the others had been, and the terror that Helen would lose the baby now, and how she could not lose her.

Helen had not believed in an afterlife before Cal died and she still did not think of it. But she listened for Cal after he died. She listened for his tread on the stairs; she listened for his advice. She listened for him pouring cereal out of a box, the clink of his spoon; she listened for the dog's nails on the hardwood as Cal set out its food in the back porch. She listened for his breathing at night. If she was lost in sewing and the kettle whistled, she expected Cal to turn it off. She asked him what he thought of the girls.

And then a murmur, a collective gasp went up, and it turned out her baby girl was fine, just fine, what a big girl, and Helen found herself thinking, Look, Cal, look. She would have liked him to tell her certain things, and she knows exactly what they are:

I'm not afraid.

Tell Helen thank you.

Tell the children I love them.

Tell Helen; tell Helen.

All the men were calling out. *We had to cut the ropes where they were iced over.* The ropes were so cold. The men couldn't hang on.

What Helen cannot fathom or forgive: We are alone in death. Of course we are alone. It is a solitude so refined we cannot experience it while we are alive; it is too rarefied, too potent. It is a drug, that solitude, an immediate addiction. A profound selfishness, so full of self it is an immolation of all that came before. Cal was alone in that cold. Utterly alone, and that was death. That, finally, was death.

Helen wants to jump into the ocean in the middle of the night when it's snowing just to see what it feels like.

Sometimes, like tonight, she is so awake she feels she will never sleep again. She feels an acute awareness of the ongoing life of the teapot. The teapot goes on, the gold vinyl sneaker belonging to her granddaughter remains a gold vinyl sneaker, the phone goes on being a phone.

It is very cold out and very dark, and Helen longs for some movement in the dark, for a taxi to go by. Out on the street the asphalt is so solidly itself. It will always be itself. The house across the street is the house across the street with its naked light bulb in the third-floor window. And there is Helen. But Helen is not sure she is herself.

She lifts her sleeping mask and the furniture buzzes and she feels pins and needles in her feet and a mounting wave of terror; she is solidly alone. She is as alone and cold and obdurately dull as the tree in her backyard, as the fender of a car under the street light, as the apple in the bowl on the kitchen table, as the church across the street, as the steeple covered on one side with snow; she is not Helen, and who is Helen? A scrap of a dream, a fragmented, a frayed — and the phone rings, it blasts into the room, it rings and rings. There is a body in the bed with her and she goes cold with terror. It is Cal. Cal is back, but he is dead.

But it is not Cal. It is not Cal.

Barry switches on the light. He is a man who wears slippers and who scuffs his feet. She can hear him pissing in the toilet down the hall. And she answers the phone and her heart leaps. What you have to become. It's John. What is it, three? Three in the morning?

Mom, John says. He is crying.

Mom, John says. We have a little baby girl.

· · · · ·

She Sees It

SHE IS THINKING again about the portal. It had a metal deadlight that could be lowered and secured over the two panes of glass, but nobody lowered the deadlight. If that metal deadlight had been lowered, the water wouldn't have gotten over the control panel.

Helen has memorized the ifs and she can rhyme them off like the rosary. If the men had the information they needed, if they had lowered the deadlight, if the water hadn't short-circuited the control panel, if Cal had had another shift, if Cal had never gotten the job in the first place, if they hadn't fallen in love. If she hadn't had the children. If.

She wants to believe Cal had time for a game of cards.

Helen knows Cal liked to have a game of 120s after supper if he wasn't on duty, and there was time for all that. The fist of ocean had punched through, yes, but there's every reason to believe from the retrieved voice recordings that nobody was too worried.

Helen wants to know exactly what happened because she can't stand the idea of not knowing. She wants to be with Cal when the rig goes down.

The public address system had short-circuited and maybe there was a subtle absence of sound the men would have noticed. Maybe Cal was dealing a hand at a card table and he would have noticed a silence like when the fridge cuts out. What she doesn't want is for him to be asleep. She doesn't want him to have woken up to the panic. If only someone could have told her where he was.

Somebody in the control room said: Let's get this water cleaned up.

Or: Get someone in here to clean up that glass.

Somebody said: The panel is wet.

Somebody said: Valves opening by themselves.

And a voice said: Working on it.

They retrieved those taped voices later on, and the men didn't sound worried at all.

Get down there and get it cleaned up, somebody said.

Here's the funny thing. The sea water hit the panel and it forced a 115-volt current to run in another direction. The current was supposed to run one way but it dug its heels in; it changed its mind.

How different is that current from a human thought or emotion, Helen wonders. A flurry of feeling. A burst of giddy indecision? A filament in one of those bulbs was shot through with an orange line of light that turned blue and then turned to ash. The filament held its shape for an instant and then lost its shape. And that constitutes the first if in a series of sacred ifs that Helen tortures herself with every time she is drowsy or alone in the car or finds herself staring into space: If the current hadn't run amok.

There might have been smoke or there might not. Maybe a few blue sparks like fireflies hover over the board for a second before they are extinguished. Helen doesn't imagine smoke, but she hears the crackle inside the teensy-tiny lights, like crunching tinfoil against a filling, a sound more like a touch than a sound. She hears this tiny sound, or feels it, deep inside her head.

The current was nervous energy that panicked and busted all the delicate filaments in its wake, and indicator lights went off on the control panel.

Or they flickered.

The PA system died. One of the guys in the control room might have asked for assistance, but the PA system wasn't working because of the water all over the control panel.

If you listen to the voices recorded in the control room the men sound relaxed, and there's every reason to believe that Cal is scooping up a handful of change on the card table with no idea of what's about to happen. Helen wants him that way, innocent of everything.

A radio handset caught stray sound floating between neighbouring rigs out on the ocean. A line or two of talk crossed wires. The men on the other vessel, the *Seaforth Highlander*, heard this talk, and they wrote down what they heard. What the men on the *Ocean Ranger* knew was the weather. They knew the waves were thirty-seven feet and the wind had reached eighty or ninety knots. Or the waves were ninety feet and the wind was gathering speed.

On one of the other rigs, a metal shed bolted to the drilling floor blew away.

We're going to need every helicopter they got, someone from the *Ocean Ranger* said. This was the line that came through. Consider the hope in it.

Or the line that came through was: Tell them to send every helicopter they have.

They said: Send everything you have. Someone listening remarked on the calm. It was a calm voice that said about needing helicopters. Of course, there were no helicopters because there was rime ice in the clouds, because of a low ceiling, because helicopters could not fly in that weather, and the men must have known it.

The men on the *Ocean Ranger* sent out a mayday. *We have a list from which we cannot recover.* They gave the coordinates. They said, ASAP. They said eighty-four men.

The men on the *Seaforth Highlander* heard the mayday and they just gave it to her. Full throttle. They were travelling eight or nine knots. They were eight miles away. They came upon the rig before they knew it. They could not see, and then they saw, and there was a lifeboat and — they could see through the murk — wavering rays of light. The men were bailing. The thing was sinking but there were men on board and they were bailing.

Someone said, Don't tow them.

Someone had been in a similar situation and knew a tow could capsize a boat like that. They'd laid out a net on the deck of the *Seaforth Highlander* and the net was gone just like that. Washed over. Everything the men did was covered in ice, and they broke through the ice. The ropes were iced over, and the men's faces. Every grimace, every gesture, broke out of the ice mask of the last yell or scream. Cheeks and eyelashes and mouths and all the folds and wrinkles of their coats and every new gesture cracked out of the shell of the last gesture and broke free to be seized by ice again. They were men in a film shot frame by frame.

But there were men, still alive, in a lifeboat, and some of them were lightly dressed. These men were bailing because there must have been serious damage to their boat, and they had a system worked out and they were doing what they had to do. They were moving slowly and with method. The method was to stay afloat at all costs. And they capsized.

These men were in the water and the men on the *Seaforth Highlander* had to untie themselves so they could reach farther, and they were in danger of going in themselves, and they threw the ropes, but the men from the lifeboat could not raise their arms. Life preservers floated within reach, but those men could not reach.

The crew on the *Seaforth Highlander* had to cut the engine because the men in the water were in danger from the propeller, they might be dragged under and sliced to ribbons. But without the propeller it was a matter of minutes before they had drifted away from the men in the water. And that is the last, Helen thinks. He is gone.

BUT THIS IS not a true account of what Cal faces, and Helen knows it. It's better to keep to the true story or it will have to be told again until she gets it right. She endeavours to face the true story.

A crevasse forms in the cliff of water and it turns, as things sometimes turn, into concrete. Is it concrete or is it glass? It's mute and full of noise, angry and tranquil.

How like itself and unlike anything else. How unlike a Ferris wheel or a dog whimpering in its sleep or popcorn in the microwave oven or watching your lover have an orgasm, the clench of a foot curled around a calf or a square of sunlight on the hardwood floor. Growing old. It is like none of these things. Not remotely like.

Or trying to hang on to an iced railing during the tipping upwards of the monstrous hunk of metal. How unlike.

This wall of water has always been. It did not design itself or come from anywhere else or form itself. There was never a forming of. It just is.

It is still and self-combusting. Hungry and glutted with love. Full of mystery, full of a void.

Full of God. Get down on your knees before this creature. It is the centre of the outside.

This wave is death. When we say death we mean something we cannot say. The wave — because it is just water after all, just water, just naked power, just force — the wave is a mirror image of death, not death itself; but it is advantageous not to glance that way. Avoid the mirror if you can. Cultivate an air of preoccupation. Get. Get out.

Death would like to be introduced. It is willing to be polite. There will be no rush. When the wall closes over Cal, he will be like a fly in amber, a riddle of time, a museum piece. He will lose the desire for escape. The obsession with living will seem like a dalliance to him then. Stillness will be the new thing.

The ocean is full of its own collapse, its destiny is to annihilate itself thoroughly, but for a brief moment it stands up straight. It assumes the pose of something that can last.

This wave has been working towards the chewing and swallowing of the world since the beginning of time. Chomp. Chomp. What is the world after all? What are sunlight and love and the birth of a child and all the small passions that break out and flare and matter so very much?

A great guzzling of itself is death, or whatever the end of life may be called, or referred to as, or spoken of. But we don't know how to name it because it is unknowable.

Except those men know it.

Cal knows it. It is a glittering thing, big and disco-ball beautiful, full of dazzle, and he left her for it.

Here is what Helen has come to think: There must be some promise in death.

If she is in a hopeful mood, sometimes she can believe in more than rot. Sometimes she thinks there must be promise.

More promise than the cold ground and a skull and the sprinkle of holy water on a casket and the gold-embroidered robes of the priest and a flock of pigeons and the street gleaming after the rain and snowbanks so bright in the evening gloom after the dark of the church that they hurt the eyes.

She heard Cal in the bathroom that night, brushing his teeth. He spoke to her, but he was not there.

He was passing through. He came to her, Helen believes. Look out the window, he said. Or he said something similar. Look out the window. The rig tips and all the water falls away from its decks and the men hold the rail. They hang on.

It tips and tips and the card table slides sideways and all the silver coins bounce across the floor, dimes and quarters and nickels, and now, at last, she is with him.

Helen is in his skin. She is Cal and she lives through this every night, or sometimes in an instant as she cleans the dishes, and the fact of it is in the faces of her children. It is the doorbell ring and the heat from the oven when she takes out the casserole, it is the smell of ketchup and the noise the ketchup makes coming out of the squeeze bottle, it is the swooshing inside the dishwasher, it is an absolute terror that she wakes to every night. A terror that has invested itself in the microfilaments of her being, in every strand and particle of thought. What will she be without it?

She is there. Helen is there with him.

But she is not there, because nobody can be there.

The dimes roll on their rims and the playing cards slide off the table and the table falls on its side. Cal is making his way up to the deck. He is hauling himself hand over hand up the stair rail. There is a monstrous crevasse in the concrete ocean and it inspires a terror that is full of calm.

They knew all along. It was decided.

One end of the rig tips and it slides in easily. It is there and it is not there.

The Royal Commission said there was a fatal chain of events that could have been avoided but for the inadequate training of personnel, lack of manuals and technical information. And that is the true story. It is the company's fault.

But there is also the obdurate wall of water, and because of it Helen will finally give up her careful recital of the fatal chain of events.

Cal is on the deck and he is almost gone. Please go, she thinks. Please go, let it be over.

Because his panic is in her skin, just as he has made love to her and just as she has had his four children, and just as she has watched him sleep and cooked his meals and made up a notion of what love might be and followed through with it.

She decided that love might look something like this: a sketch, a thing, a plan. She figured it out and then she brought it into being. Breathed life into it.

She and Cal had stayed up late and said, It must look like this. They agreed, and then they stuck it out.

If they were wrong, nobody ever said. Helen knew Cal's moods and the two of them gossiped and made up stories and held each other and fought and were careful about what they said, even in anger. And his panic is inside her. The panic of facing death.

That must be part of what they decided: If Cal died out there on the rig, Helen would never forget him. That was the promise. She will never forget him.

. . . . .

An Eclipse on the Honeymoon, February 2009

THE SUN IS a constant. The sun is not moving. It's going to take fifteen minutes. Total.

Everybody murmurs the word *total*. Everyone agrees. This is on a street corner in Puerto Vallarta. One man in the group has a toothpick. They are all heading back to their condos after a few drinks in the cafés. A few margueritas. Senior citizens. They are Americans who own time-shares, or they are, some of them, from Quebec.

Not for another thirty years, one woman says. We have to see it now. We'll be dead the next time.

Long gone, says the man with the toothpick. He lets the toothpick wag up and down.

Last chance, someone says. Everyone chuckles. The last chance was kind of a funny idea.

We're casting a shadow, a man says.

That's all, someone says. A shadow.

One man raises both his fists, and one fist slowly circles the other, and he nods to indicate where the sun is, off to the side a bit.

It's the earth moving between the sun and the moon.

Or the moon between the earth and the sun, a woman says.

It's going to be total, they all agree.

They have their arms crossed over their chests and their faces tilted skyward, and the taxis, trawling the streets, toot when the crowd absent-mindedly steps off the curb. Where the shadow has already crossed the surface of the moon there is a honey-dark glow.

Helen had married Barry in her own living room. John gave her away; Lulu wept like a fool. Gabrielle had flown in from Nova Scotia and arrived fifteen minutes before the ceremony. Cathy and her husband, Mark, and Claire. Timmy with the rings on a satin pillow. Helen had invited Patience and her mother. Patience was given a wicker basket full of rose petals that she was asked to scatter. The vast importance of Patience's job caused her to stand rigid, staring at the floor for the whole ceremony. Then she flung big squashed lumps of petal, winding up first like a baseball player. Helen's girls were happy for their mother, or they kept their opinions to themselves. It was a short ceremony.

As long as the love lasts, Helen and Barry said to each other. Cathy had written the vows. Gabrielle had designed the rings and they'd been forged by a local jeweller. Helen wore blue silk, just below the knee and unadorned because Lulu had said, Simple.

Afterwards John tried to tell Helen how to change a diaper. You're doing it wrong, he snapped. Then he nudged her out of the way.

Listen here, my son, Helen said. Don't tell me how to change a diaper.

Jane had a bag of frozen peas clutched to her left breast for the whole ceremony. She had a blocked duct. We're both exhausted, Jane said.

The baby never sleeps, John said. They had both moved to St. John's, taking two separate apartments, but John slept on Jane's couch most nights to help with the early morning feedings.

John wanted them to watch the birth video.

Jesus, not now, Cathy said.

John set up his computer and they all gathered around, except Jane, who had fallen asleep in the guest room, and Barry, who didn't want to look.

John slipped the DVD in the slot and the black screen turned blue and he hit play. There was a sudden burst of blurred green and a roar of static and the sound of ragged breath and John was saying, Okay, okay, this is it, this is it, now, now, and then he was yelling. And there was blue sky and cloud and a dipping and rising and his hands waving back and forth at the edges of the screen. He hit pause.

What the hell was that, Lulu said.

Wrong DVD, John said. It was the zip ride he'd taken in Tasmania.

After the ceremony the whole family had fish and chips from Ches's, and then Helen and Barry hurried to catch an evening plane.

Barry had said Mexico because he had never been and neither had Helen. They wanted a place that would be new to both of them.

They got a taxi from the airport in Mexico. The breeze through the window and honking traffic and pollution. The hotel was fine. Helen ripped the blanket down and the sheets were clean, and she and Barry made love and showered. Barry rubbed lotion on Helen's back and her arms and the backs of her thighs, and she did the same for him. There was loud traffic on the street outside the hotel and it was very hot, and they found their way to the beach although it was already late in the afternoon.

I'm going to get in, Barry said.

Go for a dip, Helen said. I'll watch. The ocean was green except near the shore, where the stirred sand made it the colour of milky tea. Farther out, the water was like nickel and full of glitter. Afterwards they ate at a sidewalk café and someone said about the eclipse. Someone said, Look.

We'll be gone the next time this happens, everyone on the sidewalk agrees. The women are wearing white capri pants and embroidered blouses and turquoise and silver jewellery they'd bought at the beach in the afternoon. The men are in shorts—plaid or navy—that come to their knees, and they wear loafers.

There are also buff gay men, tattooed and shiny-skulled and vaguely injured looking, and close to their chests they carry lapdogs with studded collars or bows. Or they are healthy young gay businessmen in crisply ironed shirts, cargo shorts, and gronky sandals. And there are children playing marbles on the sidewalk.

A tanned and elderly woman with a bleached ponytail smokes, and the end of the cigarette lights up orange.

It is boring to stand and watch the moon. A dull event full of majesty. There is a statuesque woman followed by her husband, and he holds the hand of a boy with Down syndrome who looks to be their son. On the corner there is a jewellery store lit up like a fish tank, and the girl behind the counter is reading the paper.

It's been going on, a man drawls, forty minutes.

I don't think total, someone says. Then, finally, the moon is gone. Blotted out. Everybody claps. They clap spontaneously. A short, self-conscious burst.

Totally gone, someone says.

But it's coming back, Barry says. He is standing behind Helen and she leans back and he draws her into him.

It's coming back.

EARLIER IN THE afternoon Barry had walked out into the water until he was floating. He bobbed up and down and a wave crashed over his shoulders. Here and there people were floating near him, and they all looked like silhouettes. The ocean was a deep navy now, and blasted all over with light. Each wave capped in silver. It was like hammered metal, sparkle-pocked.

Helen suddenly felt a shadow fall over her, and with it a chill. It was a definite shadow and it covered her towel; it was directly overhead, and the chill was uncanny, and she thought of Cal. Four men were strolling together and they had halted in front of her, all at once, and they each raised a hand over their eyes and looked at the sky just above her head. She heard a shrill whistle and it was a parasailer, a man in a harness with a parachute, coming in for a landing, and he was hovering directly over her. A group of Mexican men was running towards him, and they mimed and yelled for him to tug the rope, and the guy did and he dropped towards the ground ten feet from where Helen sat, and the Mexicans caught the man in their upraised arms and lowered him to the beach and folded the parachute as it deflated. And Helen looked out over the ocean and she could not see Barry.

She could not see him.

She looked at the spot where he had been and he was not there.

Then the wave withdrew with a roar, and there he was. He stood and he was dark against the sun except for a gleam down his arm and in his hair, and he flicked his head and the drops flew out like a handful of silver, and he dipped under the water again and waded against its pull towards shore and came back up the beach to her.

Acknowledgements

THANK YOU TO Steve Crocker, as always, for everything. Thank you to Eva Crocker and Theo Crocker and Emily Pickard for the same.

Lynn Henry at Anansi is an infinitely wise and generous editor. I am deeply, deeply grateful for having had the opportunity to work with her on this novel, for her insight and encouragement and utter brilliance.

Thank you to Sarah MacLachlan for her friendship and commitment to publishing. Thank you to Matt Williams and Julie Wilson, also at Anansi. Thank you to Ingrid Paulson for her cover design.

Thank you to my agent, Anne McDermid, for her enthusiasm and hard work and charisma.

Nan Love and Claire Wilkshire and Lynn Moore aided and abetted, cajoled and affirmed. I borrowed their eagle eyes. Special thanks.

This book had some early readers and advisers and friends to whom I offer a great big giant thank you: Bill Coultas,

Dede Crane, Eva Crocker, Rosemary Crocker, Steve Crocker, Libby Creelman, Ramona Dearing, Susan Dodd, Barbara Doran, Jack Eastwood, Mark Ferguson, Jessica Grant, Mike Heffernan, Holly Hogan, Mary Lewis, Dr. John Lewis, Nan Love, Elizabeth Moore, Christine Pountney, Lawrence Mathews, Sarah MacLachlan, Beth Ryan, Bob Wakem, Claire Wilkshire, Michael Winter. I'm indebted to these people.

I would like to acknowledge the *Royal Commission on the Ocean Ranger Disaster* written by the Honorable T. Alex Hickman, O.C., Q.C. The collection of oral stories by Douglas House, *Who Cares Now: The Tragedy of the Ocean Ranger*, was a valuable resource. Mike Heffernan's *Rig: The Story of the Ocean Ranger* is a very important and moving account of the disaster for which I am grateful. Sociologist Susan Dodd, who is also writing about the *Ocean Ranger*, was extremely helpful. I respectfully thank the writers of all these works.

I would also like to acknowledge the brave men who died on the *Ocean Ranger* and the brave families of those men.

COMING SOON
IN JUNE 2013

• • •

Read on for a preview from
Lisa Moore's forthcoming
novel, *Caught*

Searchlight

SLANEY BROKE OUT of the woods and skidded down a soft embankment to the side of the road. There was nothing but forest on both sides of the asphalt as far as he could see. He thought it might be three in the morning and he was about two miles from the prison. It had taken an hour to get through the woods.

He had crawled under the chain-link fence around the yard and through the long grass on the other side. He had run hunched over and he'd crawled on his elbows and knees, pulling himself across the ground, and he'd stayed still, with his face in the earth, while the searchlight arced over him. At the end of the field was a steep hill of loose shale and the rocks had clattered away from his shoes.

The soles of Slaney's shoes were tan-coloured and slippery. The tan had worn off and a smooth patch of black rubber showed on the bottom of each shoe. He'd imagined the soles lit up as the searchlight hit them. He had on the orange coveralls. They had always been orange, but when everybody was wearing them they were less orange.

For an instant the perfect oval of hard light had contained him like the shell of an egg and then he'd gone animal numb and cringing, a counterintuitive move, the prison psychotherapist might have said, if they were back in her office discussing the break — she talked slips and displacement, sublimation and counter-intuition, and allowed for an inner mechanism he could not see or touch but had to account for — then the oval slid him back into darkness and he charged up the hill again.

Near the top, the shale had given way to a curve of reddish topsoil with an overhang of ragged grass and shrub. There was a cracked yellow beef bucket and a ringer washer turned on its side, a bald white.

Slaney had grabbed at a tangled clot of branches but it came loose in his hand. Then he'd dug the toe of his shoe in deep and hefted his chest over the prickly grass overhang and rolled on top of it.

He lay there, flat on his back, chest hammering, looking at the stars. It was as far as he had been from the Springhill Penitentiary since the doors of that institution admitted him four years before. It was not far enough.

He'd heaved himself off the ground and started running.

This was Nova Scotia and it was June 14, 1978. Slaney would be twenty-five years old the next day.

The night of his escape would come back to him, moments of lit intensity, for the rest of his life. He saw himself on that hill in the brilliant spot of the swinging searchlight, the orange of his own back, as it might have appeared to the guards in the watchtower, had they glanced that way.

SLANEY STOOD ON the highway and the stillness of the moonlit night settled over him. The evening thumped down and then Slaney ran for all he was worth because it seemed foolhardy to stand still.

Then it seemed foolhardy not to be still.

He felt he had to be still in order to listen. He was listening with all his might. He knew the squad cars were coming and there would be dogs. He accepted that there was nothing he could do now but wait.

A fellow prisoner named Harold had arranged a place for him. It was a room over a bar, several hours from the penitentiary, if Slaney happened to get that far.

Harold said that the bar belonged to his grandmother. They had a horsehair dance floor and served the best fish and chips in Nova Scotia. They had rock bands passing through and strippers once a week and they sponsored a school basketball team.

Harold's place was in Guysborough. The cops would be expecting Slaney to be going west. But Slaney was lighting out in the opposite direction. A trucker would be heading for the ferry in North Sydney, bringing a shipment of Lay's potato chips to Newfoundland.

Slaney could get a ride with him as far as Harold's place in Guysborough, then backtrack the next day when things had cooled down a little.

He bent over on the side of the highway with his hands on his knees and caught his breath. He whispered to himself. He spoke a stream of profanity and he said a prayer to the

Virgin Mary, in whom he half believed. Mosquitoes touched him all over. They settled on his skin and put their fine things into him and they were lulled and bloated and thought themselves sexy and near death.

They got in his mouth and he spit and they dotted his saliva. They were in the crease of his left eyelid. He wiped one out of his eye and found he was weeping. He was snot-smeared and tears dropped off his eyelashes. He could hear the whine of just one mosquito above the rest.

It was tears or sweat, he didn't know.

He'd broken out of prison and he was going back to Colombia. He'd learned from the first trip down there, the trip that had landed him in jail, that the most serious mistakes are the easiest to make. There are mistakes that stand in the centre of an empty field and cry out for love.

The largest mistake, that time, was that Slaney and Hearn had underestimated the Newfoundland fishermen of Capelin Cove. The fishermen had known about the caves the boys had dug for stashing the weed. They'd seen the guys with their long hair and shovels and picks drive in from town and set up tents in an empty field. They'd watched them down at the beach all day, heard them at night with their guitars around the bonfire. The fishermen had called the cops.

Slaney and the boys had mistaken the fishermen's idle calculation for a blind eye and they had been turned in.

And they'd mistaken the fog for cover but it was an unveiling. Slaney and Hearn had lost their bearings in a dense fog, after sailing home from Colombia. They were just a half-mile off shore with two tons of marijuana on board and they'd required assistance.

There were mistakes and there was a dearth of luck when they had needed just a little. A little luck would have seen them through the first trip despite their dumb moves.

Now Slaney was out again and he knew the nature of mistakes. They were detectable but you had to read all the signs backwards or inside out. Those first mistakes had cost him. They meant he could never go home. He'd never see Newfoundland again.

Everything will happen from here, he thought. This time they would do it right. He could feel luck like an animal presence, feral and watchful. He would have to coax it into the open. Grab it by the throat.

Slaney had broken out of prison and beat his way through the forest. He'd stumbled into a ditch of lupins. The searchlight must have seeped into his skin back there, just outside the prison fence, a radioactive buzz that left him with something extra. He wasn't himself; he was himself with something added.

Or the light had bleached away everything he was except the need not to be attacked by police dogs.

There was the scent of the lupins as he bashed through, the wet stalks grabbing at his shins. Cold raindrops scattering from the leaves. Then he was up on the shoulder of the road. He batted his hands around his head, girly swings at the swarms of mosquitoes.

The prayers he said between gusts of filthy language were polite and he had honed down his petition to a single word: the word was *please*. He had an idea about the Virgin Mary in ordinary clothes, jeans and a T-shirt. She was complicated but placid, more human than divine. He did not think *virgin*, he thought ordinary and smart. A girl with a blade of grass between her thumbs that she blew on to make a trilling noise. He called out for her now.

His prayers were meant to stave off the dread he felt and a shame that had nothing to do with the crime he'd committed or the fact that he was standing on the side of the road, under the moon, covered in mud, at the mercy of an ex-convict with a transport truck.

It was a rootless and fickle shame. It might have been someone else's shame, a storm touching down, or a shame belonging to no one, knocking against everything in its path.

His curses were an incantation against too much humility and the prayers pleaded with the Virgin to make the mosquitoes go away.

Then the earth revved and thrummed. He jumped back into the ditch. He lay down flat with the lupins trembling over him. The sirens were loud, even at a distance, baritone whoops that scaled up to clear metallic bleats. The hoops of hollow, tin-bright noise overlapped and the torrent of squeal echoed off the hills. Slaney counted five cars. There were five of them.

Red and blue bands of light sliced through the lupin stalks and the heads of the flowers tipped and swung in the backdraft as the cars roared past. The siren of each car was so shrill, as it swept past, that it pierced the bones of his skull, and the tiny hammer in his ear banged out a message of calibrated terror and the rocks his cheek rested on in the ditch were full of vibration and then the sirens, one at a time, receded, and the echoes dissipated and silence followed.

It was not silence. Slaney mistook it for silence but there was a wind that had come a long distance and it jostled every tree. Some branches rubbed against one another, squeaking. The leaves of the lupins chussled like the turning pages of a glossy magazine.

Five cars. They would go another three or four miles and then they'd let the dogs out. They had taken this long because they'd had to gather up the dogs. Slaney listened for the barking, which would be carried on the wind.

He crawled out of the ditch to meet the next vehicle and he stood straight and brushed his hands over his chest and tugged the collar of the coveralls. He couldn't wait for the truck that had been arranged. Anything could have happened to that truck.

He was getting the hell out of there before the dogs showed up.

A station wagon went by with one headlight and he could see in the pale yellow shaft that it had begun to rain. The station wagon had a mattress tied to the roof. It had slowed to a crawl. There was a woman smoking a cigarette in the passenger seat. She turned all the way around to get a good look at him as they rolled to a stop.

Slaney would remember her face for a long time. An amber dashlight lit her brown hair. The reflection of his own face slid over hers on the window and stopped when the car stopped, so that for the briefest instant the two faces became one grotesque face with two noses and four eyes, and there was an elongated forehead and a stretched mannish chin under her full mouth and maybe she saw the same thing on her side of the glass.

The cop cars must have passed her already and she would have known that they were looking for someone. She exhaled the smoke and he saw it waggle up lazily. She reached over and touched the lock on the passenger door with a finger. They paused there, looking at him, though Slaney could not see the driver of the car, and then they'd sped up with a spray of gravel hitting his thighs.

Slaney had become aware of how small he was in relation to the highway and to the hills of trees and the sky. He felt the unspooling of time.

Time had been pulled up tight as if with a winch and somebody had flicked a switch and it was unspooling with blurry speed. He expected it to snag. If it snagged, it would not unsnag.

Four years and two days. Time moved evenly in prison without ever hurrying or slowing down. It was jellied and unthinking. He had timed the break so he could be out of prison for his birthday.

Slaney's sister had visited him in prison over the last year, and they'd spoken about the break, using general terms and a kind of code they made up as they went along.

She'd let him know that Hearn was planning a new trip and was expecting him. His sister was in contact with Hearn. And she was the one who told him the transport truck would pick him up on the side of the road.

The gist of it was that there would be a ride for him at the appointed time. Most escaped prisoners get caught on the first night out. Slaney had to get himself through the first night, and then he'd head west, across the country, to Vancouver, where he'd meet up with Hearn. He was heading

back to Colombia from there and he would return with
enough pot to make them both millionaires.

Easy Rider

THERE WERE TWO pinpoints of light in the distance that
dipped down and disappeared and bobbed back up.
Slaney prayed to the Virgin that these were the lights of
the transport truck with the driver who had turned his
life around and had accepted Jesus into his heart, and had
attended Alcoholics Anonymous, believing in the
twelve-step program and the ancient, sinister advice of
one day at a time.

This trucker had, according to Slaney's sister, gone to
work in a diner on Duckworth Street where ex-cons were
welcome because the owner was also an ex-con, and he'd
met a nurse there and they'd married and had a child and
bought a new house on the mainland.

Slaney's sister had put in a call and the trucker said he
would be passing through and he would pick up Slaney if he
saw him and drop him at Harold's.

The lupins on the side of the road were spilling forward,
rushing through the ditch in the reaching headlights as if a
dam had broken. Spilling all the way down the sides of the
vast dark highway in a lit-up river of sloshing purple, trying
to outrace the reach of the pummelling lights. Then the
transport truck was upon him, deafening; the long silver
flank dirty and close enough that Slaney could have touched

it. Behind the truck the lupins tumbled back into darkness, unspilling, snuffed out.

The truck had passed him and Slaney was covered in a film of wet grit. The exhaust smelled sharp in the ozone-laden air. He wiped his face with his sleeve. Slaney knew the minute he had seen the headlights in the distance that if it didn't stop he would be caught. Two possible lives formed and unformed and one of them had to do with the truck stopping and the other had to do with being caught within the next hour.

There would be the walk back down the corridor to his cell. He could summon the image of a crack in the concrete floor near his cot, or it came to him unbidden. This was a sign that the prison had got inside him. When he opened his eyes he saw the red taillights of the truck stopped a ways down the road.

He ran hard; he was afraid the driver would change his mind and take off. Slaney opened the door of the truck and climbed up into the cab. The vibration of the idling engine passed through the seat under Slaney into his thighs and ass and shoulder blades. There was a Virgin Mary statuette on the dash. She was ivory-coloured, her arms were held out, tiny palms upward. Her pale longish face tipped down, eyes closed.

About the Author

LISA MOORE IS the acclaimed author of the novel *Alligator*, which was a finalist for the Scotiabank Giller Prize, won the Commonwealth Fiction Prize (Canada and the Caribbean), and was a national bestseller. Her story collection *Open* was also short-listed for the Scotiabank Giller Prize and became a bestseller. *February* is her second novel.

Lisa Moore's books have been translated into many languages and published around the world. She lives in St. John's, Newfoundland.